SECRETS
OF THE
DEAD

ALSO BY CAROL WYER

DI ROBYN CARTER SERIES

Little Girl Lost
Life Swap
Grumpy Old Menopause
How Not to Murder Your Grumpy
Grumpies On Board
Mini Skirts and Laughter Lines
Surfing in Stilettos
Just Add Spice
Love Hurts
Take a Chance on Me

SECRETS
OF THE
DEAD

CAROL WYER

bookouture

Published by Bookouture
An imprint of StoryFire Ltd.
23 Sussex Road, Ickenham, UB10 8PN
United Kingdom
www.bookouture.com

ISBN: 978-1-78681-159-2
eBook ISBN: 978-1-78681-158-5

CHAPTER ONE

The wind tormented the branches of the trees, bending their boughs and ripping leaves from their stems. The weather forecasters had predicted a storm and this time they had been accurate. Jakub Woźniak clung to the handlebars of his bicycle as he navigated the lane he travelled every day at 4 a.m. A gust knocked into his side, threatening to sweep him into the hedgerow, but Jakub, refusing to be beaten by the weather, sank further onto his saddle and pedalled on, hunched over the bike like a vulture waiting to swoop on a dead animal.

His mind swam with troubled thoughts; his wife, Emily, had learned she was to lose her job as a receptionist, and soon there would only be his salary coming in until she could find more employment. It was so difficult to find work. In the old country he had worked as a clerk for the police in Wyszków, some fifty-five kilometres north-east of Warsaw, on the highway to Bialystok. It was not the most exciting job: he was responsible for checking various databases; recording and modifying offences in relation to road traffic incidents; logging collisions and accidents and corresponding with the insurance companies. However, he earned a decent salary that, over there, would have fed a family, paid for a house and allowed for holidays each year.

Love had caused him to leave his homeland and follow his heart to the Staffordshire countryside where he had queued with other world-weary hopefuls at the social welfare office every week for months, looking and hoping for employment, only to be turned away. Week after week, he scrolled through websites and sent off his CV to be considered for a position, yet he never even made it to an interview. Gradually, his enthusiasm had been sucked away. It hadn't helped that he'd found the English language almost impossible to learn. Even after eighteen months in the country, he could still only master basic sentences. Luckily, Emily had found him this position or he might have given up altogether and returned to Poland.

He reached the end of the lane and, avoiding the whipping branches that hung near the brick-arched entrance to Bromley Hall, he entered the grounds. He recalled the first time he had set foot here. He had been overwhelmed by the quintessential English countryside surrounding the Hall. The Hall, and its grounds, represented everything he loved about the UK – the smell of freshly cut grass and the gentle hum of bees buzzing between brightly coloured blooms.

The Hall had been a family home in the late nineteenth century, and was Elizabethan in style with curved gables, chimney stacks that resembled classical columns and large mullioned windows of the period. It boasted an ostentatious entrance hall and a magnificent oak-panelled Long Gallery, over a hundred feet in length. Now, it was a world-renowned hotel and spa, frequented by celebrities and those who earned far more than he ever could.

Jakub would not be using the entrance hall this morning, nor would he ever be invited to the balls that took place each Christmas in the magnificent ballroom. He navigated his bike through some of the fifty acres of grounds and along the sweeping drive. The wind had ripped the last remaining leaves from the trees and hurled them onto the ground where they had clustered and now spun in small, rustling whirlwinds that chased about the car park. Jakub buried his neck further into his scarf, cursing the weather. Of all the times for his car to break down and need a new head gasket. These were now the darker months, when winter was beginning to set in and the clocks had been turned back, so mornings were dark, and afternoons were dark and everything was gloomy.

He was surprised to spot chef Bruno Miguel's striking yellow Citroën DS. Bruno, who, in Jakub's opinion, was one of the better-tempered commis chefs, had purchased it in September on a finance plan, and was terrified the brand new vehicle would suffer damage in the staff car park, so he stationed it as far away from the other cars as possible. Ordinarily, Bruno didn't turn up until six o' clock, leaving most of the preparation to the younger chefs. Jakub dismounted, bending to remove the cycle clips that protected the bottoms of his jeans from the filthy pedals and oily bike chain. He wheeled the bike to the rear of the Hall and into the alleyway that led to the kitchens. Now that he was protected from the wind, he removed his gloves and the beanie hat that had been pulled well over his ears. He hated late autumn in this country; it was cruel, especially when your only transport was a two-wheeled, second-hand bike.

Above him, in the Hall itself, the pampered guests would be fast asleep under Egyptian cotton sheets, heads resting on goose-feather pillows. They wouldn't have to worry about getting up at three thirty every morning to come to work in the foul weather to clean up the mess that had been left by the guests, collecting wet towels discarded by the pool, washing out showers smeared with soap and expensive body lotions, or cleaning toilets till they gleamed – all for a pittance; then, aching from scrubbing floors, tiled bath surrounds and glass-fronted cubicles, having to pedal three miles back home again in atrocious weather conditions. No. They wouldn't have to do any of that. They'd get up when they felt like it, take a shower or bath, don the luxurious white cotton robes and fluffy slippers in their bedrooms, then wander down to breakfast. They would spend the rest of the day loafing beside the pool, reading books, snoozing or basking in the famous spa area, being pampered by an entire team of therapists and fitness gurus.

He felt the rage that sometimes consumed him mount as he unlocked the kitchen door and entered the darkened hallway. He shrugged off his outer garments and hung them by the door, on one of the many pegs used by the employees. He walked past the kitchen where two of the chefs were preparing breakfast. An aroma of bacon wafted out, and he swallowed the saliva that collected in his mouth; he had only grabbed a cup of coffee before setting off. If he were lucky, he'd be able to blag some toast or even a slice of bacon from Bruno, although these days it was more difficult to get free food or titbits. Management had really clamped down on such things, and all food now had to be accounted for – no more cheap or free meals for the staff. That was only one of the austerity measures they had implemented. The staff cuts were the most recent. He growled quietly. Management, in its wisdom, had fired his wife who earned a good salary working full-time on the front desk, meeting and greeting clients, yet he, who earned the minimum wage, had been kept on. If he could find another job he'd ditch this bunch immediately.

Bruno was one of the friendlier chefs. The rest were a bunch of sour-faced wannabes, who all hoped to go on to bigger and better establishments. Jakub couldn't stand any of them. He was here to do a job and that's all he did. He came in, he worked all day and he went home again, home to a miserable wife who now had no job and who, only the day before, had discovered she was expecting their second child.

Jakub collected the cleaning equipment from the cupboard. He would start in the men's changing room before starting on the spa. He might only be a cleaner, but he was thorough. A job was a job, and he would do it to the best of his ability, even if that job were beneath him. It paid some of the bills and, heaven knew, they needed his wage now more than ever.

He wheeled out the cleaning trolley and paraphernalia that accompanied it. The floor cleaner was a large industrial machine that had seen better days, but it still worked. It made a racket so it was best to use it while the guests weren't present. Nothing spoils a relaxing stay at a luxury spa more than someone attempting to clean around you with a machine that sounds like a band comprising several kettledrums and a whole army of bagpipe players.

The spa itself was housed in a purpose-built extension, adjacent to the Hall, that featured a twenty-six metre saltwater pool with two large whirlpools. It boasted several bio thermal rooms designed to invigorate and relax, an arctic cold ice room with an ice fountain, steam rooms and a sauna. Each of the zones was designed to stimulate different senses. Finally, there was the aspen wood sauna, subtly hidden away within the suite. Jakub had never tried out any of it, even though he was often alone at work. The CCTV cameras that whirred quietly were watching his every move, and he would most certainly be spotted if he suddenly decided to jump into the pool for a swim or enjoy a spell in one of the solariums.

Jakub was not impressed by the opulence here. Poland had many equally impressive resorts and spas that had been enjoyed by Europeans for centuries. A flame of fondness for his country flickered in his chest.

The men's changing room smelt of stale sweat and testosterone. It always seemed to reek that way, no matter how often it was cleaned. The air con hadn't been working in there for some time, even though Jakub had reported it, and the stench lingered in spite of air fresheners positioned around the room. Jakub emptied the bins and cleared away the dirty towels that had been dumped on a bench, before cleaning the toilets and showers. It was the same routine every day.

He ought to persuade Emily to return to Poland, although it was unlikely she would want to leave her family who lived nearby in Stafford, only twenty miles away, especially with another baby on the way. There were days when he was homesick, but he reasoned that to return so soon after leaving would be to admit defeat. His family had not wanted him to leave Poland. Still, he was young at thirty and had time. He would go back when he was ready, although he was less sure about how long he could bear to stay at Bromley Hall. His temper might just get the better of him if he wasn't careful.

He shut the cubicle doors to the showers and moved into the spa area, donning the obligatory protective footwear. The sound of the water being pumped around the pool echoed eerily as he padded past it, pushing the heavy cleaning machine in front of him, in the direction of the saunas and steam rooms. He put on the necessary headphones that shut out the constant noise generated by the machine and thought about his son, now almost two years old, who wanted to go on a steam train like Thomas the Tank Engine for his birthday at the weekend. Jakub wasn't sure they'd be able to get to the Severn Valley for such an outing if his car wasn't mended. Head gaskets were very expensive parts to replace.

As he moved the cleaning machine around in a circular motion, his eyes alighted upon a pile of clothes, folded and left outside the aspen sauna on one of the 'relax' beds. He scowled. Some guest had not read the rules. It was forbidden to enter the spa area before 8 a.m. He was tempted to pick up the clothes and hide them in the changing room so whoever was in the sauna would be obliged to race around naked, hunting for them. He sidled up to the clothes. There was a suit and shirt, and an expensive watch had been left on top of the pile.

Jakub sneered. A watch like that cost a lot of money, and yet the owner didn't seem to care that it might be stolen. They were either naively trusting or didn't give a damn about the cost. He struggled with his conscience before deciding the owner would not miss the watch. They would merely claim its value from an insurance company and purchase another. Jakub checked the camera above him. It was pointing in the opposite direction, focusing on the ice room at that moment. It would gradually move to cover the whole of the area. The guest could well afford to lose it and Jakub needed the money. He checked for anyone watching him and was about to slide the watch into his pocket when he stopped. He had never been a thief. He couldn't stoop so low as to steal from someone, no matter how tough times were.

He moved away and edged past the sauna with the machine. No doubt the occupant would complain about him making a row. It was five thirty. He would stand up to management if they took him to task about it. As he moved past the glass-fronted door of the sauna he stopped, all thoughts of management forgotten. A dark-skinned man was curled on the floor in a foetal position. Jakub gingerly opened the door, recoiling from the tremendous wave of heat. His mind could not comprehend what he was seeing. The body was not, as he had first thought, a dark-skinned man. It was charred. Large chunks of skin lay on the floor. Jakub stared at the body, which resembled a large piece of *przysmak piwny* – beef jerky. Suddenly, he remembered the watch on the pile of clothes. He had seen it only recently, on the wrist of the man who had fired his newly pregnant wife for no other reason than cost-cutting. Jakub had taken issue with him and asked for Emily to be reinstated. The man had fobbed him off and checked the time on his watch, as if he had somewhere more important to be. Jakub had thumped the desk and blown his top before being sent away with the threat that if he did not cool down, he would be joining Emily on the dole queue. This wasn't a guest in the hotel. This was the hotel manager. The broiled body on the floor was that of Miles Ashbrook.

CHAPTER THREE

DCI Louisa Mulholland's honey-coloured eyes blinked in surprise. 'I don't know how these things get out. For the record, I have been invited to consider applying for the position of superintendent. However, it would mean moving to Yorkshire. It's a fair distance from my friends and family.'

'Nice walks in Yorkshire. The Dales are beautiful.'

'Nice walks here too, DI Carter.'

'True. So, no plans to race off up north?'

'I'm not sure yet. As soon as I am, I'll let everyone know rather than rely on the gossips to decide when the news should be made public. So, tell me. What happened?'

Robyn explained the unfortunate incident of chasing the wrong man.

'And how are you going to resolve this one, Robyn? We can't make an additional appeal tonight.'

'We had another breakthrough. A call from a woman who thinks the robber is her live-in boyfriend, Wayne Robson. She was rooting through a cupboard searching for stuff to donate to a charity and uncovered a backpack filled with cash. She's currently hiding out at her sister's until we bring Robson in. Scared of what might happen if he finds out she rang us. Says he's got a temper.' She waited for Louisa to comment, but she didn't.

'Carry on.'

'I've sent PC David Marker and Sergeant Patel to bring him in for questioning.'

Louisa Mulholland nodded approvingly. 'Let me know when Wayne Robson has arrived. I'd like to observe the interview and hear what he has to say for himself.'

'Does that mean I'll have to be extra polite to him, ma'am?'

'Indeed, DI Carter, it does not.'

It was well after 9 p.m. when Robyn left the station and headed for the gym. She no longer felt tired or disheartened. Wayne Robson had been officially charged and was sweating it out in the cells, waiting for his case to come up. Robyn felt a weight had been removed from her shoulders. It could so easily have gone the other way, and she could still be scrabbling about hunting for the man who stole for the thrill of it and thought nothing of those victims he had mutilated.

She shook herself and tried to clear her thoughts. She changed into her gear, noting that Tricia was in again. Her Adidas bag was resting in its usual spot in front of locker fifteen. The woman was never out of the place. Ever since her divorce she had become a gym junkie. Robyn didn't have much to do with the woman. In fact, Robyn didn't have much to do with anyone. When she was in the gym she was completely focused on her training, and tonight would be no exception. She had signed up for the Staffordshire Ironman Triathlon event, taking place on 17 June, and she was determined to win it.

As she pulled on her Lycra shorts she asked herself why she felt this constant need to prove herself. She glimpsed at her lean frame in the mirror and saw what her team must see every day – a woman with large dark circles under her eyes, who had the hungry look of a bird of prey. She had not aged much, and although she was in her forties, her posture was that of a much younger woman. Robyn was not hung up on looks or ageing. As long as she could do her job and train as hard as she did, all was as well as it was ever going to be. She studied her hands and removed the ring she always wore, putting it safely into her purse before locking it up in the locker. It had been given to her by Davies, and she refused to hide it away. It was almost two years since he had been killed in an ambush in Morocco. Davies, a military intelligence officer, had been her rock, her man, her true other half. He had died unaware she was pregnant. Robyn wished he had known about the baby, even though it had not been born. The miscarriage had been another damaging blow and almost cost Robyn her sanity. She banished the sad memory. Tonight she would drown out all thoughts of the past, all thoughts of her job, and concentrate on improving her physical condition.

There was no one in the gym at all. Tricia must have finished her routine and gone to the swimming pool. Robyn was glad of the solitude.

She set up the squat rack with a freestanding barbell and grunted her way through six sets of varying weights and repetitions, starting with just the barbell as a warm-up and moving up to the final couple of sets using 80–85kg weights. By the time she had completed the final set she could feel the lactic acid building in her arms and sweat beginning to trickle down her back. She wiped her hands on the towel she always carried and shook the lactic acid away, striding about the gym, avoiding her reflection in the mirrors.

Next on her agenda was a Romanian dead lift. She completed three sets of eight to ten repetitions, using 50kg weights, followed by the same number and sets of shoulder shrugs.

Immediately following this, she did three sets of dead lifts and was moving onto the cable hamstring curls when she spotted Tricia observing her. She lifted her hand when she saw Robyn had noticed her and hurried over. 'Look, I know it's bad form to interrupt when someone's training, but I need to talk to you.'

Robyn wiped the sweat from her face. Some had already got into her eyes and it was stinging like crazy.

'I've got about another half an hour to do.'

Tricia chewed on her lip. 'If you don't mind, I'll wait for you.'

Robyn gave her a curious look. This was most unlike Tricia. Ordinarily they nodded or exchanged a brief 'hi' and, at a push, pleasantries. They'd only had a few conversations in the past year, and one of those had been about Robyn's job after Tricia had seen her on television. Robyn decided it must be important if she was willing to hang about and wait. 'Okay. I'll catch you in the changing room. What's so urgent?'

'I'll tell you when you're finished. I'll wait for you there. I want to talk to you in private,' she added, as one of the regulars entered the gym.

CHAPTER FIVE

Cassidy Place was only a ten-minute walk from the gym, so Robyn left her car in the car park and strode towards Tricia's house. Tricia lived in a trendy area made up of terraced Victorian houses that had been renovated in recent years. Each house had a tiny front courtyard that was only big enough for a couple of large flower tubs. Tricia had opted for two bay trees in pots on either side of a cheerfully painted red door. Robyn pressed the buzzer and pulled up her coat collar around her neck. After the stormy morning, it was now an icy, cold, starlit evening. Robyn began to wish she had driven here. Her hands were beginning to numb. She rang again. There was no answer.

She was about to leave, cursing the woman for messing her about, but thought she would try the handle first, just in case Tricia was in the bathroom and hadn't heard her ringing.

The door opened into a carpeted hallway and a staircase. She called Tricia's name. Once again there was no response. The sound of a television, showing some sort of cop movie with gunfire and sirens, told her someone was in the house and that something was definitely awry. Tricia was not here to greet her, and yet the woman had wanted to talk to her. There was no way she would leave her house unlocked like this if she were not here. Robyn edged towards the sound of the television, her senses on alert as she approached the sound of wailing sirens. She nudged the door open with her foot and peered into the room.

On the settee sat two teenage boys, game controllers in their hands, completely absorbed in shooting at villains, who were racing muscle cars. Neither noticed her presence. She was about to call out when she heard Tricia behind her.

'Did they not let you in? Hey, you two. Turn the bloody set down. I told you to listen out for the doorbell. You wouldn't hear it if it was as loud as Big Ben.'

One of the boys twisted in his seat and grinned sheepishly. 'Sorry, Mum.' He had Tricia's fair hair and long face, while his brother had a round face covered in freckles and a cheeky smile that endeared him to Robyn immediately.

'Soz, Mum. I wanted to catch Josh. Hi.' He nodded at Robyn.

'That's Joshua and Ryan – the terrible twins. They're supposed to be doing their homework,' she said in a no-nonsense voice. 'Aren't you, boys?'

Ryan nudged his brother, who reluctantly paused the game and dropped the controller onto the settee. 'I haven't got much. Can we finish our game afterwards?'

'No. You should have done it ages ago when I was out. You know the rules – homework first. You can play again tomorrow. It's already late and you have school in the morning. Go on, hop to it.' The boys sidled out, leaving the women in the lounge.

'Sorry about that. They're good lads, really. They get a bit carried away once they're playing on the Xbox. It's addictive. I was up in the loft and didn't hear the doorbell. I wanted to get this photograph album to help explain.'

Robyn was surprised that Tricia was a mother to two boys. It had never crossed her mind that she would have a family as she seemed to spend all her life at the gym.

The front room was welcoming. Two large plump settees with several flattened cushions on them were facing a large television screen. A black cat lay zoned out on one of the settees, oblivious to

Robyn's arrival. There was a glass-fronted cabinet housing a variety of medals and trophies, presumably won by Tricia's children, and on the wall hung three black and white photographs of her with her two boys, all beaming at the camera and striking a range of poses. It was a far cry from the sort of place Robyn had imagined Tricia living in – a sterile flat with just the basics, much like her own home.

'Sit down and I'll explain.' Tricia dropped onto the settee next to the cat. 'I know this is going to sound far-fetched, but I genuinely believe Miles Ashbrook's death was no accident.' She took a breath and began her story. 'I met Miles when I was at university, way back in the nineties. We were on the same business studies course and ended up next to each other in a lecture one day. It was a dreadfully dull lecture and, halfway through, he passed me piece of paper with a noughts and crosses grid on it. I filled in my space and he filled in his and somehow we managed to spend the entire lecture playing the stupid game. At the end of the hour, we were told we were getting tested on the contents of the lecture the following day. Since neither of us had a clue what had been said, we had to ask for help from our fellow students. We managed to blag some notes from one of the really clever students, photocopied them and arranged to do a cramming session back at my flat. That's when it all began. That was the night Miles fell in love.'

Robyn watched as Tricia's face took on a faraway look. She opened her album and passed it to her. 'That's Mark.' The photograph was of a handsome young man with a chiselled jawline, a mane of blond hair that was swept back with some strands falling forward, and deep navy-blue eyes. Robyn was struck by the similarity between the man in the photograph and Tricia.

Tricia gazed at the picture. 'He was my brother – my twin brother. Twins run in the family. You've seen my pair. Mark and I were twins. We were very close, which was surprising given we

She tapped on Mulholland's door, unsure of what to expect. Louisa Mulholland was staring out of the window, hands behind her back. Her short dark-blonde hair, lit by the sunlight, revealed several grey strands. She turned to face Robyn, her face unreadable. Robyn noted the fresh frown lines that seemed to have appeared overnight. Louisa's eyes held hers.

'Go on, spit it out. I have a good idea what this is about. Let's hear your side of the argument.'

Robyn outlined her meeting with Tricia and her belief that the death of Miles Ashbrook warranted further investigation. When she had finished she remained standing. She had not been invited to sit. Louisa Mulholland nodded gravely before speaking.

'Here's my problem, DI Carter,' she began. 'Last night we had an incident in town where several victims were stabbed. I have been led to believe that it was not a random act and there is some sort of turf war going on between groups or gangs of young people. This is one of many senseless acts of violence that take place regularly on our patch. We also have several burglaries to handle, not to mention the numerous incidents which we are called to daily. Only yesterday you made an error of judgement when you went off half-cocked after a perp who turned out to be a visually impaired innocent.'

'I'd like to point out that I actually prevented officers from halting the vehicle, ma'am,' Robyn interjected, earning a steely look from her superior.

'Fortunately for you the matter was resolved, yet it is another example of you following an instinct which is not always accurate. Now, this woman you know might have cause for concern, but I put a highly respected officer onto that case and he informed me that Miles Ashbrook walked into the sauna of his own volition. I have also received the report from the autopsy, and Miles Ashbrook died of a heart attack most likely brought about by high temperatures and humidity from the sauna.'

Louisa's fingers interlocked and she tapped her thumbs together rhythmically.

'If you were me, DI Carter, would you allow your officer to hunt about on what is likely to be a wild-goose chase or would you deploy them elsewhere, possibly to one of the many areas where they are needed more urgently?'

Robyn squared her shoulders and regarded her superior with a confident air. 'I would allow the officer to follow their hunch and, if they did not turn up anything, send them elsewhere.'

Louisa breathed in deeply. 'You are not making this easy for me, DI Carter. I have already had DI Shearer in here complaining that you are not following procedure and that you have suggested he has not done his job properly. I don't want any bad feeling among my officers. I need you to work as a team. If I am seen to give you the go-ahead, it will appear I am choosing favourites, and there are no favourites in this station, just hard-working individuals.'

'Excuse me, ma'am, I spoke to DI Shearer before I came to see you about this. I most certainly did not suggest he had not done his job properly. I merely pointed out that there had been concerns, from a third party, that Miles Ashbrook had not gone into the sauna willingly. I didn't want to be anything other than open with him. I didn't do this behind his back.'

'I understand.' Mulholland turned back towards the window. 'Sorry, DI Carter. There are several case files for you to chase up on your desk and I'd like you to attend to them. I want them resolved. I can't allow you to pursue any line of enquiry into Miles Ashbrook's death during valuable police time.' She let her words hang in the air.

'Yes, ma'am, I understand,' replied Robyn, with a thoughtful expression on her face.

Soon afterwards, Robyn strode back into her office. Mitz was typing a report. Anna was working through some files.

'Anna, isn't it your day off tomorrow?'

'It is. I'm taking my dog for a walk on Cannock Chase, and after that I'm having a pamper afternoon – bath, book and wine – lots of wine.'

Robyn grinned at her. 'I have a better idea. It's my day off too. Why don't I treat you to a spa day?'

CHAPTER SEVEN

'This isn't quite what I had in mind,' complained Anna as she and Robyn squeezed into the office at Bromley Hall.

'I'll make sure you get a proper spa day if we uncover anything,' replied Robyn. 'Right. You're the computer whiz. Rewind the video surveillance footage right back to the night Miles Ashbrook died.'

'You're lucky they have this much footage. Normally it would have been wiped after twenty-four or forty-eight hours.'

Anna whizzed through to the section where Miles placed his clothes on the lounger.

'Those are the worst underpants I have ever seen,' she commented. On screen, Miles, with his back turned to the camera and in a pair of Union Jack boxers, strode to one of the showers outside the sauna.

'They're certainly unusual.' Robyn noted the times as the camera swivelled again to show an empty pool. 'Is that when he went into the sauna?'

'No, I think we see him again. I spoke to PC Gareth Arrow on DI Shearer's team and he said Miles was seen actually going into the sauna.'

The camera panned back to the ice room and then to the entrance to the sauna. Miles was walking towards it. 'There.' She paused the footage. 'That's him again in his jazzy pants.'

Robyn drummed her fingers soundlessly on her leg. 'Isn't it weird to shower in your pants? You'd think he'd have brought swimming trunks.'

'Must have forgotten them.'

A small sigh escaped Robyn. She couldn't put her finger on what it was that didn't feel quite right.

A man appeared at the door. 'Everything okay?' he asked. Robyn swivelled in her chair to speak to him. 'Fine thanks. DI Carter, Staffordshire Police,' she replied, digging in her trouser pocket for her warrant card. 'This is PC Anna Shamash. Just going back over footage for the night Miles Ashbrook died.'

'I thought Miles had a heart attack,' he said, casually.

'Just making sure we have covered all angles before we finalise the report, Mr...?'

The man extended a hand. 'Scott Dawson. I'm the temporary general manager. Also, the gym manager. Poor Miles,' he added.

Robyn shook his hand, noting the firm grip and clean, neatly cut nails on his tapered fingers. Davies had always had neatly cut nails too, she mused.

Davies always believed you could tell a lot by a man's hands and his shoes. Scott was shorter than her, with short, fashionably cut hair, spiked with gel, sharp facial features and light-grey eyes. His T-shirt, emblazoned with the hotel's logo, hugged the contours of his well-defined pectoral muscles. Anna threw him a glance and smiled at him.

'Have you reason to suspect his death was suspicious?' he asked.

'We're just covering all angles, Mr Dawson. How well did you know Miles Ashbrook?'

'As well as anyone can know a person who spends most of the day behind closed doors, running through budgets and targets. Miles wasn't one for socialising. It would have been difficult anyway, given he was brought in as an axe man. Everyone was wary of him. None of us knew who was next to get the chop.'

'Not an easy job. So, you didn't really know him?'

'Apart from the monthly meeting for managers, when we had to go through numbers, costings and so on, I rarely saw him. All the staff take meals in the canteen, so I bumped into him on a few occasions when I was on late shifts and he was eating dinner. He joked he had to eat at the Hall because he was a hopeless cook. I told him I ate here because Alex, my wife, is a hopeless cook. She isn't really. She's a great cook, but I can't go home at eleven p.m. and expect her to feed me. Besides, after training all day, I'm ravenous. I'd eat us out of house and home. The food here's very good, puts me back on track. I didn't banter with Miles much. He was the quiet, serious sort. He chatted about football though. Supported the same team as me – Wolves.' His face softened for an instant.

Robyn noted his wedding band. 'I expect, like for us in the force, the shifts can really eat into your home life at times.'

'Yeah. I'm lucky that Alex is in the same industry, so she understands. She's a beautician here, although she's part-time at the moment. One of us has to be able to look after George, our three-year-old. He goes to nursery in the mornings.' He twisted a leather-woven clasp bracelet on his wrist. 'So, what are you looking for?'

'As I said, Mr Dawson, just going over the footage.'

Scott nodded seriously, his eyes drawn to the monitor. He suddenly drew himself up as if realising he ought not to be intruding. 'I'll leave you to it. If you want me, I'll be in Miles's office. I mean, my office. It seems odd. One minute I'm running a gym, and now an entire hotel and spa. I don't think it's me. I'm happier shouting instructions to a group of exercise junkies, not staff and friends. Let me know if you want to go into the spa and I'll show you around.'

'Thank you. Actually, would you mind if I took a look on my own now?'

'I think we have several guests at the moment, although if you don't mind using protective footwear, you can wander about.'

Robyn winked at Anna. 'You'll be okay here, won't you?'

Anna nodded. 'Much more fun than sitting in a jacuzzi or lying in a steam room,' she replied, maintaining a serious face. Scott

in her head, then departed before it could settle. She eased open the door to the sauna and held her breath. The room smelt sickly and she was convinced she could detect the stench of burnt flesh. She glanced around, noting the stains on the floor where flesh had made contact with the hot wood and stuck to it. Lorna was correct when she said no one would want to take a sauna in here.

Robyn left the sauna and shut the door. It fitted snugly, but there was no lock to it. If Miles had felt ill, he could have opened the door and escaped the heat. The heart attack must have happened so quickly it had prevented him from doing so.

Robyn surveyed the scene once more. Attached to the wall of the sauna was a box, a temperature regulator, its display no longer lit. Robyn turned about once more. The humidity in the spa was getting to her. She needed to clear her head. A cough interrupted her train of thought. Anna stood by the exit to the changing room. 'Sorry, guv. Mitz rang me. He says DI Shearer is on the warpath. He's found out we're here.'

'How?'

'Mitz doesn't know. He says Shearer's got a face like a bulldog licking piss from a thistle.' Anna's mouth twitched.

'DI Shearer always looks like that. Did you find anything useful?'

'Didn't have enough time. I copied it all onto a USB stick to go through back at base.'

'Excellent. Okay, let's go.'

Robyn couldn't understand how Shearer had found out about her being there unless someone had alerted him. Either Shearer had charmed someone here and made a friend, or somebody didn't want her snooping. Her senses told her it was definitely the latter. Shearer couldn't charm anyone even if his life depended on it, which made this all seem even more intriguing.

CHAPTER EIGHT

Rory Wallis was having the day from hell. Not only had bloody Suzy phoned in at the last minute to say she couldn't do her shift, but then the Carlsberg had gone off and, while he was going into the cellar to change the barrel, he'd slipped on one of the steps and sprained his ankle so now it throbbed like crazy. The pub was hosting a party of revellers on a stag night. Rory wished they'd bugger off to one of the nightclubs. They'd been in the pub for the last three hours and had consumed so much alcohol it was amazing they could still stand. There were twenty of them and they were now playing yet another drinking game that involved raucous laughter and the downing of shots. His Friday night regulars had left much earlier, fed up with the noise the young men were making. Rory hadn't tackled them about their obscene language or the row because not only did they all look like front-row rugby props who would give him a good kicking if he yelled at them, they were spending money like it was going out of fashion, and heaven knew he needed that till to ring.

Business had been pretty lousy recently. It had been lousy all year, ever since people discovered coffee shops and started buying cheap booze in supermarkets. Two more coffee shops had opened near him in the last three weeks. There were now more cafés than actual shops in Lichfield, or so it seemed. And he couldn't blame the fact people weren't frequenting the Happy Pig on lack of income. They all had ample money when it came to buying takeaway coffees at two pounds fifty a go. He had to face up to it – spending habits were changing, and people today would rather have a *frappé latte* and a muffin than come into the pub for a quick pint. He raked a hand through his shoulder-length blond hair and heaved a sigh. The old days were gone, and now he was reduced to hosting themed nights to drag punters into the Happy Pig pub. The last bloke he had hired as Elvis had been dreadful. Even Rory could do a more passable impersonation of the great man.

It was impossible to keep turning a profit. Even a well-known brewery was shutting one of its pubs in the city. If they couldn't make it, what hope was there for the Happy Pig? Truth be told, Rory couldn't last much longer. The Happy Pig's days were numbered no matter what new idea he came up with: quiz nights, events or happy hours. The brewery had pretty much told him that unless takings went up in the next month, he was out on his ear and the pub would be sold.

Part of him didn't care. It was a nightmare working late some nights, then navigating his way back to the car park. Gangs of youths holed up in shop doorways would look at him through glazed eyes, bristling with testosterone and resentment, brains befuddled by alcohol. There seemed to be a fight kicking off most nights. They didn't try it on with Rory. He had adopted a look and stance that kept potential attackers away from him. Besides, most knew he ran the Happy Pig and might not ask them for ID if they went in to buy alcohol. He had to take business where he could, didn't he?

At last the stag party decided to move off, shouting and cheering as they half-carried the groom-to-be, now dressed in a pink tutu, through the door

'Thank you, gents,' he called after them. 'Come back again soon.' Rory breathed a sigh of relief. He would lock up and stack the glasses. That lazy cow Suzy could wash them when she came on shift tomorrow. She'd better show up or he'd give her her marching orders. He'd already made plans for his Saturday off. She was always taking liberties and calling in sick with 'women's troubles'. What about 'men's troubles'? He had plenty of those.

He bolted the front door. His ankle pained him further as he limped back to the bar, collecting a few empties half-heartedly as he went. He dropped the glasses on the bar with a clatter. On the counter stood an opened bottle of Moët & Chandon, and beside it a glass of champagne, bubbles rising. Someone was still in the pub – probably one of the stag boys playing a trick on him. He was about to call out in what he deemed an authoritative way, a 'no-nonsense yet able to take a joke sort of voice', when he felt warm breath on the back of his neck. For a second he wondered if he was imagining it. Before he could react, a voice whispered, 'Drink it.'

'Are you having a laugh?' he retorted, bravado building and masking his initial fear.

'Drink it.' The voice was more of a growl this time.

'Now look here,' began Rory. The rest of his words died on his lips as a knife was thrust into his line of vision. He recognised it. He had used it only that evening to chop limes for the stag's tequilas. 'You can take whatever you want from the till. I had a good night. Take it all and I won't say a word.'

'Drink it!' The voice – a man's voice – rose in anger. Rory picked up the champagne glass and downed it.

'Again. All of it. Drink all of it.'

Rory's hand trembled as he poured glass after glass, drinking every one of them in turn, each becoming more difficult to swallow, until the bottle was empty. His stomach gurgled in protest. He didn't much care for champagne, and certainly not in that quantity nor consumed at that speed. He belched. The champagne tasted sour in his mouth.

The man spoke. 'You have now made your payment in full.'

Emboldened by the alcohol, Rory was about to ask what the heck was going on when he felt the sharp point being pressed against his throat. Rory's brain scrabbled to comprehend as he felt his hair being tugged aggressively, forcing his head backwards. Rory felt a sudden warmth, as if he had spilt coffee down his front. He watched, eyes wide, as crimson spray misted the bar top and several glasses he had just collected. He wondered what it was, then slowly he realised it was his own blood. His attacker was sawing at his throat. All his terrified thoughts collided and Rory let out a high-pitched scream of terror that rapidly turned into a gurgle, before he slumped to the floor in a pool of warm sticky blood.

CHAPTER NINE

DCI Louisa Mulholland's office was on the fourth floor, overlooking the staff car park. Outside, PC David Marker was leaning against one of the pool cars and talking to Mitz. Periodically, small groups of dead leaves, fallen from the oak tree that stood outside the station, were being picked up by the wind and whisked past the pair. David was waving his hands while Mitz stood patiently, nodding from time to time. David was no doubt talking about football. A keen supporter of Stoke City, he could talk forever about the Potters. There was a transfer window, so he was undoubtedly pontificating on that subject or giving Mitz a minute-by-minute analysis of the previous week's match between Stoke City and Bournemouth.

Robyn continued to stare ahead. She had been listening to Louisa Mulholland although she didn't intend to take what her boss was saying too much to heart. This wasn't the first time she had been called out for taking matters into her own hands. Mulholland had lambasted her for involving Anna in her 'informal investigation' and warned her that as a DI, Robyn was expected to set a good example. Robyn thought solving crimes and thinking outside the box encouraged good policing, but she kept that thought to herself. Louisa Mulholland was saying this more for Shearer's benefit than her own. The man needed his ego massaging and Robyn would just have to put up with being in the doghouse for the moment.

Beside her, Shearer appeared to be having difficulty breathing. He blew his nose on a tissue and turned rheumy eyes in her direction.

It seemed he had lost a battle with the cold he had mentioned the day before and it was now taking a full hold of him. It had certainly not improved his mood.

'So, in brief, I expect my senior officers to try to get along, or at least appear to get along. I do not expect them to bicker and snipe, nor do I expect them to be anything other than exemplary in their conduct. Your officers look up to you. They respect you. Give them no reason to think otherwise. That's all.'

Robyn stared at Mulholland and gave a curt nod. Mulholland had a job to do. That was all. In her eyes, there was no time for office politics or infighting. There was enough fighting on the streets, as DCI Mulholland had been explaining at length. She had read through the list of unsolved crimes and even Shearer managed to look a little shamefaced at having brought his petty complaint to the chief officer rather than getting on with cracking some of them.

Mulholland dismissed them both and, once outside the office, Robyn held out her hand to Shearer. 'I didn't deliberately undermine you.' She meant it. She wanted to be fair. She had not intentionally set out to prove Shearer incompetent. She had merely wanted to do right by Miles Ashbrook, but Louisa Mulholland had given her a pasting about going off-piste with her investigations into Miles Ashbrook's death and made it clear that she was not, under any circumstances, to do so again. The case was closed, and Miles Ashbrook would be laid to rest in due course. Shearer grunted and accepted her hand.

He walked away. She called after him, 'Try a steam inhalation. It'll help with the breathing. Hot water in a bowl, and hold your head over the bowl, cover it with a towel and breathe in the steam. Add some eucalyptus drops to the water. They'll clear you up in no time.'

'Or, I could just hang out in the steam room at Bromley Hall,' he replied, with a small twitch of his lips.

'Might be dangerous,' she quipped. 'Don't want you to keel over.'
He snorted and blew his nose again.

Robyn left him to it and joined her officers. Anna was on the phone. 'Got that. She's just walked in.' She waved Robyn over. 'Matt's at the Happy Pig pub in Lichfield. Looks like the barman's had his throat cut.'

'Tell him I'm on my way.'

Robyn snatched up her car keys and sprinted from the office, all thoughts of Shearer and Miles Ashbrook gone. She yelled at her officers still chatting outside. 'David, jump in. We've got a body. Mitz, work with Anna and drag up as much information about the barman at the Happy Pig as possible.'

As she and PC Marker headed for the car she spotted Shearer standing by the front door. He snuffled into a tissue and dabbed at his streaming eyes. He seemed so miserable she almost felt sorry for him. That was before she remembered his torrent of abuse earlier. With luck, he had flu and would be off work for a few days. She had a sudden thought. *She* might not be able to investigate Miles Ashbrook's death, but she knew a man who could.

CHAPTER TEN

Ross Cunningham slammed down the phone receiver and fumed. It was times like this when he really needed a cigarette but, since his health scare two years ago, he had been adhering to a healthier lifestyle. Not only had he given up working for Staffordshire Police and set up a private investigation agency, he had also given up smoking and even allowed his wife Jeanette to change his diet. Gone were burgers and chips while out on a job surveilling a fraudulent insurance claim, and in were neat Tupperware boxes of salads. It was one of the Tupperware boxes he had picked up and hurled against the wall of his office beside his desk. It broke open, allowing the beetroot and quinoa salad to drip down the magnolia paint. Immediately he felt saddened. Jeanette had prepared it especially for him, had kissed him on the cheek as she passed it to him, informing him, 'If you eat up your salad, you'll get a special surprise tonight.' She'd accompanied it with one of her sexy winks.

Ross ignored the purple stain and lumps of what resembled tiny eyeballs on the wall, slumped onto his battered leather chair and reached for the bottom drawer. At this precise moment, all he needed was a cigarette. He was sure he'd left an emergency packet in the drawer. One wouldn't hurt.

As he rummaged for the elusive fag, his mobile rang. He snatched at it.

'Ross, if I asked you to do something that would really cheese off DI Shearer and probably Louisa Mulholland too, would you do it for me? I'll even foot the bill for your time.'

water and added some suds to it. He'd better clear up the mess he'd made. He examined the food, now mostly on the floor, and sighed. It wasn't like him to lose his rag. Still, it wasn't every day someone deliberately slammed into your car and made off with your laptop, which contained highly sensitive material.

CHAPTER ELEVEN

It was another grey, dull day. He blinked his eyes, sticky with sleep, and groaned. He hated grey days. They affected his moods badly, and today, he reflected, was one of those days where the clouds were so thick and heavy they felt as if they were actually resting on top of your head. He had forgotten to draw the curtains before he went out last night, and outside the morning commuter rush was well under way. Derby ring road was full of ordinary people, going about ordinary lives, oblivious to him.

He drew back the duvet reluctantly. The cold air rushed up to meet his bare legs as he sat up, stretching and yawning and trying to get some sensation into his mouth by smacking his lips together. His head was muzzy; his tongue felt as if it had been knitted out of coarse yarn. He remembered returning to his bedsit in the early hours, jubilant, blood coursing through his veins, and for a while he had felt more alive than he had since he had lost her. He had poured a glass of vodka, then another, and at some point his mood had changed and he had taken his pills. Had he drunk any more? He padded to the kitchenette adjacent to the bedroom-come-living room. The empty bottle of Grey Goose was lying beside the sink. He couldn't remember finishing it. He couldn't recollect how many pills he had taken either. All he could recall was the burning rage that consumed him from time to time, and that had flared up from nowhere and spoilt his happy mood.

He stretched his sore hand. His knuckles were grazed from where he had repeatedly hit the wall. A flash of memory. A neighbour yelling, 'Keep the fucking noise down.' More rage. He had been going downstairs to knife the bastard when he remembered the plan. He shouldn't draw attention to himself. He had to learn to keep a lid on his temper.

He blamed the vodka. It had always been the same when he drank. Some inner demon escaped and transformed him into an uncontrollable maniac. He had always had a temper. It went hand in hand with the huge 'black hole' days. The days when he no longer cared about his life, or anyone else's for that matter. Black hole days were the worst. He dreaded them. He never knew when they would appear, and when they did he was always powerless to fight against them. They sucked him in, drained him of all emotion except despair, and made him want to die. *She* had been able to keep him from falling into the black hole. Even the thought of her smile had always brought him back from the edge. Her laugh had kept black hole days away. She had been his very own guardian angel.

He ran the tap, stuck a dirty glass under it and drank the tepid contents. He needed to focus. The vodka had been a mistake. He had stolen the bottle from the bar after he had murdered Rory Wallis, unable to resist taking a souvenir of his first kill. He wouldn't make the same mistake next time. No more heavy drinking. Not until it was all over.

a large brown bib. His blond hair was hanging over his face and his head had fallen forward on his chest, as if he were snoozing.

Robyn knelt down beside him and examined the gash that began on the right-hand side of his neck. Pieces of jagged flesh hung from it. Whoever had done this had not been careful, or experienced in cutting throats. It had been hacked. Robyn lifted his hair from his face, trying hard to concentrate on her actions rather than the smell of defecation and urine. The man had been terrified. She studied his face, which was locked in a grimace, but she knew this was likely to be down to the facial muscles contracting, rather than fear. Rigor mortis had not yet fully set in, so she could assume Rory Wallis had been dead less than eight hours; however, the pathologist would confirm that.

She didn't want to move the victim's head before the pathologist examined him, so she got David to take photographs of his body. Then, as she stood to move out of his way, a stub of paper caught her eye. It stuck out from between the man's fingers.

'David, get pictures of this,' she said, before prising the slightly rigid hand open and sliding the paper out. She carefully unballed it. It appeared to be a bill. She held it up and read it. A gentle whistle of air escaped her lips. 'Okay, chaps – we've got something here. It's a typed receipt. It doesn't say what for:

INVOICE ONE: RORY WALLIS
PAYMENT NOW DUE
THE SUM OF TWO HUNDRED AND FIFTY THOUSAND POUNDS
£250,000

'Someone's scrawled "paid in full" in red ink over it.' She passed it to Matt. 'Bag it.'

Robyn walked the crime scene with her officers methodically to ensure they didn't miss anything that might be relevant.

'I want that champagne flute and bottle collected and checked too. This doesn't look like the sort of place you'd come to for a glass of champagne, and why only one glass? Bubbly is usually something you have for a celebration. You wouldn't come here alone to celebrate.'

The door opened, bringing in some daylight and Sam Gooch, a forensic photographer. Robyn was pleased to see him. In spite of his curmudgeonly ways, she had always got along with him.

'Well, if it isn't DI Carter and her merry men. I haven't seen you since we discovered that chap at the boarding school last year.' He was referring to a case in which a missing person had turned up dead with his genitals removed and stuffed in his mouth. It had been Robyn's first case following a year off. It had been what she needed to get back into policing.

'How are you, Sam?'

'Can't grumble, but will anyway. My joints hurt, I hate the cold and I'm sick of my grandkids turning up at the house every weekend and plonking themselves down as if they own the place.'

The fat grin on Sam's face told a different story. He meant none of it. He adored his grandchildren – two girls aged six and seven.

He pointed at Rory. 'This one's unpleasant. Haven't seen one like this in a very long time.'

Sam unpacked his equipment and began photographing the scene, turning the camera this way and that, moving in for close-ups as if he were taking photos of a model, not a body. The door opened again and a bald-headed man with a ruddy complexion entered.

'Morning, Robyn, Sam, chaps.'

Robyn had only met Harry McKenzie on a couple of occasions, and liked the Scotsman's approach to work. He was a highly regarded pathologist who treated all the victims he encountered with respect, as if they were in a doctor's surgery being examined for an illness. He rustled over in his paper shoes and knelt before the man.

'Sharp-force injury. The wound starts below the ear and ends on the opposite side of the neck, lower than its point of origination. In this case I would suggest the neck incision is compatible with a cut throat from behind by a right-handed person,' he said, talking to no one in particular as he studied Rory's neck.

Robyn waited with hands on hips. 'What weapon are we looking for?'

McKenzie carried on as if he were addressing a group of students attending a lecture. 'This looks to be an incised wound caused by a sharp weapon such as a knife, glass or metal.'

Anna nodded gravely. 'Can you tell from the wound exactly what weapon was used to kill him?'

McKenzie shook his head. 'I can't call that one yet. I'll examine the tissues and take measurements of the wounds.' He produced a rectal thermometer and began work on the body. Robyn moved off to allow him space to concentrate.

Sam padded about the room quietly, his camera making no noise as it snapped away at the gory scene.

David, who had been searching behind the bar, called out. 'I've got something. It's a knife.'

'Don't touch it! Sam, would you photograph the knife and entire bar area please?'

It was a serrated bar knife, about four inches long, with a pronged end. Its blade was stained brown.

'Good job, David. When Sam's finished, bag it and send it for blood analysis and fingerprints. Any idea of time of death, Harry?'

'Some time between ten p.m. and one a.m. would be my guess. His body is in the rigid stage. The body's muscles have contracted and, as you know, this normally lasts anything from eight to twelve hours, before the body becomes completely stiff.' He squinted at the man's face and sniffed. 'I can smell alcohol.'

Matt scribbled in his notepad. 'Probably had one or two while working. Must be hard not to when you're in this line of work.'

Someone tapped on the door. It was PC Howarth. David spoke with the officer, and returned a few minutes later.

'Got a statement from Suzy Clarke. She can't tell us much, except Rory Wallis was single and lived on the Boley Park estate. He'd been the manager here for four years. The pub is having difficulties and the brewery's threatening to close it. Both she and Rory had been looking for other jobs. There are only three members of staff who work here and the third member is on holiday in Tenerife at the moment. Suzy was supposed to take over from Rory at eight last night but she had stomach ache and called in sick. Rory wasn't happy and complained the place was heaving for once and a stag party was in. She could hear their noise in the background. Rory told her she owed him and that was that. She came in early to take a delivery from the brewery, unlocked the door, walked in and thought it smelt odd. She saw the lights on over the bar then spotted the body. She knew it was Rory because she recognised his hair. She belted out, locked the door and called the police.'

Harry squatted on his haunches, glasses perched on the end of his nose. 'Mr Wallis had a fall. His ankle's swollen. I think that happened some time before he was murdered.' He continued examining the body. Robyn joined him again. 'I suggest his neck was pulled back, making the trachea more prominent. The assailant ran the knife along the left-hand side of his victim's throat. There are incisions – hesitation marks – and then he or she sliced or sawed through the neck muscles, blood vessels and the common carotid artery which would have killed him. He might have lived one or two minutes after it was severed. There is damage to the rest of the throat area, but our victim bled to death from that wound.' He pointed to the large gash in Rory's neck.

Robyn nodded. 'Can we definitely deduce our assailant is right-handed?'

'It would appear so.'

Robyn faced the bar thoughtfully. 'Our perp might have appeared from behind and slit his neck. Harry, would blood spray from the wound?'

'In all probability. Once a carotid artery has been severed there is a likelihood of spray, especially if the victim's heart is racing. It would not last long.'

'Long enough to spray over the glasses. I'm going to leave all this to the forensic team. Matt, you stay here and assist when they arrive. I'll head back to Stafford and start gathering information about Rory Wallis. Thanks, Harry.'

Sam checked the quality of his shots. 'I'll come with you. I'm done here. Nice to see you again, Robyn. You were fortunate to find a weapon.'

'I always get nervous when things seem to be too good to be true. I bet we don't find the perpetrator's DNA on it.'

'You never know.'

David Marker appeared and cleared his throat. 'One last thing – Suzy told PC Howarth that Rory was teetotal. He never drank.'

'Yet there's alcohol on his breath,' replied Robyn. She shrugged off her protective clothing and rubbed at her forehead. 'Get that bottle and glass checked out as a priority.'

She left the building. In the street, officers were still keeping people at bay. In spite of the grey day, it felt lighter and brighter out here. She breathed in the air, dispelling the stench of death that had lingered in the Happy Pig. Robyn had the feeling that despite the clues, this would prove to be a difficult case to crack. She spotted a familiar face in the crowd: Amy Walters, a journalist with the local paper, was trying to attract her attention by waving at her. She ignored Amy and, stern-faced, got into the squad car and left the scene.

CHAPTER THIRTEEN

'I'm not going to report it to the police, so drop it.' Ross was visibly annoyed.

Robyn knew that Ross was not only worked up about the damage to his car and the loss of a laptop containing highly sensitive material, but was also furious with himself for not working out he had been set up.

'So, who could it have been?' she asked quietly.

'Given I'm working on an infidelity case, my money's on the cheating spouse. I reckon the guilty party got wind of his wife hiring me and sent his goons after me.'

There was more to this than just an annoyed husband. Robyn pushed him further.

'Who, Ross?'

He was reluctant to tell her. 'Never mind,' he replied.

'Ross, who is it? Come on, tell me.'

'Jason Nuttall,' he snarled.

'Jason Nuttall who runs the boxing club in Derby? Jason "Nutter" Nuttall?'

Ross crossed his arms. 'That's him.'

Robyn pursed her lips and exhaled slowly. 'Wow! That was brave of you, taking that job on. He's an out-and-out thug. He's got previous, Ross. What were you thinking?'

'Paying my mortgage, Robyn,' he replied. 'It's what I do. I get hired to solve problems – investigate infidelities, fraudulent claims. And Nuttall was a job.'

'Does Jeanette know?'

Ross shook his head. 'I didn't tell her about the case. I told her I got rear-ended and both the car and I are okay. That's all she needs to know, so don't say anything to her.'

'I won't, but only if you promise not to go after him. Tell Derbyshire Police what you know and leave it to them. Who dealt with it?'

Ross opened his hands in a resigned gesture. 'They're not likely to believe me now, are they? I didn't report the shunt. There were no witnesses. I was at the station roundabout when a black Audi drew up and hit the rear of my car. I got out to swap details and the car reversed. I thought it was going to pull into the side and we'd assess damage and sort it out, so I walked up to it. A bloke wearing a balaclava jumped out, thumped me in the gut, winding me completely, and then got back in the car and drove off. When I'd recovered my breath, I returned to my car only to discover my laptop had been nicked. I guess he had an accomplice who grabbed it while the man in the balaclava was thumping me. Good thing I had my mobile in my jacket pocket or they'd probably have taken that too. The police are not going to chase after Nuttall on that evidence alone. It could have been anyone. And, if they did interview Nuttall, can you imagine he'd suddenly confess to nicking my laptop? Come on, Robyn. You know as well as I do how this works – even if I tackle him, he'll claim to know nothing about it and probably send his goons around to smack me about a bit. I'll have to let it drop.'

Robyn suddenly wanted to punch Nuttall herself, yet Ross was right. It was wisest to walk away. 'And what about the whole infidelity business?'

'I'll tell Sheila Nuttall that I'm not able to continue working for her.'

Robyn felt for Ross. He wanted to do right by people, and she was sure Sheila was someone Ross would want to help out. Sheila was a quiet, petite woman who had fallen for Jason when she had been a teenager. Now, at twenty-five, she had four children under ten and another baby on the way. Sheila had brought them up single-handedly while her old man was in jail.

'What if we handled it differently?'

'How? If I stay on the job he'll find some way to punish me. This time it was the car and my laptop. Next time it might be me, or worse still, Jeanette. I'm going to drop it. Sheila will have to hire another private investigator.'

Ross ignored the look she gave him and pulled at a hangnail. 'Okay, tell me about this case. I could do with a distraction from this.'

Robyn explained what she had found out from Tricia and what little she had gleaned from the spa.

'Why are you so certain Miles Ashbrook was murdered?'

'Firstly, Tricia was convinced he would not go into a sauna. He refused to travel to hot, humid climates with her brother when they were an item. Secondly, he had a heart condition. If he'd intended to kill himself that way, he would not have undressed. He would have gone into a hot sauna fully clothed. And thirdly, the footage of him showering is plain bizarre. Why not get undressed in the changing room first?'

Ross flicked imaginary braces. 'Flimsy evidence, DI Carter, flimsy. Tricia might be right, but how do you know Miles just didn't like hot climates or travelling? If someone asked me to go to Borneo or Singapore, I might also refuse on the grounds of it being too humid. Not everyone likes humidity. He might well have a heart condition, yet is it likely that a few minutes in a sauna would aggravate it? He might have had a stressful day in the office and thought he'd unwind. He might have done this regularly, yet on this occasion he had a heart attack. Lastly, he might have wanted to keep his clothes nearby in case anyone spotted them and wondered what he was up to. I'm guessing it would be frowned upon for managers to be found enjoying the facilities at Bromley Hall out of hours. I rest my case, your honour.'

Robyn chewed at her bottom lip. 'Damn, you're right. Am I reading too much into this situation because I want Shearer to be wrong?'

Ross shrugged his shoulders. 'Far be it from me to say, but he does have a way of winding you up. And others.'

'I don't suppose it would hurt for you to go to Bromley Hall and get a feel for it yourself. Chat to Scott Dawson. He's taken on the role of general manager. See if you can get any information about the place or the people that might help me. At best, you'll uncover a possible suspect or reason for Miles Ashbrook's death, and at the very worst, you and Jeanette will have a nice weekend together.' She punched him lightly on the arm. 'It'll take your mind off "Nutter". You could do with a couple of days relaxing. It's not every day you get the chance to go and chill out at a top spa for free. All expenses paid. My treat, remember?'

Ross forced a grin. Robyn was giving him what he called a cheeky sparrow look, head bobbing from side to side. She may have very little evidence pointing at a murder, but she really did have a brilliant sixth sense. If she suspected foul play he would do his best to help her prove it. Besides, he wasn't one of Tom Shearer's fans either. He had had several run-ins with him in the past. Shearer was abrasive and cocksure. It wouldn't hurt if he were to be taken down a peg or two. He smiled at the prospect.

'Agreed. Now, I'd better go home to prove I am fit and well and have not been injured in my "accident".' He drew quote marks in the air with his fingers.

CHAPTER FOURTEEN

His head throbbed again and his entire body felt sluggish, as if it could no longer be bothered. He almost turned over and went back to sleep. The dream world was far better than the real one.

He'd been dreaming about her. She was running towards him at Stowe Pool. He was trudging around the reservoir, now used only for recreational purposes, ignoring the ducks that waddled around the edge of the water, quacking noisily as he strode past. His eyes were on the cathedral with its three spires. He wasn't at all religious; in fact, he was mentally scoffing at those poor misguided individuals who believed in a deity. As far as he was concerned, you lived and you died. There was no mystical power to direct, comfort or look after you. He'd proved it two nights earlier when he'd whacked his neighbour's cat over the head with a spade. That'd stop it crapping on his lawn. Where was God then? Certainly not looking after his creatures.

He dug his hands into his pockets and hunched forward to make himself a smaller target for the increasingly cold wind that was blowing in his face, causing his eyes to water, and continued on the path towards Lichfield centre. He wished he were wearing something warmer. The bloody weather forecasters had promised a mild day and he had left home in unsuitable attire – a pair of grey tracksuit bottoms and a light, long-sleeved top. He hadn't intended being out long. He had an appointment with the bank about debt consolidation again. There was no need to make an effort for the dopey twenty-year-old who would no doubt be assigned to deal with his 'problem'. He fished about in his pocket for a cigarette, then out of the corner of his eye spotted her. She was dressed even more unsuitably than him, in a tight fuchsia-pink jogging vest that read 'Believe in Yourself' and black leggings. Her glossy blonde hair was held back in a pink headband. He noticed her because she smiled at him as she ran past. Not many people smiled at him, and certainly none like her. She radiated warmth and kindness, and he knew from the second he saw her that he wanted her.

He woke with a jolt, perspiration on his face. No, they were tears. He'd been crying in his sleep again. The ache of seeing her in his dream and the torture of knowing she was gone had been too much for his confused mind.

Focus. He needed to focus. He didn't have much time. He rubbed at the damp patches on his cheeks, now angry. They owed him. They had to pay for their actions. And today was a pay day.

CHAPTER FIFTEEN

Robyn peeled off her running kit, dropped it into the wash pile and headed for the shower. Usually a run helped her think. Most of her best decisions and hunches had come to her as she pounded the streets. Tonight, the rhythmical slap, slap, slap of her trainers on the damp pavements had only served to remind her of Davies.

She enters the flat, face red from her efforts, and slips off her trainers. Davies is on the settee and greets her. A wrapper belonging to a family-sized bar of chocolate is beside him, and he has a giant grin on his face. She drops down beside him.

'I don't know how you stay so lean when you never seem to exercise.'

Davies pops the last piece of chocolate into his mouth and smirks. 'An overactive metabolism,' he replies. 'Or, too much stress.'

'You don't get stressed. You're the most relaxed man in the universe.'

Davies sits further back on the settee and drops an arm around her shoulders. He massages them, gradually easing the tension. 'You make me feel relaxed.'

Robyn laughs. 'Impossible, you calm me down. If it weren't for you, I'd be permanently wound up, like a giant coiled spring.'

'Then it's a good thing I am around. Can't have you uncoiling in the middle of a case.'

She feels the knots in her muscles being teased out and thanks the universe for giving her such a man.

*

Once showered, she dried off and, twisting a towel around her head, turban-like, entered her bedroom and sat on the edge of the bed.

She bent down and pulled out the drawer under her bed. The box was in the same place she had put it two years ago when she had tried to block out what had happened.

She lifted it onto the bed and ran a finger over the label on the lid: 'Family Photographs'. She had little family apart from Ross and Jeanette. Her chance to have her own family had been snatched from her. She opened the lid and removed the first few pictures. They were of her and Davies in Paris, taken on a Valentine's trip. Davies had surprised her with tickets and whisked her off on Eurostar for a romantic weekend that hadn't disappointed.

Robyn felt the warmth of happiness that accompanied the memories, tinged with a sadness that they could never be recaptured. However, Tricia had been right about having proper pictures rather than those on a phone or a laptop. The sheer fact they were tangible made the memories seem more real. She gazed at Davies's face, so calm, contented and dependable. She picked up the photograph, kissed her fingers and touched them to his lips. 'Who's going to stop me uncoiling now?'

She pulled out another, a photograph of them both with Amélie on holiday in Devon: Amélie standing on a pebbled beach, holding a bucket in the air. She'd been searching in rock pools and found a medium-sized crab that had waved its pinchers at her. She had triumphantly captured it and dropped it into her bucket, releasing it some time later. She was so like her father – curious, interested and always up for a challenge. That gave Robyn an idea for an outing with her. It could be ideal.

They had often had the girl to stay with them. Davies's divorce from Brigitte, Amélie's mother, had been amicable, and Brigitte had been extremely magnanimous towards Robyn when she learned she and Davies were dating. Amélie had taken to her too, and Robyn grew fond of the girl.

She replaced the photographs, unable to look at them all, and padded into the kitchen. On opening the fridge she decided she didn't fancy the paltry offerings inside. Instead, she got a cereal bar from the cupboard and sat down at the kitchen table, blank A4 sheets in front of her. She picked up a black pen and began writing. Davies had taught her to write down everything she knew when puzzling over a case. 'It'll focus your mind,' he had said. She began with the name Rory Wallis and the word 'invoice'.

CHAPTER SIXTEEN

Robyn had gathered her team together in her office at the station. She had spent most of Saturday night and all day Sunday wrestling with the Rory Wallis case. It had been forty-eight hours since he had been found dead and she was struggling to come up with a motive or find a suspect. Her deliberations had also been punctuated with thoughts about Miles Ashbrook and DI Shearer. She was taking too much on. She knew she was, yet she couldn't stop herself.

David Marker was the last to join them. He slipped in, mouthing 'Sorry.' She nodded at him and stood up. That was all the signal they needed. They sat quietly while she presented the facts.

'Rory Wallis.' She pointed to a photograph of a man with shoulder-length blond hair and green eyes, grinning widely, 'Manager and barman at the Happy Pig. You're all up to date with the basic details. What we don't have yet is our perp. Let's see where we are with this. Anna?'

Anna flicked through her notes and spoke with assurance. 'We spoke to his next of kin, Mrs Annette Wallis, his mother. She couldn't think of any reason he would be attacked. According to her, he was a quiet man who visited her every week and took her shopping on a Saturday when he wasn't working. He wasn't in any relationship, nor had been for a year. His girlfriend of ten years went to Australia after they broke up in 2013, and he's not had a serious relationship with anyone since. He didn't seem to have much of a social life either. He was a gamer and spent almost all of his free time online. His best friend, Stephen Cross, is also a gamer and lives in Barry, Wales. They only met up once or twice a year, although they were often online together. The world of gamers is vast, and Rory appears to have formed friendships online with people all over the world. Stephen confirmed Rory was very much a loner and had become something of a hermit after his girlfriend left him. Rory has a Facebook page, but he hasn't posted for over two years, so no leads there.

'He recently applied for a couple of positions at pubs in other areas. He was obviously thinking of moving on, which coincides with Suzy's statement. Both were looking to find new employment. The Happy Pig has been having difficulties for a year, and Rory received written confirmation that the brewery was considering shutting its doors.

'We interviewed regulars who frequent the Happy Pig and tracked down the stag party that was in the pub on Friday night. The group consisted mostly of local lads and we took statements from them all. We have yet to interview two members of the stag party, William Dixon and Kyle Copeland, who both live in Shropshire. They went to Amsterdam on Saturday night and are due back later today. In spite of being drunk that night, the majority of the young men were able to confirm that they left the pub at about eleven p.m. and moved on to Shenanigans nightclub. They were the last ones to leave and said the barman definitely locked the door behind them because they remember banging on it, for fun, asking to be let back in for one last drink.'

'So our victim was alone in the pub that night,' Matt commented. 'Or was apparently alone. At some point, he might have let someone in.'

'Or, someone else was already in the pub when he closed up?' Mitz fiddled with his pen.

Anna nodded. 'That's possible, Mitz. There is a back door that leads to a yard, although it would be almost impossible to scale the high wall and come in that way without being spotted. The wall backs onto a car park. The only keys to the back door were on the same key ring used for the front door.

'We took statements from the regulars. Most of them left early Friday night thanks to the noise from the stag do. None of them claimed to know Rory well. Comments ranged from "Barely spoke to him" to "He could be a surly bastard some days." One person said Rory seemed to have lost his passion for the job and that he used to be more enthusiastic. Most preferred it when Suzy was on shift. All in all, no one seemed to know much about his personal life, or had a lot of good to say about him.' Anna put the notes back on her desk.

Robyn spoke to the group. 'The coroner's report came through earlier and confirms Rory Wallis died through blood loss caused by a knife wound to the neck that sliced his carotid artery. The forensic toxicology report verified he had a very high blood-alcohol concentration, and there was sufficient evidence to suggest Rory Wallis had consumed several units of alcohol shortly before he was murdered. The bottle of champagne and glass both bore his fingerprints.'

She paused to let them digest all the information before pointing to the photograph of the invoice, also stuck on the whiteboard, along with the other crime scene pictures. 'We have a typed invoice for Rory Wallis for the sum of £250,000 and the annotation "paid in full". It would suggest that Rory paid the amount with his life. I want to know why. Who did he owe money to?'

Matt lifted his pad and spoke. 'We ran a credit check and came across nothing out of the ordinary. He had a mortgage that he paid off regularly, and he owed a couple of hundred pounds on his credit card, but nothing stands out. I searched his computer and smartphone history and he didn't frequent any gambling sites. He seems squeaky clean.'

Robyn stared at the board. 'Anyone got anything else on him?'

David Marker coughed to draw attention to himself and spoke quietly. 'I checked his employment history earlier. He completed a degree in social science at Keele University before taking a year out to travel. He returned in 2005 and worked at a pub in Hoar Cross and became bar manager at Bromley Hall in 2008.'

Robyn perked up. 'Bromley Hall?'

'He left there in 2013 and took up the position at the Happy Pig.'

'Did you find out why he left?'

'No, boss.'

She pondered this new information and wondered if the two cases could be linked in any way. It had to be nothing more than a coincidence. Rory would not have known Miles Ashbrook or come across him. Robyn was letting her desire to get one over on Shearer blind her. However, she didn't trust coincidences. This might be worth prodding.

'Look into that, please, and find out if Rory knew Miles Ashbrook socially, or from the past. Check with his mother and Suzy Clarke. Thanks.' She got back to the matter in hand. 'Rory Wallis was attacked and murdered by a person or persons unknown late on Friday night. He cleared the pub of customers by eleven p.m., then drank an entire bottle of champagne. Suzy confirmed they do not sell champagne, so either Rory or his assailant brought the bottle and glass into the pub. We have no idea of its significance. Were they celebrating? Did both drink from the bottle and afterwards did his attacker dispose of their glass? Or did Rory drink alone? Either way it seems odd, especially as he was teetotal.

'We have recovered the weapon that was used to kill him.' Again she pointed at the board and a photograph of a knife. 'The weapon had been wiped clean, so there were no fingerprints, full or partial, on it. No glove prints either. The lab confirmed there were traces of blood on the blade, along with ascorbic and citric acid.

The blood type was A-positive, not an uncommon blood group. The coroner confirmed Rory Wallis's blood type was A-positive. There is also a possibility the knife was one used by the bar staff. We asked Suzy Clarke to identify it and she admitted it looked exactly like the knife they use to cut lemons or limes. For the moment, this is all we have.

'I'm going to request a reconstruction of some of the events that night, to see if it jogs any memories. There must have been a few people out on the town who maybe saw somebody acting suspiciously, or spotted them enter the building after closing time. I want you, Mitz, to interview the regulars again and all the men on the stag night, including William Dixon and Kyle Copeland. They might have seen someone hanging about and forgotten about it. David, find out some more about Rory's work at Bromley Hall. Anna, could you check with the brewery? Ask about their relationship with Rory. I'm trying to establish if there was anyone at the brewery who might have dropped by to speak to him. Long shot, I know, but we need to look at every possibility, however bizarre. When you've done that, double-check Suzy's alibi for the night. Any questions?'

She dismissed her team and called Matt Higham over.

'I have one thing I can't work out. Can I run it past you?'

He nodded.

'Suzy was supposed to be on shift that night. How did the assailant know she wasn't?'

Matt pondered her question.

'Rory invited his attacker to the pub?'

She shook her head. 'He didn't make any phone calls from his mobile or the pub phone. The only call came from Suzy at seven thirty.' She leant back in her chair and tucked an invisible hair behind her ear. Matt thought some more. 'The perp was obviously casing the pub. He had been watching for the right moment. He didn't know it was Suzy's night to work. He saw an opportunity and took it?'

'That's what I thought. I think he seized an opportunity, which leads me to believe he didn't plan this.'

'What about the champagne?'

She tapped her fingers on her chin. 'If he suddenly decided to carry out the killing, on a whim, and his plan involved champagne, surely he would buy it from somewhere near the pub. He wouldn't be carrying it around for days waiting for a chance to carry out his plan.'

'Unless he had a car and kept it in the car.'

She cursed. 'You're right. He might have driven into town. Let's check the car park CCTV for that night and see if any there are any number plates that crop up regularly. Before you do that, see if any off-licences, pubs or restaurants sold a bottle of Moët & Chandon that night.'

'Okay, boss.'

She leant back in her chair again and shut her eyes. She couldn't get a handle on this case. She had no idea why somebody would murder a man and leave an invoice for such a large amount in his hand. A voice in the corridor made her sit up again, eyes now trained on the door. She watched as Shearer scurried past her office, talking into his mobile, looking very calm and efficient. She thought about Mulholland's words. She would make more of an effort to get on with Shearer, even though he really needled her. She ought to forget him altogether and focus on her case, and that was the problem. Although she was deploying all her team and they were doing what they could, it was becoming a frustration. She couldn't settle. Why had someone left a demand for quarter of a million pounds? What could Rory have bought or done to warrant that? Had he borrowed money from some moneylender who couldn't wait any longer to be paid? If he had, what had he used it for? There was no sign he had spent it. There were too many questions at the moment. She breathed in deeply and tried to clear her mind. What she really needed was a breakthrough in this case. Her thoughts skipped briefly to Ross. She knew she should be concentrating on the murder in Lichfield, yet she hoped Ross would uncover something useful at Bromley Hall.

CHAPTER SEVENTEEN

Linda Upton wrestled with the sleeve until a pudgy hand appeared.

'There, it's on. Now let's do it up,' she said brightly to her four-year-old son, who managed to look sulky and cute at the same time.

'Don't want to go,' he repeated for the fifth time. He held on to a toy dinosaur that he brandished at his mother. It was the same routine every Monday morning but Louis was being especially awkward today because of the plastic dinosaur skeleton that had just been delivered.

'Louis, you love school. And you have art with Mrs Simmons today. Maybe you could draw me another lovely picture, perhaps of a dinosaur for the fridge.'

The fridge was filled with colourful pictures of dogs, dinosaurs and cats that all looked very similar, with stick legs and brown ears. He gave her a pensive look. 'A big dinosaur. A terryansaurus.'

'Tyrannosaurus,' she replied, smiling at him as he screwed up his face to try the word again. He got it right and beamed at her. She gave him a squeeze.

'How about you draw me a big dinosaur at school and tonight we'll make up the skeleton together? Look, let's lay out the pieces on the table and you can put it together as soon as you get in from school.'

Louis gave her another heart-warming grin and collected the box containing the precious skeleton. He tipped the contents out, carefully positioning them on the table, studying the larger pieces of white plastic.

'There's lots of bones,' he remarked.

'We'll soon work out how they fit together,' she replied. 'That one looks like a long leg bone.' She pointed out a femur. Louis nodded wisely. He pulled out the instructions and laid them next to the plastic pieces.

'I get to make it and you can be my helper. You can read the destructions.'

She laughed. 'Deal. And they are instructions not destructions.'

She bustled the boy out of the house. He held her hand and chatted animatedly. She loved that he still wanted to hold her hand. One day, he wouldn't want to. However, no matter how old he was, he was always going to be her little boy. It was only a ten-minute walk to his school, and one of the reasons Linda and her husband had settled in Kings Bromley. She thanked her lucky stars that they had found a house so close to such a charming village school with nursery classes. Only seventy pupils, most of whom were local to the area, attended it, and it had excellent Ofsted reports year after year. Linda checked her watch. They were running late. It was almost 9 a.m. Louis's teacher was on duty in the playground. She had shepherded all Louis's classmates together and they were about to enter the school. As Louis entered the gates, a loud buzzer sounded marking the start of the school day. He scurried over to his teacher and joined the group.

'Hi, Louis. What's that you've got?'

Mrs Simmons was in her fifties – a rotund, motherly figure whose eyes crinkled with pleasure whenever she spoke to her pupils.

'Tyrannosaurus,' replied Louis with pride, waving the toy dinosaur at his teacher.

'Wow! We'd better take him inside before he scares all the children, eh?'

Louis joined his friend Harry and prodded him with the dinosaur. They fell about laughing and roared at each other. Then he headed inside, his mother forgotten as he entered the building. At the last minute he remembered, and turned and waved. Linda blew him a kiss, waiting for him to disappear from sight before she headed home, a smile playing on her lips. Her husband would be home tonight. He'd been away all week on business and she'd missed him. She opened her garden gate and walked up the path, thoughts on dinner, Louis and the dinosaur skeleton they were going to make up when he returned that afternoon. She wasn't aware of the man until she had put the key in the lock.

'In,' he whispered. 'No screaming or I'll kill you, and later today, your kid.'

He forced her roughly through the door and, dragging her by her arm, pushed her onwards into the lounge. She lost her balance and crumpled in a heap on the floor next to the table.

'What do you want?' she asked, voice quivering.

'Payment,' he replied.

Her face stared blankly at the man. There was some mistake. She didn't owe any money. Neither did her husband. They were fairly well off. No debts. This was a mistake. She was going to tell him so until she saw the look in his face. He was no debt collector. He was a killer.

'Please,' she began, heart pounding so loudly she thought even he would hear it. 'My little boy. He needs me. He's only four. Please don't hurt me. I'll do whatever you ask.'

He ignored her pleas and her eyes now filled with frightened tears. He had a job to do and time was running out. He cocked his head to one side, dark eyes glittering, and pretended to consider her request. For a moment, she believed he would let her go. She had no idea why he was doing this. She didn't recognise him. Who was he? Had he made a mistake in choosing her? Then, as he delved into his backpack, her brain registered the fact he had allowed her to see his face, making no effort to conceal his identity. There was only one reason for that. It made no difference to him if she could describe his appearance to the police. He was going to kill her. She had to act fast.

A dramatic burst of adrenalin fuelled her and she leapt to her feet while he rummaged through his backpack, knocking into the table covered with bits of plastic skeleton, and made a mad dash to the front door. She fled through the hallway, stumbling frantically, and put out her hand to grab the door handle. She was in reach. She had used the element of surprise. Once outside she'd scream as loudly as possible and rouse her neighbours, a retired couple, who were at home. As she touched the handle with her outstretched fingers, she felt a severe pain behind her knees, causing them to buckle completely. She fell headlong into the door and smacked her face on the floor. Her nose crunched sickeningly. Waves of agonising pain burned behind her knees. The fight drained out of her. Reality sank in. She was going to die and she didn't know why. Hot tears rolled down her cheeks. The man stood over her, brandishing a baseball bat. His mouth twisted into a cruel smile.

'Tut, tut. Naughty girl. Now you've just made it worse for yourself.'

'Why?'

'Your payment is due.'

'What payment? I haven't bought anything on credit.'

He pondered her response, tapping the head of the baseball bat against the palm of his hand. She hoped he was going to say she wasn't the person he thought she was. That he had made a mistake and he would let her go if she kept quiet about it.

'I won't tell anyone if you let me go,' she managed to blurt out.

He ceased his tapping as if coming out of a trance.

'If you've got me mixed up with someone else—'

He silenced her with a wag of his finger and whispered, 'Shh!'

She fought back the waves of nausea. The pain was terrible, although nowhere near as bad as the icy fear that flooded her body. He stared hard at her and tutted again.

'You owe payment. You haven't given it a thought since it happened, have you?'

She shook her head. It seemed to be the response he wanted. Her hands and body were shaking so badly she could barely react. She feared she might actually shut down, and if she did there would be no chance of talking her way out of this. He prodded her with the baseball bat and smirked.

'You've got a wonderful life and future with your little boy.' A snigger escaped his mouth and he shrugged his shoulders. 'Except there is no future for you, Linda Upton.'

She let out a squeak. He knew her name. There was no mistake. She babbled, 'No… Please, no. I'll make it better.'

His features changed again. He was bored with talking. He raised the bat and brought it down on her shoulder, making her scream out.

'Shut up,' he hissed. 'You can't make it better. It's too late. However, you can pay for it.'

Linda drifted towards unconsciousness and was only aware of him lifting her from the floor and carrying her upstairs. There was no point in struggling. She was dead already.

CHAPTER EIGHTEEN

Ross Cunningham chatted convivially to the porter who escorted them to their room. The man was in his mid-sixties, as he had been proud to tell Ross's wife, Jeanette. Jeanette had arrived at Bromley Hall in full 1940s outfit with faux fur collar over her tweed jacket and a retro victory roll hairstyle, which had provided a conversation starter with the man called Charlie. She now held onto her husband's hand tightly, squeezing it now and again to show support. She'd been in this sort of situation before, playing the quiet companion while Ross was on a case. She may have come across as the silent partner, but she was also taking in everything she saw or heard, ready to share information with him when they were alone.

Charlie talked enthusiastically about the history of the Hall, and had been most informative, although Ross had yet to find out anything to help him ascertain if Miles Ashbrook had been murdered. His efforts to steer the conversation in that direction had failed until Jeanette spoke up.

'I still can't believe you're sixty-five. Surely you must be thinking of retirement?'

'I wasn't, because I love this place, but I've been forced into it. The powers that be are doing away with us porters. They say guests don't need us to meet them, and gone are the days when we used to be really busy. I was forever organising limousines or trips into town for guests, or collecting them in the golf buggy from their helicopters. The management has already cut us down to two porters, and we're both part-time. You might have noticed Dan, the other porter. He was standing by reception when you came in.'

Ross recalled the solemn-faced young man whose arms had seemed too long for his sleeves and who wore a black beanie hat pulled tightly over his head. Ross had tried to engage him in conversation but the man had been called away by a member of staff, and Charlie had been sent across to accompany them to their room. Charlie carried on, 'Dan and me, we don't have the same sort of duties as we used to. We're more dogsbodies now. It's unusual to have us both on duty but we had to chauffeur one of the regular's wives about today in the boss's car. I let Dan do it. He's good at that sort of thing. He doesn't like chatting to guests so he's happy to drive them about in silence. I like people. I like getting to know the guests. Can't help it. I'm like that,' he said with a grin. 'These days though, I spend far too long hanging about the door doing nothing. Shame, really. I preferred it in the old days when we were always busy. There used to be two porters on every shift. The reception staff are going to take over the meeting and greeting part, and guests will have to wheel their own bags to their rooms. Dan and I are both leaving at the end of the month. It's all right for me cos I can draw my pension and enjoy some time off with the other half and the grandkids, but he's only in his thirties. He's a bit quiet like, you know? He doesn't sell himself very well. I can't see him easily getting another job. I don't know what he'll do after this. There aren't many jobs like this one about today.'

Jeanette patted the man's arm in a friendly gesture. 'It will take away some of the class not being met by someone like you.' He gave her a smile.

'It's lovely to meet someone as stylish as yourself, Mrs Cunningham. Took me right back to my dear mum. She was always dressed smartly like you, even when she was doing the housework.

Her hair was always immaculate, and when we went out she was a right bobby-dazzler.'

Jeanette chuckled at the old-fashioned expression.

'There've been a few changes the last few weeks. It affects the atmosphere, you know?' He whispered, 'You can tell when someone's been told they're getting the chop. They walk around with glum faces, or moan the odds about being let go. Me and Dan, we've kept quiet about it. We haven't told any of the staff here. We're not ones to socialise with them anyway. We're only the porters, after all. Besides, there's no point in dragging morale down any further. It's been depressing working here some days. There are still guests coming and they don't want to be greeted by miseries, do they?'

'Times are changing.'

'As they are everywhere. I don't mind. I've seen this place during its heyday. What's the reason for you coming here? Is it to de-stress?' he asked Ross.

'It's a belated anniversary treat. Thought we'd have a couple of days away together. It was Jeanette's suggestion. She said I'd benefit from time off work and being pampered. Never been to one of these places before. I always thought they were too girlie. What's the routine?'

Charlie gave a genial smile. 'You just pretend you're the lord of the manor for a while and enjoy yourself.'

'I'm not used to that. I'm not even lord of my own manor.' He laughed loudly, then whistled. 'This is very plush, isn't it?' as Charlie took them through the Long Gallery, a stately room with wooden panelling and large paintings of serious people. 'It's a proper palace. This is way out of my comfort zone.' He stared open-mouthed as they passed huge oil paintings and velvet-covered settees. 'I'm not sure what I expected.'

'Lord and Lady Bishton bought and restored it as close to the original house as they could,' Charlie explained. 'It took two years to get it to this standard. They had tremendous taste in furnishings and were heavily into antiques and period furniture. It was their passion. Lady Bishton travelled abroad regularly to find the perfect furnishings and the marble for the floors. They spent months researching the interior and took on a top designer to help them plan the perfect spa. Bromley Hall featured in all the glossy magazines when it opened up. We had some very special guests for the grand opening night.' He ran through a list of high-profile names, and Ross whistled again.

'You got anyone famous staying at the moment?' Jeanette asked.

'No. There's a minor royal from Saudi Arabia in the penthouse with a few of his entourage who's leaving today. He's been here a couple of times. No one ever sees him. He has a personal trainer, eats his meals in his room and his wives are escorted to the beauty salon by a bodyguard. Apart from them, there's no one well-known here now.'

'Do Lord and Lady Bishton still live here?'

'They have a house just outside the grounds, although they spend most of their time in Thailand now. They sold the Hall in 2014, after the new spa extension was built. It's not been the same since they left.'

'See, I'd have kept it just like this. It's a lovely hotel.'

'There's more money to be made if you can offer beauty treatments and a spa experience as well. Guests today want more than just a nice, comfortable room and a full English breakfast. The new owners took it on in the belief the spa and luxury hotel mix would be big selling points. For some reason it hasn't done as well as they hoped, hence the redundancies. The last few weeks quite a few heads have rolled. I shouldn't talk about it, but hey, I'm off soon, so what the heck!'

'I think it's beautiful,' said Jeanette, taking in the gold and red wallpaper, and the antique tables in the corridor. 'I quite like the idea of old and new.'

Ross gave a little laugh. 'I imagined spas just involved sitting around in a thick towelling gown, reading magazines or getting bored in a warm, chlorinated pool, watching my swimming trunks losing their colour and my skin wrinkle like the skin on custard, all while drinking glasses of vegetable juice. Jeanette says I'm a blinkered old dinosaur about such matters and she wants to prove me wrong. So far, I'm impressed.'

Jeanette smiled. She knew where the conversation was leading, and took her cue as they had discussed on the journey there. 'I told you – women and men come to spa hotels, Ross. It's quite normal. I don't know where you get your antiquated ideas.'

Ross nodded in agreement. 'I guess I just find the whole idea alien. Do you get many men coming here, Charlie?'

Charlie chuckled. 'I know what you mean. I've been here years and I've never actually experienced a spa day. There are more male visitors than you'd expect. The younger generation are far more open-minded about having facials and treatments than my genera-tion. We also get quite a few couples, like you, who come along and spend some time chilling – that's the modern-day expression for it, isn't it? I often see the men using the gym more than the women. They also seem to like the sauna and steam rooms. They're supposed to relax you. You'll have to try them.'

Ross lowered his voice. 'Not sure if this is true, but I overheard someone say that one of the chaps here had a heart attack in the sauna.'

Charlie frowned. They reached their room and he showed them in. 'It wasn't one of the guests,' he replied after the door shut behind them. 'I'm not supposed to talk to the guests about it, but I don't want you put off by what you heard. It wasn't a guest who died. It was the manager of the hotel. He had a sudden heart attack. I don't think it was related to anything to do with the sauna.'

'Gosh! I bet that upset the guests who were in the spa at the time. What a dreadful thing to happen.'

Ross pulled out a ten-pound note and handed it to Charlie, who refused it.

He shook his head. 'That's too much, sir.'

'Go on, put it towards buying something for the grandchildren for Christmas.'

Charlie pocketed it with thanks and continued talking. 'It happened late at night, so no one knew about it until the following morning. The spa is out of bounds after seven, so nobody came across his body until the cleaner found him. It's okay though. The sauna has had a deep clean and you wouldn't even know it had happened.'

'I'm not squeamish. I'll give it a go. However, if I fancy nipping to the pool for a spot of skinny-dipping after seven, I can't?' He grinned at Charlie, who responded with a chuckle.

'That's right. The spa is open from nine a.m. to seven p.m. The door automatically locks out of hours, and only staff with access keys can get in, so I wouldn't go skinny-dipping if I were you, Mr Cunningham.'

'That's scuppered my plans for the weekend,' joked Ross, slapping Charlie on the back. 'Unless you have an access key?'

'Sorry. I'd have to be management to get an access key. We're like you – we only have day passes.'

'It was worth asking. Thanks for making us so welcome. I think I'll be okay here. I thought I'd feel like the proverbial fish out of water.'

'I'm sure you'll enjoy it. What with this lovely lady to share it all with,' he said, bowing to Jeanette. 'The bar opens at six and dinner is at eight.'

'No vegetable juice?'

'Only if you request it. They have a good selection of beers in there.'

Ross kept up the camaraderie. 'Excellent news. I know where I'll be hiding out this weekend. Thanks, Charlie.'

Charlie grinned back before leaving with a cheerful 'Enjoy your stay, Mr and Mrs Cunningham.'

Once the door had shut, Ross peered out of the sash window at the manicured lawns below. 'Tasty here, isn't it?'

'Very nice,' replied Jeanette. 'What are you planning on doing?'

'Continuing my "hapless husband who isn't sure what to expect" routine and seeing if I can get any info on Miles. There are twenty-two rooms and, according to Charlie, only eleven are occupied, including the penthouse. Some of those guests have been here a few days. I'll work on the gym staff and find out some more about Miles. I'm booked in for a personal training session in half an hour. The things I have to do in the line of duty,' he sighed, dropping onto the king-sized bed.

'Think of all the dessert you'll be able to eat tonight if you burn off enough calories,' replied Jeanette, unzipping one of the bags Charlie had deposited on a stand, and pulling out a swimming costume. 'I'll start in the spa. I'm sure I'll find someone to chat to. Who knows, they might have been here a couple of days and like to gossip.'

'That's my girl.'

At the gym, Ross was met by Brad Turnpike, whose wide smile and upbeat nature was infectious.

'Mr Cunningham?' he asked, holding out a huge hand that completely enveloped Ross's. 'I'm your trainer today. I'll have to run through a few preliminary things first to make sure you're okay to train, and we'll get started.'

Brad turned out to be far cagier than Charlie, and all Ross learned was that the gym had three members of staff, recently reduced from six. They took instructions from Scott Dawson, the gym manager, who – Brad let slip – had not always seen eye to eye with Miles Ashbrook, the manager who had been responsible for the sackings.

Brad had been at the gym for four years, the longest-serving member of the team apart from Scott. After half an hour, he revealed he too was planning on leaving and was waiting for the outcome of test results to get into the fire service. 'Pay will be double what I earn here,' he confessed, as Ross persisted in questioning him. 'It's a pittance here – little wonder staff don't stay. Shame, because we used to have a decent team, until management began axing the staff and messing about with work schedules. I don't think I'll be sad to leave now.'

Ross left the gym sweating profusely and under the distinct impression that Miles Ashbrook had made quite a few enemies at Bromley Hall.

CHAPTER NINETEEN

Robyn pinched then rubbed the bridge of her nose. 'Nothing? Nothing at all?'

Mitz continued in his usual calm voice. He knew his boss was getting angry at the lack of progress in the case, but he could only present what he knew. The two men they had interviewed had been nonchalant and cocky. They hadn't cared that a man had been murdered. They had sat in front of Mitz with sneers on their faces. It had not been an easy interview, even though neither of the men were suspects. 'Dixon and Copeland couldn't remember much about the night. They recalled a "grumpy bastard who told them to keep the noise down" and they remembered being hauled out of the Happy Pig by their mates and mooning in the street at a couple of girls. However, they couldn't even describe the women.'

'Useless! I suppose they were too far gone to pick up on any strange activity. So, we have no witnesses at all. There's nothing untoward on the car park CCTV. What the heck happened? How did the attacker get in the pub and why did no one see him going in? We'll have to hope the TV reconstruction this evening brings in some information.'

She crossed the room to her desk. All her officers were working flat out. If they couldn't unearth something soon, she didn't know what she'd do. She didn't want to stand in front of DCI Mulholland and say she had no idea why Rory Wallis had been killed. Her phone rang and she answered curtly. She recognised Shearer's voice immediately. His words sent an icy frisson through her. 'Carter, I have a body that might relate to your investigation. Care to join me?'

It was an average-sized bathroom, clean and fresh with fluffy blue towels hanging on a rail beside a cream bath. A wind-up frog and submarine were propped up on the side of the bath, waiting for their owner to play with them. A plastic bottle of bubble bath was lying in one of several small puddles on the floor, a plastic fish and several colourful plastic boats were scattered about, and in the bathtub now half-filled with water lay Linda Upton, still in her underwear, her lips a shade of blue, and her bloodshot eyes wide open.

'Judging by the mess on the floor, she struggled hard.' Shearer's face seemed more lined than usual. 'Pathologist reckons she suffered several injuries before the assailant hoisted her into the tub. She was hit behind her knees and across her shoulder with some force by a blunt instrument. There's no weapon in the bathroom, although we'll obviously conduct a thorough search of the entire house inside and out.'

She was overcome by an overwhelming sadness. This was a defenceless woman who had been brutally attacked and killed – a woman with a young child. She couldn't understand the mentality of someone who could be so barbaric.

Shearer sensed her mood and did not come out with any of his usual quips or comments. 'We shall have to wait for the forensic post-mortem to establish the cause of death. I think at this stage we can assume she drowned in the bath, and that it was no accident.' He folded his arms and waited for her to respond. A small cough alerted her to the presence of Harry McKenzie. He stood by the door. When she turned, he spoke. 'Mrs Upton had been fully clothed, including outdoor clothes and shoes. These were clearly removed by force. They were left in a pile in the bedroom. As you

can see, she's only wearing underwear. It is difficult to say if she was
sexually assaulted without proper examination. Her body displays
several areas of haemorrhaging where she was attacked with a blunt
instrument. When I arrived, she was lying on her side as she is now,
but I believe she was held face down underwater until she was dead.
Judging by the angle and swelling, her nose was broken before she
drowned. A forensic toxicology report will determine if she had
been taking any pills or alcohol and accidentally drowned. I think
it is unlikely she drowned herself. There is significant evidence that
she was hit, injured and attacked before entering the bathroom,
although at this stage we have to take everything into account until
the evidence speaks to us. I'll get on to this immediately.'

Shearer nodded. 'Thanks, Harry.' He and Robyn moved away
from the bathroom and into the hall, where she spotted a sit-on
toy fire engine. She felt her heart sink further. Some child was now
without his mother. She couldn't shake the sorrow that accompanied
that thought. Shearer spoke. 'My lad had one like that.'

'Fire engine?'

'Yes, when he was little. He loved watching *Fireman Sam*. We
bought him a fire engine just like that and he went up and down
the house on it all day. He used to make a siren noise too. Drove
me mad.' His eyes told a different story. She had no idea he had
a son. This was a Shearer she didn't know. She felt compelled to
continue the conversation.

'How old is your son now?'

'Nineteen. He's at university. Doing some pretentious subjects
that'll land him a job in politics. He went off fire engines. I don't
understand his world any more. He's into rap artists I've never heard
of, and technology that is beyond me. They all grow up too soon.'

'What about the boy here? Where is he now?'

'With his dad and grandmother. His teacher alerted us. Linda
didn't come to collect him at home time. Mrs Simmons, the teacher,

became concerned and rang Linda's mobile. When she couldn't raise her, she walked here, saw Linda's car outside and rang the doorbell. When she got no answer from that, she phoned us. The front and back door were locked when we arrived. There was no sign of a forced entry. The neighbours saw her accompanying her son to school. They didn't see her return because they were watching breakfast television. My team is doing door-to-door questioning.' Shearer shifted uncomfortably. 'I found this around her neck. I spoke to Mulholland and she told me to call you.'

He passed her a red plastic waterproof container on a red cord. 'It's for storing cards, money and keys when you go swimming to keep them dry and safe. Open it.'

She popped open the container and withdrew the piece of paper inside. She had already guessed what was written on it. She unfurled it and read,

INVOICE TWO: LINDA UPTON

PAYMENT NOW DUE

THE SUM OF TWO HUNDRED AND FIFTY THOUSAND POUNDS

£250,000

She sighed deeply. This was undoubtedly related to the killing of Rory Wallis. Robyn studied the demand left with Linda's body. The fire engine on the landing was a stark reminder of how great the loss would be to this small family. How many more motherless and fatherless children, and how many invoices were there going to be before she tracked down the killer?

She descended to the lounge, where scattered pieces of plastic lay on the rich burgundy carpet. The room was tasteful and homely, with light-grey walls and comfortable settees. She sighed again when she spotted a teddy bear sitting in the corner of a chair, another sign that this was a family home. She steered around the pieces of plastic and noted the diagram of a dinosaur skeleton on the table. The more she searched, the more evidence she saw of the boy: children's DVDs stacked neatly on shelves, and toy cars parked alongside china ornaments. There were photographs of the family lined up along one shelf: auburn-haired Linda with a healthy glow, arms wrapped around a small boy, both giggling; pictures of the three of them at the zoo, in front of an elephant enclosure. There were other photographs of her and her husband on a beach, eating dinner at a restaurant and at a friend's wedding, and one of Linda with a friend in running gear, holding up medals after a Race for Life event. In it, Linda had shorter hair and was plumper. Her friend was willowy and blonde-haired, with the body of an athlete; both wore pink ribbons in their hair.

Robyn turned away from the photographs and took one last look around. The whole house would be taken over by forensic officers now. She would leave them to it. She glanced once more at the broken pieces of the dinosaur, wondering who could be so cold-hearted as to murder a woman who had a child. Whoever he was, she vowed to catch him.

CHAPTER TWENTY

He was growing ever closer to her. He knew it in his heart. He could feel it in the very marrow of his bones. He could hear her calling. The pills that eased the pain in his head had made him drowsy and he couldn't focus on the television programme. The presenter's face seemed familiar – blonde hair to her shoulders and fine features just like hers. The more he squinted at her, the more convinced he became that it was his love. He blinked several times; however, his vision remained blurry. He shouldn't have mixed his pills and beer. At this rate, he'd end up killing himself and wouldn't fulfil his promise to her.

His mobile showed it was 9 p.m. The fact the room was in darkness also proved it was nine at night. He'd taken some tablets and washed them down with some beer. He couldn't recall why. Was it something to do with hurting somebody? Ah yes, Linda Upton. He savoured the sketchy memory of raising the baseball bat and the sound of her shoulder shattering, her weak cry. She was so feeble. She gave in too easily.

As he'd carried her upstairs, she'd been no more alive than a marionette. No doubt she had thought he had wanted her body. That made him wince. He'd never wanted anyone less. Even when he yanked at her clothes, turning her this way and that, removing the garments one by one, tearing at the buttons of her blouse that would not undo easily, revealing a lacy bra, he had not desired her. Then, when she had stared blankly at him and shuddered at the thought he might force himself on her, the rage descended. How dare she! He had grabbed a handful of her hair, yanked her from the bed and into the bathroom. She'd whimpered like a child and obediently waited on her knees while he ran water into the bath, desperately trying not to launch a volley of blows on her feeble body. He had to control his urges until she climbed into the bath at his demand, uncomprehendingly. Maybe she'd hoped he would let her go. She had knelt in the bath as he commanded, and only when he shoved her face in the water had she put up any fight, although by then it was too late. He forced her head into the tub, bashing her already broken nose into it and ensuring she took great gulps of water until she kicked and flailed no more. The memory made him smile again. She'd got her comeuppance. On getting home he'd had a drink to celebrate and then another, and he'd fallen unconscious in front of the television.

He couldn't remember when he'd last eaten. It might have been the day before or maybe the one before that. Sometimes he lost track of normal actions like eating. He ought to eat. It was Monday night and he had work the next day. He shuffled into an upright position and his head swam. He wanted to lie back down on his couch and return to the dream world, but he couldn't. On the television, the presenter was smiling, revealing teeth so white they hurt his eyes. Now he could see properly, the presenter was trashy in her glittery dress, with her breasts straining out of the low top. In an instant, he became angry. How could he have thought this woman even looked like his beautiful angel? He hurled the remote control at the television and it hit the screen with a thud and fell to the floor. There was no damage. He wouldn't have cared if there had been.

He pushed himself onto his legs and swayed. The room spun for a moment. How many pills had he taken? Six cans were strewn on the floor and the smell of stale beer hit his nostrils, making him want to gag. The room was in darkness apart from the television, whose blue light flickered on and off like a lazy disco light, throwing random shadows against his walls. He stumbled against a small table and swore. Reaching out a hand, he fumbled for the light switch and shut his eyes when the bulb that hung above the couch lit up. He glanced around the room, making a mental inventory, reminding himself of what he had become: beer cans, a faded couch with worn-out patches, a second-hand television, a small, scratched table. He didn't care for possessions – the most precious thing he had ever owned had been taken from him, and nothing would ever replace it. The television flickered, spreading light over the walls and the hundreds of photographs of the woman covering them.

He shuffled into the kitchenette – a galley kitchen just off his bedroom. It contained the bare essentials: a sink, a fridge, a microwave, a gas cooker, a kettle and a toaster. He opened the fridge and wrinkled his nose at the sour smell. He had forgotten to throw away the out-of-date milk again. A piece of unappetising cheese, a half-eaten can of beans and a Cornish pasty sat on the shelf. He grabbed at the latter, removed the cellophane wrapping and bit into the pasty, chewing thoughtfully as he tried to focus. He had been out of it for over a day. He had to build up his strength. He glanced at the calendar beside the fridge – a large, red letter 'X' was placed beside the twenty-seventh of November. He chewed some more. The pasty tasted of cardboard. He ran the tap and tried to wash down the lumps of meat and pastry stuck in his mouth. After a while he gave up and put the remainder back in the fridge. He drank some more water, slowly tracing the letter X with his finger. He didn't have long left.

CHAPTER TWENTY-ONE

Mitz took the call from journalist Amy Walters.

'I wondered if you could give out any details about the murder of Linda Upton?' she said smoothly. 'DI Carter was seen at the scene of the crime, which begs the question, is it linked to the murder of the barman in Lichfield, Rory Wallis, four days ago?'

Mitz growled 'No comment' and slammed the phone down. 'How did she get through?' he asked Anna.

'Who?'

'Nosy Walters, the journalist for the *Lichfield Times*.'

'Talk to reception 'bout it. They're not supposed to redirect journalists' calls to us. She must have blagged her way through. You'd better warn the guv. She won't be pleased.'

Mitz strode past her desk and leant against the door jamb, a cup of coffee in his hand. His brow was furrowed in concentration. It had been a long few days and the briefing earlier had been disappointing. They had not come any closer to establishing a link between Rory Wallis and Linda Upton, nor had they any leads on who might have committed the heinous acts.

The office was empty apart from Mitz and Anna, who was reading through statements relating to the Linda Upton case. Heaving a deep sigh she said, 'I can't believe that nobody spotted a stranger in the area. It's a village, and I thought people in small villages always knew what was going on. They're usually tight communities, aren't they?'

'Times have changed. Villages like Kings Bromley are now filled with people who used to live in cities like Birmingham. Some don't even know who their neighbour is. Gone are the days when they all used to hang out at the village hall for community events and knew the moment there was a birth or death.'

'It's almost unbelievable. We have two murders and no one saw a thing. They didn't notice a strange car. That can't be possible. I always spot if someone parks in our "owners only" car park.'

'That's because you're an observant police officer,' replied Mitz with a grin.

Anna ignored his comment, lost in thought for the moment. 'There must have been people walking their dogs, or coming back from school having dropped off their kids, or driving by or catching a bus…' She stopped mid-sentence. 'Buses,' she repeated, slowly. 'I need a bus timetable.' She leapt across to the computer and bent over it, typing furiously. Mitz joined her. She pulled up the bus routes and read through them.

'There aren't many services through the village. There's a bus to Burton-upon-Trent at seven forty-five in the morning, another at midday and two in the afternoon. There are buses going to Lichfield at seven ten, another at ten fifteen, and two much later in the day. What if our perp arrived or left on a bus, and was seen at the bus stop in the village? How far away from Linda's house is the bus stop?'

'It's near the crossroads on the A513 and her house is in the other direction, off the A515. It's not far. It's about five minutes from her road.'

'I know it sounds crazy, but we ought to take a look at it and maybe even speak to the bus depot. Many of the passengers on these local routes are regulars. There could be a chance a driver recognised a new face.'

Mitz patted her on the shoulder, a warm gesture. 'Good work. I wouldn't have thought of that. Fancy going to check it out?'

Anna scraped back her chair. 'You bet.'

*

Robyn was with Mulholland in her office. Shearer had been gracious for once and had handed over his findings from Linda Upton's house without hesitation. 'Good luck,' he had said. 'Not that you'll need it. You'll find whoever is doing this.' She reserved judgement. Shearer was not normally this accommodating, nor was he one to mellow with age.

It was too warm in the office. She was feeling uncomfortable and wanted to get back to work, not hang around. She hated wasting time, and every minute in front of Mulholland was a wasted one. She'd rather be with her officers.

Mulholland crossed her legs and tapped the Rory Wallis file with her finger. 'Not much progress then, DI Carter?'

She stared at the photograph of PC Louisa Mulholland receiving a medal for bravery. She was twenty years younger in the photo-graph, petite and almost frail. Little would anyone imagine she would go on to be the chief inspector of a busy station. Mulholland had faced many challenges in her life, including being widowed at an early age, but she continually threw herself into work and was obsessive about results and catching criminals. It dawned on Robyn that there was hardly any difference between them. Work had become their lives and their driving force. It was what made them get up each day and what occupied their thoughts. She understood the tone in Louisa's voice – it was impatience mingled with hope. She knew Mulholland was counting on the famous gut instinct she was renowned for, although on this occasion the familiar voices that guided her remained silent.

'I'll admit that, right now, I'm at a loss. I've got my officers going back through statements and tracking down anyone who might have been in town the night Rory Wallis was murdered. We've spoken to all the off-licences in the vicinity and even the large supermarkets at the top of Green Hill Road to see if anyone recalled a man buying a bottle of Moët & Chandon. We've interviewed every possible person who was in Lichfield that night. Similarly, we've interviewed all the residents in Linda Upton's street and along the main road in the hope they spotted a stranger's vehicle or unusual activity. Anna's been through mobiles and laptops, from both victims, trying to establish if there was any communication between the pair, and searching for anything that might help us. Matt's tracing the owners of the vehicles that were in the car park at about the time Rory Wallis was murdered. The television reconstruction we set up at the Happy Pig didn't herald any useful leads and we wasted manpower chasing up every call we received.'

Louisa Mulholland shook her head at this news. 'I'm not sure how much longer I can keep a lid on what's happening. The press are baying for information, and I don't want to have to admit the two cases are linked at this stage. Amy Walters from the local paper has called twice today. Each time I told her I was not willing to talk to her, or to any member of the press. People will get very nervous if they believe there's a serial killer out there. Tell me you have something, anything, so I can throw them a crumb to keep them appeased.'

The room felt stuffy, even though it was November and cold outside. Robyn suddenly had the urge to get some air. She needed some space. Everything was happening too quickly, and the killer wasn't giving away anything to help them find him. She felt a prickle on the back of her neck. That was it; the killer was working quickly. There were only three days between murders. This debt he felt people owed was now due, and he wasn't wasting time in killing those people who owed it. She had to work out what it was that he valued at £250,000 per death. She licked her lips and pressed them together. 'Give me twenty-four hours and I'll have something.'

Mulholland stared hard at her. She picked up the files and passed them over. 'Twenty-four hours and that's all. We need to be seen to be on top of this. If you can't bring me anything, I'm handing the case over to DI Shearer.'

Back in the office, Robyn slammed the files onto her desk. Her twenty-four hours had begun. She hoped she hadn't taken on too great a challenge. If so, she would have handed her case and any chance of promotion over to Shearer.

CHAPTER TWENTY-TWO

She ran towards him, her face glowing, arms outstretched. He waited by their bench; the place where they had first sat and chatted. It had been another cold day and he had already walked the dog around Stowe Pool four times in the hope of seeing her. He was beginning to feel a familiar drumming in his temple which heralded one of his headaches. If she didn't turn up soon, he'd get the red mist. Stacey had been surprised and suspicious when he offered to walk the dog. Ordinarily he couldn't be bothered with the stupid animal. Stacey cheesed him off with her silly girlie voice and the way she hugged the animal, calling it 'baby' all the time. Although she was slightly wary of his motives in taking it out, she let him, grateful for some respite from him.

He dragged the dog – a white, West Highland terrier – down to the pool, impatient to see her again. The dog trotted eagerly by his side, small pink tongue out. He was ambivalent to the creature but today he needed it to play its part in attracting her attention. He dragged on a cigarette to calm his nerves as he stood by the bench. Alfie the Westie sniffed about the grass and pulled on the lead. He was fascinated by the ducks that waddled near the water's edge, their green and blue feathers glossy in the morning sunlight. He was banking on Alfie.

Suddenly she appeared from the direction of the cathedral as she always did, and turning right, began to run around the pool. She would not have spotted him yet. She would round the boathouse and pass the playground before she would have him in her sights. Timing was everything. He opened the plastic bag of bread he had prepared earlier and threw the crusts to the ducks. With frantic quacking, they waddled towards the food, pecking and quacking in excitement. Their noise alerted more ducks, who flew and skidded along the water, wings flapping wildly in their haste to join the others feeding. He counted silently. He knew how long it would take her. He had watched her many times. Thirty-five – she would have passed the boathouse now. Forty-four. She'd be running past the playground and be only ten paces from rounding the bend and spotting him. He bent down and unclipped an excited Alfie, who had been tugging at his lead to reach the ducks, and whispered excitedly, 'Ducks, Alfie. Fetch!' Alfie raced off yapping and scattered the ducks. There was a cacophony of noise with Alfie, in his element, racing about and ducks quacking. He called out, 'Alfie, come here!' The dog ignored him. The ducks were now obstructing the path and she was forced to slow to a halt. He gave her an apologetic smile. 'I'm so sorry. I don't know how he got off his lead. He's normally so good.' He called the dog again, shaking a bag of dog treats at it. It ceased its game and raced back to him, sitting obediently and holding a paw up to shake hands. It was one of the tricks Stacey had taught him.

He gave Alfie a treat. The woman smiled at the dog, who held up the other front paw.

'He doesn't really deserve a treat for chasing ducks,' he said. 'He's so cute, though, I can't refuse him. Want to see him do naughty dog?'

'Go on.' Amusement sparkled in her eyes.

'Alfie, you naughty dog.'

Alfie dropped to the ground, eyebrows waggling, and covered his eyes with his paws. She burst out laughing. 'Oh, that is adorable.'

They got talking and she sat on the bench beside him. She told him about the dog she'd owned when she was a girl. He let her give Alfie treats in exchange for tricks. His heart hammered in his chest as he caught a waft of her perfume, a mixture of floral scents. He gazed into her soft grey eyes and had a strong urge to stroke her perfect face with its neat nose and beautiful bow-shaped lips. Never had he wanted someone so much. After a while she moved off, waving as she left him on the bench. He floated back home and for once he didn't feel the urge to kick Alfie when they got there.

Now she ran towards him again, her arms open wide, eager to hold him. He reached for her, desperate to envelop her in an embrace. She seemed so alive. He understood why, and why she appeared to be so happy. It was because of him. It was because he was settling the debt at last, a debt that had to be paid in full. Once it was, they would be together again. She was so close he could almost touch her hands. His heart flipped with joy.

The sound of an ambulance siren woke him with a start and he lay there, numb. It had felt so real. How could it have only been a dream? He refused to believe it was only his imagination; it was a sign from her. She wanted him to continue, and he would. He wouldn't stop until the debt had been erased.

His mouth was dry. He trundled to the bathroom and popped two pills. They were becoming less effective these days. He'd need a couple before he could show up at work. His job served a purpose. He didn't enjoy it. However, it was all part of the big picture. He closed his eyes and thought about her bright smile, how much brighter it would be if he succeeded in pulling in another debt. He hadn't planned on working through them so quickly, but now he wanted to be with her more than ever. He opened his eyes and saw what his work colleagues saw every day – a grey man, a man to whom no one gave a second glance. Yes, it would be easy to wipe off another part of the debt. Tomorrow was Wednesday. He would do it tomorrow.

CHAPTER TWENTY-THREE

Robyn pounded the street. The cold rush of the air soothed her mind and the rhythmic motion of running helped her collect her thoughts. After leaving Mulholland's office she pulled on the running kit she always kept in her locker and headed out. A run would be better for her than lunch.

She ran directly to Victoria Park, a pleasant, award-winning park in the centre of Stafford. She chose the entrance nearest the large aviary, which was filled with many different birds, including peacocks and gloriously coloured budgerigars.

She ran faster to shake the ache she was beginning to feel in her chest. She often felt that way when a memory of Davies sideswiped her. She focused on the killer. Two hundred and fifty thousand pounds was a very specific amount. Had he lost some sort of lawsuit? Had he suffered an injury and made a claim? If he had, how would that be linked to Rory Wallis and Linda Upton? That needed checking. She made another mental note to add to her growing list. Her mobile buzzed in her pocket and she stopped beside a group of bare-branched trees to take the call. The morning frost had cleared, although under the trees a white carpet twinkled at her as she held the phone to her ear. It was Tricia.

'Sorry, I know I shouldn't pester you when you're working. I was hoping for news about Miles. I've been going over it and over it and I am more certain than ever that he did not decide to take a sauna that night.'

Robyn felt guilty that she couldn't devote more time to Miles Ashbrook, although she'd done the next best thing by asking Ross to look into it.

'I'm not able to look into myself, so I have an undercover detective working on the scene.' There was no need to tell her it was a private investigator not actually associated with the force. 'As soon as I hear anything at all, I'll let you know.'

Tricia sounded tearful. She sniffed. 'Thanks. I'm at his mum's house. We're sorting out funeral arrangements. There's a service next Wednesday at his local church. This has brought back so many memories of my brother Mark. Miles's mum is in bits. She can't understand why her son went into the sauna any more than I can. I'm going to sit down with her later and go through his personal possessions that were sent from Bromley Hall. She doesn't want to look at them on her own. I hoped maybe you had found something that would help us gain some closure on Miles. At the moment, we can't reconcile ourselves with the fact he's gone.'

Robyn understood the emotion behind her words. Burying someone was only the beginning. It took so much time to come to terms with the fact that the person was never coming back. Ross would call as soon as he had something. The fact he hadn't yet didn't bode well. Tricia might have to let go of her belief that Miles was murdered.

'If there's anything that is remotely suspicious, we'll jump on it and I'll call you. Please send my condolences to Miles's mother. We will do our utmost.'

She ended the call and began running again. A mother and a small child were throwing bread for the ducks that swam on the River Sow which ran through the park. She concentrated on the evidence she had. Rory Wallis had been alone in the pub when he had drunk a bottle of champagne and then had his throat cut. Linda Upton had not drunk anything; the toxicology report had been negative on drink and drugs. She had been drowned in her bath, at some point during the morning between 9 a.m. and 12 noon. The slap, slap, slap of her feet on the concrete path as she ran around the park circuit again calmed her mind and she found herself in the zone where this became a puzzle she could work out. She only needed one piece to guide her on her way. A flicker of enlightenment came a few minutes later, accompanied by a crawling sensation in her scalp, only to be extinguished almost immediately. The killer had removed Linda's clothes, although not her underwear. Why had he not stripped her completely, or left all her clothes on? Similarly, it was unlikely Wallis would drink a glass of champagne, let alone a bottle. The man was teetotal. This had to be significant. The answer was still beyond her reach. There was a pattern of sorts, if only she could see it and fathom out what it meant.

CHAPTER TWENTY-FOUR

The heady perfume from the scented candle and the background soundtrack of a rainforest had almost sent Ross into a heavy slumber, coupled as it was with a deeply relaxing massage. Lorna, the woman currently working the knots from his shoulders had, in his opinion, magic fingers – firm, strong and able to locate every tight muscle, pummelling it into submission until it felt warm and relaxed. Up until now he had almost forgotten why he was at the spa.

'Would you mind turning over?' she asked quietly.

He obliged, and now facing upwards, it was easier to talk to her.

'Have you worked here long?'

'Six years,' she replied.

'Like it here? It seems a really nice place to work.'

'It's okay. We're a small team but we get on well.'

'Get many famous clients in from the hotel?'

'We used to have quite a few pop stars and television personalities. I'm not supposed to gossip about them. We're supposed to respect every guest's privacy, regardless of who they are. Back in the day when Lord and Lady Bishton ran the place, we had celebs arriving every weekend. They used to land their helicopters on the helipad or arrive in limos. It was fantastic. We were even allowed to meet them in the bar after work. Lord B. knew how to attract the big names.' She dropped her voice to a whisper and told him the names of some famous guests who had stayed at the Hall in the past.

'It was different then. Nowadays, we get well-off people, although far fewer celebs. When Lord Bishton sold the place, it all changed. The consortium that purchased the Hall made some changes and now we have an additional fifty members who can use the facilities during the day, as well as hotel guests. It's all about money these days,' she huffed. 'I preferred the place when it was smaller and more intimate. The Bishtons added this new extension purely to make the place saleable. I liked working in the Hall. We had individual treatment rooms on the ground floor that were created from the servants' quarters. I loved the old red and gold decor. You felt like you worked somewhere special. This could be any modern spa.'

'What was it like before the extension?'

'The Hall had the twenty-two rooms it has today. Downstairs, the Long Galley was a grand dining room, and off it was a champagne bar. Nowadays the Long Galley is only used as a ballroom for the annual summer ball. They turned the old ballroom into the dining room that hotel guests use at night. When we had pop stars visiting, they'd sometimes give an impromptu concert after dinner. The spa area was actually below that floor. Now that's all changed and become a staff canteen and the laundry rooms.

'It used to be a breathtaking, oval-shaped swimming pool. The sides were made up of hundreds of coloured mosaic tiles, and there were jets of water and waterfalls that massaged your back and neck. It was very grand, with large stone pillars by the steps, and statues of lions. If you pressed the right button, water used to flow from the lion's mouths. It was like being in an Egyptian palace. Not that I've been in one,' she giggled.

'It must have cost a fortune to drain and fill in the area. Seems a crazy idea when they could have put a canteen in the extension instead.'

He felt the pressure on his neck and shoulders change. Lorna lifted her hands from his body.

'That's the end of your session, Mr Cunningham. Wait for a few moments before you get up and don't sit up too quickly.'

She left him to get dressed. He didn't move immediately. His brain had begun to stir into action. The rainforest sounds were beginning to irritate him. He sat up on the couch and shook himself from his reverie. Was it his imagination or had Lorna suddenly clammed up?

Jakub had cleaned the changing rooms and was sitting in the staff canteen with a coffee when the guest turned up. The man came across as vaguely ridiculous, in his huge white dressing gown and complimentary slippers, and very uncomfortable, as if he felt out of place. His hair was awry but his eyes were bright and sharp. He lifted a hand and joined Jakub at the table.

He smiled genially. 'I seem to have got lost. My wife told me the restaurant was down here.'

Jakub shook his head. 'No, here is staff. Restaurant not here.'

The man pulled out a stool and sat opposite him. 'What a fabulous place! I'm glad I came here. My friend came a few years ago. I think it must have changed since he was here. He told me there was a swimming pool here.'

'Pool gone,' said Jakub, wishing the man would go. He liked to enjoy his coffee break in peace. 'In new part,' he added, pointing at the door that would lead to the new building, hoping the man would head off and look for it. He didn't. Instead the stranger pulled out a packet of chocolate biscuits from the pocket of his dressing gown and offered one to Jakub, who refused.

'Sure? They're very good. I'm addicted to them.' He tipped one out and bit into before passing the packet over. 'Go on. Take one. They'll go well with your coffee.'

Jakub grunted thanks and extracted one from the packet. He hadn't eaten breakfast again, and Bruno wasn't on duty to sneak him any toast or leftovers. His stomach gave a growl of appreciation.

'You been here long?'

'Five years.'

'You knew the place before they built the extension?'

Jakub nodded and chomped on his biscuit. The man was right. It was very tasty.

'Pity they got rid of the pool. It sounded lovely: pillars, lion statues, jacuzzis.'

'Yes. Very pretty, like spas in Poland.'

'Yet they filled it in. Madness. What made them do that, eh?' Ross's eyebrows rose in mock surprise, two dark circumflexes over bright eyes. Jakub studied the man's face. He wasn't the usual sort of guest, and guests didn't ordinarily engage Jakub in conversation, especially about an event that had occurred in the past. He popped the rest of the biscuit into his mouth and drained his coffee.

'Must go. Work. This is canteen for staff. You go too, please.'

He pushed back his chair and left the man in his dressing gown.

Ross pulled out another biscuit and bit into it. His hunch was right. No one wanted to talk about the old spa. Could there be a link between it and the death of Miles Ashbrook? He would have to box clever to get information out of these folks.

CHAPTER TWENTY-FIVE

Robyn had returned from her run and now sat with Post-it notes laid out on her desk in rows. She had written down her thoughts on separate yellow squares, and was studying each in turn when a pink-cheeked Anna rushed into the office. She waved her notepad.

'Might have a lead in the Linda Upton case, guv. We've got a sighting of an unknown man waiting for the bus to Lichfield.'

She read out the information on the pad. Flora Mackay, who lived at the Thatched Cottage in Manor Road, was walking to the post box at approximately ten fifteen yesterday morning when she'd spotted a man wearing a blue coat waiting by the bus stop. He was partly hidden from view by some overgrown bushes near the stop. She paid him little attention other than to cast a disapproving look as he tossed a cigarette butt onto the pavement and trod it down. The village had won the Best-Kept Village competition that year, and as she was on the parish council it was her job to ensure that standards were maintained. The council aimed to keep Kings Bromley neat and tidy all year round. She was about to speak to the man about it when the bus pulled up and he got on it. Flora picked up the cigarette butt herself and threw it in the nearest bin.

Anna's words tumbled out: 'The man wasn't a local. Flora has a good idea of who lives in Kings Bromley. She's lived there all her life and is a member of the parish council and the local church. The man might have nothing to do with Linda Upton, but it's something to go on. Mitz is at the bus depot waiting to talk to the driver who was on that route yesterday. Apparently, the bus is rarely busy at that time and they are considering reducing the timetable to only two buses a day, so we might get lucky.'

Robyn studied her young colleague, keen and anxious to make the right impression, and was reminded of herself when she first joined the force. She chewed on a ripped thumbnail. It was possible that Linda's attacker had casually left the scene of the crime and caught a bus out of the village, rather than risk his own vehicle being seen. Maybe he didn't even drive. Anna had followed her instinct, and who was Robyn to criticise that? At the moment, it was all she had. She couldn't discount any theory. She gave up on her nail and stared at her own notes, each one a theory, an idea – no more than a hunch.

'No chance you found the cigarette end?'

Anna shook her head. 'I headed straight to the bin but it had been emptied.'

She nodded approvingly. 'If Linda Upton was attacked shortly after she took her son to school, it is feasible that this man is connected to her murder or saw something that might help us. I see Flora describes the man as "in his thirties, wearing a dark blue jacket and jeans".'

'She apologised for not being able to be more helpful. She didn't really take much notice of him. It was only when she spotted the cigarette being dropped that she paid attention. The words she used to describe him were "scruffy" and "wild-eyed".'

A smile twitched Robyn's lips. 'There's an expression you don't hear every day. Good job, Anna. I'll leave you and Mitz to pursue this line of enquiry. I've tried to uncover a link between Rory Wallis and Linda Upton, and I can't find anything. Matt has brought over her mobile. Did you look at her social media sites and emails to see if there's any link to Rory Wallis – if they're friends on Facebook or if she was following him on Twitter?'

'I checked everything. It didn't take long because her husband handed over her passwords. There's nothing of note on her call log or emails – even deleted stuff. She seems to have texted a couple of women in her village now and again, had a network of friends on Facebook who are also mothers, and was a member of a couple of health-conscious groups. She was into keep fit and did Pilates and a few classes at the local village hall. I couldn't find anything on Rory's devices other than calls to his mum or work-related numbers. He was quite a loner. He didn't bother with Facebook, and his browsing history was mostly to do with gaming websites.'

'Blast! I was hoping you'd found something. Okay, thanks. I'll let you get on with this hunt for the man at the bus stop. If anyone wants me, I'll be in the village about three miles away from Kings Bromley. It's right next to the A38. Place called Alrewas – I'm going to chat to Linda's husband.'

Late-blooming roses arched over the thatched cottage doorway, clinging onto their pale pink petals that were now twisted and browned by the first frosts of the year. The house was chocolate-box perfect, nestled between two charming white and black timber-framed buildings. The lane behind Alrewas village church had been a revelation to Robyn: quintessentially English, with perfect front gardens, now neatly trimmed, ready for winter. She knocked on the front door of Blossom Cottage and was greeted by a tall, thin man in his thirties. His face was drawn and his eyes bruised with tiredness. She recognised him as Robert Upton. She held up her warrant card and he motioned her inside.

It was dim in the hallway, although the smell of fresh baking from the kitchen made the place seem cosier. Robert opened a door and ushered her into a room with low wooden beams, filled with antique furniture, where a log fire roared in a grate. Shining horse brasses hung over the fireplace, and in niches in the brick wall there were photographs of smiling people, much like those she had seen in the house at Kings Bromley. Robert invited her to take a chair, and no sooner had she dropped onto the wide cushion than the door opened and a woman, smartly dressed in tailored trousers, cashmere sweater and expensive loafers appeared, her ash-blonde hair held back in a large, tortoiseshell hair slide.

'Mum, this is Detective Inspector Carter.'

A look of anguish crossed the woman's face. She whispered, 'Is it about Linda?'

Robyn nodded.

'I'll keep Louis occupied,' she continued. 'He keeps asking when she's coming back.' Her voice faltered for a second and she turned to leave. As she did, a cheery-faced boy carrying a toy dinosaur wandered into the room. He studied her. 'Hello, I'm Louis and I'm four years old. How old are you?'

'You can't ask a lady her age.' Robert's mother put a hand on his head. He twisted away from it.

'Why not?'

'It's rude to ask.'

'Why? I don't think it's rude.'

'Well, it's what we call personal.'

'My dinosaur is hundreds of years old,' said Louis, ignoring his grandmother and coming further into the room to show off his toy. Robyn took in his auburn hair, much like his mother's, his round cheeks and bright eyes. No one had yet told him his mother was never coming back. 'I have lots of dinosaurs and a dinosaur skellyton. Mummy is going to make up it up with me when she gets back. She had to go away urgently. I can't wait for her to come home. I really want to make it up and take it to school but Daddy can't do it, so I have to wait. Are you any good at making up things?'

Robyn held her hand out for the dinosaur. 'This is one of the most terrifying dinosaurs in the world.'

His head bobbed up and down in agreement. 'It is. It's a tyrannosaurus.' He grinned a gap-toothed smile in delight at having pronounced the name correctly.

'And you're not afraid of it?' she asked. 'It's a big monster.'

The boy shook his head. She handed it back to him. 'Then you are a very brave boy.' She smiled at him, her heart heavy.

He grinned. 'I am brave. Mummy told me I was brave when I fell over and cut my knee.' He showed Robyn a small scar on his kneecap. 'I didn't cry.'

His grandmother took him by the hand. 'Come on, Louis. The lady wants to talk to your daddy. Let's go and get the cake out of the oven.'

'It's going to be a dinosaur cake,' Louis said happily, swinging his dinosaur by the leg and disappearing from view.

Robert's face had turned grey. She understood why. 'He doesn't know, does he?'

Robert swallowed a sob and shook his head. 'We're going to tell him later today. I just wanted him to have one last day before we shatter his world. He and Linda were so close. He was everything to her, and she was such a good mum.'

'I'm so sorry for your loss. I completely understand what you're going through. I can't make it better for you, but I can try and find whoever is responsible.'

'And what have you found out so far, detective?'

'It's still early on in terms of identifying a suspect. We have several leads, and some new information has recently come to light. I assure you we are all working flat out on this.' There was no need to tell the man any more than that. Even if – when – they found the murderer, it wouldn't help Robert Upton or his son. Nothing would compensate them for losing Linda.

'Would you mind answering a few questions?'

'About Linda?' Robert blew his nose on a handkerchief. The reality of her death was beginning to hit home. 'I can't arrange a funeral until her body is released, you know?'

'That's normal procedure, sir. They'll release her as soon as they can.'

He eyeballed the mobile lying on the table, as if Linda might ring him. Suddenly he spoke, his eyes moist. 'I was on my way back from Dubai. I'd been away for a week trying to help negotiate a new engineering contract with my boss. I only spoke to her yesterday morning to tell her my flight was on time and I'd see her for dinner. She was in a fluster. Louis wouldn't get ready for school and wanted to play with his dinosaur. She had to rush off and I didn't even get to tell her how much I loved her.' He stopped and swallowed quietly.

'I'm sure she knew.'

He nodded an affirmation. 'What do you want to know?'

'Did your wife ever go to Lichfield? For a meal or a night out?'

He rubbed at his eyes. 'She used to shop now and again in Lichfield. I'm sure she'd have gone there for coffee with friends from the school or village. She's even been with my mum, although they both prefer shopping in Burton. She wasn't one for going out at night, unless it was with me. We only moved into the area five years ago. It was Linda's idea. We were trying for a family. She wanted to bring a child up in a village rather than a busy town. She had an image of inviting local kids around for afternoon tea and play dates. She was an only child, and it was pretty lonely growing up, by all accounts. She wanted our children's lives to be different. It helped that my mum and dad live here in Alrewas, so we moved from Sutton Coldfield and came to Kings Bromley. Her old friends still live around and near Sutton, although she hasn't stayed in touch with them. You know how it is; you get married, have kids, move away and move on.

'When we first moved to Kings Bromley, she joined a running club in Lichfield. She got heavily into it and used to run almost every day and go out with the girls three times a week. She became good friends with Harriet, one of the girls who was the same age. They broke away from the original group and started training together. They did a couple of fun runs and a half marathon. Then Harriet died and Linda stopped running altogether. A few weeks after Harriet's death, she discovered she was pregnant. After Louis was born, she became involved with a mums' group in the village, and she seemed quite content to be part of that and occasionally go to the local exercise class in the village hall. She knew everyone at the class, if that's any help. I'm sure they'll be able to tell you more.'

'They'll be interviewed in due course.'

Robert dragged his hands through his hair. 'She was one of the best. She was one of those people who was content with everything in life. And she adored Louis.' His eyes became moist and he gulped back the tears that threatened.

Robyn wasn't sure she was asking the right questions. Nothing so far helped her. She had ruled out Robert as a suspect since he was on a flight back at the time of Linda's death. As for a connection between Linda and Rory, it was possible that Linda had met Rory in Lichfield, but certainly not through running, and it was unlikely that Linda would frequent a pub alone or with a child in tow. That was confirmed a few moments later when she learned Linda was, like Rory, teetotal.

'She gave up drinking about the time she found out she was pregnant and has never drunk since.'

Robyn could gather no more useful information or establish any connection to Rory Wallis. She was about to leave the house when she spotted the same photo of Linda with a female friend that she had seen in the Uptons' house – the one with the two women showing off their medals and wearing pink ribbons in their hair. She pointed at it. 'Is that Linda's friend, Harriet? Did she have cancer?'

He shook his head. 'No, Harriet's death was an accident. She and Linda went away for a girls' spa break. Harriet got drunk and went for a swim on her own after Linda had gone to bed. She slipped on the tiles by the pool and cracked her head, tumbled into the water and drowned. Her husband, Alan, was devastated. He and Harriet used to come around for the odd dinner party before the accident. We used to play Trivial Pursuit. Linda loved that game. She always won the pink wedge because she was heavily into entertainment. Loved watching movies, especially romantic comedies. Invariably sobbed at a happy ending.' He smiled at the memory. 'The Hall owners paid Alan compensation for her death. He never divulged the sum. How much value do you put on the life of someone you love dearly? He sold his house and moved away to Knowle, over Solihull way. He severed contact with us. Linda was never quite the same afterwards. She took it really badly. Luckily, Louis helped bring her back out of herself.'

Sharp tingling pinpricks ran up Robyn's spine. She thought of the dinosaur skeleton lying in pieces on the floor of the Upton's lounge. She was about to pick up the first piece of her own puzzle. She spoke calmly, even though her heart was racing. 'Which hotel spa did they visit?'

'Bromley Hall. It's about twenty miles away.'

She said her goodbyes and raced off to her vehicle, boots crunching conspicuously on the gravel in the drive. She was sure she was on to something, but the euphoria of knowing that was tempered by the thought that Louis would soon learn the dreadful news that his mother was not coming home and would never be able to make up the dinosaur skeleton with him.

CHAPTER TWENTY-SIX

Jeanette dropped onto the bed beside her husband. 'I have gossip.' Ross pushed himself into a sitting position and propped a large pillow behind his back.

'I have stiff joints and I've decided I'm allergic to exercise and healthy living. I have, however, spent the most of the day mooching about Bromley Hall and chatting to some of the employees. I also got a free sample of bread and butter pudding in the kitchens, so it wasn't all wasted. Robyn is right about the CCTV cameras. They seem to be focused on areas in the spa and pool area that I can't access or check out fully, not without someone seeing me. So, Mrs Cunningham, what have you uncovered?'

'I've been talking to one of the guests who was here at the beginning of the week, Fiona Maggiore. She's a regular visitor. At first I thought she was a bit stuck up, but she's actually okay. She's married to some filthy rich property dealer, but I get the impression it's not a happy marriage. She told me that there have been changes going on here over the past few weeks, and none of them for the better. Quite a few of the staff have been made redundant, and those who are left are not happy bunnies.'

'How does Mrs Filthy Rich know all this?'

'She's got a special relationship with one of the staff here.'

'You mean she's bonking someone?'

'You have such a way with words, Ross.'

'Well, is she?'

'That's the impression I got.'

'Did she say she was?'

'We women have a way of communicating hidden meanings to other women without words.'

'Like mind readers.' He grinned at her. She thumped him playfully on the arm.

'She says there'd been a lot of ill feeling towards Miles Ashbrook since he began laying off people willy-nilly. He started hiding out in his office so as not to be verbally attacked by anyone, but the day he died somebody was overheard yelling at him in his office.'

'Who?'

'Apparently it was Jakub Woźniak, the man who is responsible for cleaning the spa. There was some hoo-ha over Miles sacking Jakub's wife, Emily. She worked on reception. Two weeks ago, a few of the women who worked the front desk and in the back offices were called into Miles's office and given instant dismissal with a redundancy package. When they challenged it they were told they could either take the money while it was offered or leave when the place was shut down due to lack of funding. He was brutal about it. The women accepted the offer and left that same day, but Jakub Woźniak took the news of his wife's dismissal very badly. He and Emily then discovered they have a second child on the way and need the income more than ever. Anyway, last Wednesday morning, he marched into the office and threatened to kill Miles.'

'Hmm. It could be heated words that didn't mean anything.'

'Fiona is completely convinced he meant it, and I thought it was worth mentioning. We had quite a chat in the spa whirlpool. She loves it here, and knows almost everybody. I'm certain she doesn't come here for the treatments alone. You ought to check it out.'

'I shall. I spoke to Jakub Woźniak earlier. He seemed a little brusque. I'll have to try and talk to him again. I don't suppose you could get Fiona to divulge who her source is?'

'I might. I've invited her to join me for champagne at six at the bar. I'll see if I can coax it out of her.'

'Super. Not so super is that I have another training session with a different instructor. I'm going to try some ju-jitsu class with Scott Dawson. I can't wait! I've tried to talk to Scott but he's always busy. This seems to be only way to get to him. I hope to grab him for a few minutes after the class if I haven't seized up completely and can still walk. Brad told me Scott's been here since it opened, and I'm sure he'll have some opinion on the subject of Miles Ashbrook. I'm also a little curious why everyone is cagey about the original pool and spa being sealed up. Maybe Scott can enlighten me. I had hoped to talk to Charlie about it, since he's happy to talk about anything, but he's off today and tomorrow.'

'You don't need to ask Charlie or even go to your class and pester the trainer about the old spa. I know why the pool was filled in.'

'How did you find out?'

Jeanette tapped the side of her nose. 'I have my ways.'

'Come on, tell me.'

'There was an accident in the old pool. A woman drowned.'

'Why did they fill it in?'

'According to Fiona, the Bishtons paid out a large amount of compensation to the husband of the woman, Harriet Worth, who also wanted the pool filled in as part of the settlement.'

He pursed his lips, impressed by his wife's findings. 'Very interesting. That's one mystery solved. Now I only need to track down Mr Woźniak and see whether he really hated Miles Ashbrook enough to kill him.'

'Aren't you forgetting something?' Jeanette smiled.

'Thank you. You have saved me wasting time on that particular puzzle.' He put his hands together and bowed dramatically and kissed her hand. 'I shall now look forward to mastering the techniques necessary for *mata leon* – the lion killer – or for a sliding choke hold, which might be useful for when clients refuse to pay me.'

'I meant, aren't you forgetting to hand over your credit card so I can buy some champagne for my new friend?'

CHAPTER TWENTY-SEVEN

Robyn threw down the newspaper and rubbed the back of her neck. The photograph of Linda Upton's face stared up at her.

'Bloody Amy Walters. What's she playing at? This is an ongoing investigation.'

Matt, the only other person in the office, picked up the paper and read:

> Villagers in Kings Bromley were devastated to learn of the murder of a well-respected resident and mother, Linda Upton (34). Full details have not yet been disclosed, but one resident said, 'Everyone here feels nervous now. It's scary knowing someone could be watching you, hunting you down.'
>
> Mrs Upton's murder is the second in the locality in less than two weeks. Manager and barman Rory Wallis was found dead at the Happy Pig in Lichfield last Friday. Suzy Clarke, barmaid at the Happy Pig, told the *Lichfield Times*: 'I can't go back there. I keep imagining someone is watching me, waiting to pounce on me like a big cat when I go through the door. I've had terrible nightmares since it happened.'
>
> Until more information is released, residents are going to continue to worry that they too might come under

attack from the killer who is being called the Lichfield Leopard.

Matt put the paper down and shrugged. 'That's sensationalist nonsense.'

Robyn continued to rub the back of her neck. 'And that's what sells papers.'

Matt sneered. 'Someone needs to gag Amy Walters before she ruins things. Want me to deal with her?'

'I'll sort it, thanks. I'll tell her to wait until we have something to say and to stop stirring. This is not what we need. The Lichfield Leopard. I could bloody strangle the woman.' Robyn cricked her neck side to side but she couldn't shift the tension in her muscles.

Matt read the article again. 'If it's any consolation, she hasn't made the front page with it.'

Robyn huffed noisily and stood in front of a whiteboard on which were pinned photographs of Rory Wallis and Linda Upton. She wrote a name beside Linda's photograph. Everyone knew that she preferred to write in black marker pen rather than give PowerPoint presentations. She felt it helped if you could see links in black and white.

'Can I run some thoughts past you?'

Matt put his work to one side. 'Sure. Go ahead, guv.'

Robyn indicated the name she had written. 'Robert Upton was married to Linda. He was on the way back from Dubai at the time of Linda's death, so he's not a suspect. I spoke to him and to his mother and have no reason to believe he is involved in any way in Linda's murder. With him ruled out, I don't know where to look next.' She tapped the board with the end of her pen. 'We have a seemingly ordinary, contented family who have no debts, no hidden secrets we can uncover and no enemies that we know of. All of this leaves us with the question of who? Who would want Linda dead?'

'A disgruntled lover?'

'Again, there is no evidence at all to suggest Linda was having an affair. Nothing has been flagged up on phone records or emails. She was a contented housewife who had a small circle of female friends and spent most of her time with her son and husband.' She pointed at the photograph of Rory Wallis.

'And then there's Rory Wallis, who was, by all accounts, someone who kept himself to himself, had no girlfriend or partner and few friends. We have turned up absolutely nothing from our enquiries. He worked, played video games and rarely socialised. And he was teetotal, which is ironic given he worked in a bar. There is nothing peculiar about either of these people.'

She drew a line between the photographs and wrote the words 'Bromley Hall'. 'This is the sole thing we have to connect these people. Remind me, Matt, when was Rory at the Hall?'

'From when it opened in 2008 until 2013. He was bar manager at what they called the Champagne Bar.'

She waved her pen, and under Bromley Hall wrote the name Harriet Worth.

'Now I'm going to begin speculating. This lady was Linda Upton's friend. Harriet died during a spa weekend at Bromley Hall after drinking too much, falling in the pool and drowning.'

'Then they're both linked to the place in some way. What else connects the pair of them?'

'I can't think of anything else. We've been through everything and there isn't any other connection apart from one – they might both have been at the Hall the night Harriet Worth died in July 2012, and she might have met Rory Wallis at the Champagne Bar. I'd need his work schedule to confirm that he was on duty that night. I just want to be certain I'm barking up the right tree before I say anything to Mulholland.' She paced in front of the board and spoke again. 'What if somebody is now seeking revenge for the death of Harriet Worth? What if that someone believed others were to blame for her death, and by others I mean Linda Upton, who went to the spa with her friend, and Rory Wallis who may or may not have served her alcohol the night she died? Does that sound too far-fetched?'

Matt shook his head. 'No, it doesn't. It sounds logical, especially as there were invoices on both bodies for £250,000 pounds each.'

'My thought exactly, Matt. It smacks of somebody seeking payment for her death. I could be wrong, and the invoices might relate to something else altogether, but for the moment, it fits. However, what I can't get to fit is Miles Ashbrook. We have three deaths, all somehow connected to Bromley Hall, and I'm unable to establish a link between these two deaths and Miles Ashbrook. He wasn't at the Hall when Harriet Worth drowned, and there was no invoice on or near his body.'

Matt pulled a hand through his hair. 'The invoice might have shrivelled up in the heat of the sauna, although that's unlikely. If you want my opinion, I think Miles Ashbrook died of natural causes, and if there's no invoice, the cases are probably unrelated.'

'Again, I hear you, and still I can't shake the feeling they're related in some way.'

'I'd stick with what we have and hope something comes to light that confirms your suspicions. You'll only wind people up if you try to bring up the Miles Ashbrook case again, and you'll get Shearer baying for your dismissal.'

Robyn sighed. 'You're right, I suppose.'

Matt cocked his head to one side. 'What if Harriet Worth's husband has suddenly decided he wants revenge? Maybe the money is no longer enough and he wants blood? Okay, that's a long shot,' he said, noting the surprised look on his superior's face.

With her lips pressed together, Robyn turned over this new idea in her mind. 'No, it's worth considering. You know me. I'll act on any leads or hunches. Can you drag up the Harriet Worth case for me and email me details? I want to know what happened that night and how much compensation her husband received. I'll see if Mr Worth is at home and surprise him with a visit. Send the information over as soon as you've got it. By the way, you don't know where Mitz is, do you?'

'Anna was joining him at the bus depot. They're trying to track down the guy at the bus stop in Kings Bromley.'

'Get him to call me if he has anything, and if Mulholland wants me, tell her I'm out chasing a hot lead, and that we've made progress. I need to keep her off my back for as long as possible.'

Matt grinned. 'I'll keep her sweet.'

The bus station was filled with schoolchildren and shoppers waiting to go home. Anna wasn't keen on crowds at the best of times, and the older, cockier kids were getting on her nerves with their loud music bursting from iPhones and their fake cries as they jostled and punched each other before yelling, 'Help, police! My mate pushed me.'

She was glad when the bus she was waiting for pulled in and a uniformed man in his sixties emerged, bag over his shoulder. His shoulders were slumped, the top button on his shirt undone and he walked like a man who wanted nothing more than to go home and put his feet up. Anna sympathised with him. She'd been working almost non-stop for several days and could do with time off too. She was also concerned about her colleague Sergeant Mitz. He had left her and rushed off home to his parents' house, where he also lived. 'It's my gran,' was all he had said. Anna knew how important family was to Mitz; he had spoken frequently about his wonderful granny, who gave all her money to charities and people who she felt were worse off than her. Anna had met her only a couple of weeks earlier when she went to collect Mitz, and had fallen for the old lady's charm.

The bus driver ushered her to a room behind the bus station with grubby whitewashed walls. There were several notices for staff on display, and a table and five plastic chairs. 'It's quieter in here. Call me Bill.' He dropped his bag down on the floor.

'We're looking for a man wearing a blue jacket and jeans who we believe boarded the Lichfield bus at Kings Bromley yesterday morning at ten fifteen.'

'Unshaven bloke who looked like he was on something? I remember him. He just about managed to grunt at me. People these days can't be bothered with anyone, can they? There was a time when I used to say good morning to everyone who boarded my bus. Nowadays, they glower at me or ignore me altogether, and I haven't the heart to engage them in chit-chat. Some of the elderly people are still polite. I prefer that particular village route because I often get the older locals on board, especially on market days. They can be quite chatty.'

Anna felt a frisson of excitement rising in her chest. She had been right to explore this avenue of enquiry. 'I expect you know where he got off.'

Bill gave her a grin. He had a front tooth missing, which made him all the more endearing.

'Indeed, young lady, I do. He got off just up the road at the marina. There isn't a bus stop there but he asked me to let him off. I'm not supposed to drop people off willy-nilly. There was no one else on board that day, so I did. It's a long walk to the marina from Kings Bromley, and part of me felt a bit sorry for the guy. He seemed really downhearted. I can't tell you much more than that. The bloke jumped on board, sat in the front seat, took a phone call and pointed to where he wanted dropping off. He managed to say thanks.'

The euphoria Anna had just experienced disappeared quickly. The marina was vast and it would take a lot of manpower to track down the man.

'If it's any help, I think he's called Peter,' continued Bill. 'His phone rang and he answered it with, "Yes, this is Peter…" I didn't catch his surname. I only picked up on it because my grandson is called Peter. Do you want me to come to the police station and identify anyone for you? I'm good with faces.'

His enthusiasm to assist was refreshing and his shoulders slumped in disappointment when she told him that wouldn't yet be necessary. As soon as she left the bus station she dialled Robyn's number, stopping before she pressed the call button. She didn't have very much to tell her boss. It would be better if she tried the marina first and tried to locate the man. That would show initiative. She'd ask about and find out where this Peter lived before calling for back-up.

CHAPTER TWENTY-EIGHT

They are sitting on the bench beside the reservoir. Alfie has a dog chew and is patiently working his way through it, gnawing it until it is in minuscule pieces. He licks his paws and huffs contentedly. Stacey has no idea he has her dog again. It's the only way to get the beautiful woman to stop and speak to him. She likes the wretched animal. Today, he took one of Alfie's favourite squeaky balls with him on their walk. He left early to make sure he was in position when she appeared for her morning run. He knew her route now. She started from her house at Cathedral Rise and jogged along the lane towards the lake, taking the first entrance, past Friary School and down the lane flanked by large bushes that hid the school playing fields from view. She turned left and entered the circuit, running the one-mile exercise loop around Stowe Pool and Stowe Fields five times before stopping at the all-weather gym where she would do various exercises on the machines before jogging to the far end of the reservoir and exiting near the church. From there she would run back home. If he positioned himself on a bench after the playing fields, she wouldn't see him until she rounded the bend and ran past where the fishermen sat.

It was a wet, murky morning – one where the clouds hung so low in the sky you felt you could put your hand up and touch them. He had been woken very early by the sound of a car engine struggling for life, churning and churning until the noise grated on his nerves so much he wanted to scream. Then Alfie had started barking in his high-pitched, irritating manner. Eventually Stacey got up and dealt with Alfie, and he heard the sound of the kettle as she made a cup of tea. It was Thursday and she was on an early shift. She would be gone soon and he would be left in peace to do whatever he wanted with his day, and he would spend it with the woman he loved. With that delicious thought, he put his head back under the bedcovers and tried to doze off again, but he could only think about his potential new girlfriend – the woman who jogged around the reservoir.

He'd arrived too early and had to walk Alfie back and forward around the lake, anxious he would attract attention from the two mothers who were gossiping while their toddlers squawked and squealed as they played on the climbing frame. It was early spring, and clumps of purple and yellow crocuses were pushing through the grass. Soon the park would fill up with walkers and people playing football or cricket or throwing frisbees. Once that happened, it would be impossible to get her on her own. As it was, there were several fishermen hunched under umbrellas, staring into the water hoping for a catch. The reservoir was filled with all species of fish. He'd never understood the mentality of those who could sit for hours waiting to hook one. The wait would be too much for him. He wouldn't be able to stand the hours wondering if a fish would nibble at the bait. He was a man of action, and his beloved had not yet appeared. He shuffled from foot to foot. Alfie pulled at his lead and whined. He jerked the lead and gave the animal a soft kick with his foot and growled at him. 'Shut up. Sit!' Alfie whimpered and lay down, head on paws.

He watched the all-weather gym next to the children's area furtively, and he hoped she wouldn't forgo her run. St Chad's church clock chimed nine. It was getting on. His knee bounced up and down restlessly. Just when he thought he would explode with anticipation, he spotted her as she jogged onto the circuit. She was in a tracksuit that hugged her shapely form; it was nothing like the baggy sack of an outfit that Stacey wore as she slumped about the house. He smiled as he watched his woman run upright, with her head up, hair held in a ponytail, swishing from side to side. He wondered what it would be like to stroke it. He was certain it would feel like silk.

She was near the grassy area called Stowe Fields and it was time to put his plan into action. He picked up the squeaky ball and gave it a squeeze. The sound made Alfie sit up, his ill-treatment forgotten. The man unclipped the dog's lead and held the ball up, waving it at the animal. The dog's eyes sparkled in delight at seeing his favourite toy. The man squeezed the ball again and it let out a loud squeak that made Alfie bounce on the spot in excitement. He squeaked it several times more before throwing it with some force. The ball went deep into the bushes and Alfie scurried after it.

The timing was perfect. No sooner had the dog vanished than she appeared. He stumbled onto the circuit and feigned surprise at seeing her. She was forced to stop, and seeing his distraught face asked, 'Is everything okay?'

He gulped, his head twisting this way and that. He held up the lead, tears in his eyes. 'I've lost Alfie again. I've been searching for over an hour. He ran off and I don't know what to do.'

'Where did you lose him?'

'We were on the playing fields. I was throwing his ball and another dog arrived – one of those huge Alsatian types. I couldn't spot an owner for it. It began worrying Alfie. I tried to yank it away by its collar, but it snarled at me. Then it continued pestering Alfie, barking and darting backwards and forwards and nipping at him, before racing off with the ball. Alfie chased after it. I haven't seen either of them since. What if the dog's attacked him or he's run into the road?' His eyes opened wide as if this idea had only just occurred to him.

'It's okay. I'll help. If we can't find him around here, we'll go to the police station.'

Although that was the last place he'd go, he threw her a grateful look. 'Would you? Thank you so much. I'm almost hoarse with shouting.'

She called the dog's name loudly. He kept his fingers crossed that Alfie was still looking for his ball. He'd thrown it right into the prickly bushes and hoped it had got stuck in there. She held her hands to her mouth to call. Her nails were pearl pink and manicured. He gazed at them, imagining them caressing his face, his chest. He dragged himself away from his thoughts and called, 'Alfie, come on, boy.'

They walked back towards the playing fields, shouting. After a few minutes, he gave her a look filled with sorrow, mentally congratulating himself on his magnificent performance. He swiped at his eye. 'Thank you, but it's hopeless. I've lost him. I just hope nothing terrible has happened. I couldn't bear that.'

She placed a hand on his arm, a friendly gesture, and said, 'Don't worry. He'll probably be playing and will come home when he's ready.'

He nodded slowly, not wanting her to remove her hand. The warmth of it surged through his body. How he wanted this woman.

'You're very kind.' As he finished his sentence, there was a volley of squeaks as Alfie appeared, ball in mouth, and dropped it at her feet.

Alfie!' he shouted and fell to his knees, hugging the little dog, who squirmed away, tail wagging, wanting the ball to be thrown again. She gave a laugh that lifted his soul.

'You naughty doggie,' she said, playfully. 'You gave us such a fright.' He sat obediently at the sound of her voice.

The man feigned relief and gratitude. 'I must thank you. It's down to you that he's come back. Look at the little chap. He's completely taken with you.'

She laughed again. 'He's such a funny little dog. Is he okay? The other dog hasn't hurt him?'

'He seems fine. He must have chased after it, retrieved his ball and come looking for me.' He rubbed the dog's head affectionately. 'I must thank you in some way. There's a coffee shop nearby – let me buy you a coffee.'

She shook her head. 'Sorry, I can't. Thanks all the same. I have to get on. I've got an appointment at eleven and I need to shower beforehand. I'm just glad Alfie is okay. I'd better be going. Be good, Alfie. No more chasing after big dogs.' She patted the animal.

'Thank you again… uhm, I don't know your name.'

'Harriet. You're welcome. See you again. Bye.'

She jogged out of the park, not completing her usual circuits. He clipped the lead back onto Alfie and left in the opposite direction. He felt warm, light and hopelessly in love. 'Harriet,' he whispered, letting the name rest on his lips before repeating it. He would win her over very soon.

CHAPTER TWENTY-NINE

The inland marina at Bromley Hayes was even larger than Anna expected. She'd never been interested in canals or boating, but the array of beautifully painted narrow boats with pots of chrysanthemums on their decks, and names like *Dragonfly*, *Free Spirit*, *Serendipity* and *Blue Moon* conjured up a romance. She could see the appeal of travelling the canal network or living on one of these boats, snuggled in a little cabin with a roaring log burner keeping her warm rather than being bedraggled from the drizzle that was now falling. She pulled at a strand of hair that had stuck to her face, tucked it behind her ear and headed for the main office.

The marina was quiet and no one was about, not even on the service quay where folk could obtain the necessary fuel for their boats. The weather was maybe keeping people inside. The berths were set in two landscaped basins connected by a bridge. Anna could envisage how pretty it would look in summer, with the wooden pontoons to the boats bordered by tall grasses and shrubs, and the rhododendron bushes filled with pink or blue blooms.

There was a facilities block in the distance, and a summerhouse that appeared to be a fresh addition to the site. She had heard that the canal community was a friendly one. No doubt they spent warm summer evenings chatting over wine and discussing trips they had made.

There was a light on in the office so she tapped on the door and entered. A woman reading a magazine and sitting next to an electric heater commented, 'Dreadful day, isn't it?' Her eyes widened in surprise when she saw Anna in uniform. 'Good afternoon, officer. Has there been some trouble? None of the boats have been stolen, have they?'

Anna slid her warrant card over the desk. 'It's nothing like that. I'm trying to locate a gentleman who was seen heading in this direction. We think he might be staying on a boat here and that he might be able to assist in our enquiries.'

The woman scraped her glasses onto her tawny-coloured hair, and peered myopically at Anna. 'Oh, okay.'

'I'm looking for a man called Peter.'

'I'll get my book out. We keep the key fobs here and a list of boat owners. Bear with me.' She slid down her glasses and ran a finger down a list of names, muttering quietly as she did, and copying her findings onto a piece of paper. Eventually she pushed her glasses back onto the top of her head.

'There are four Peters registered here. She pointed at the first name. 'Peter Arnfield's not here. He left in August and moors his boat here empty over winter. He won't be back until April. Peter Howes isn't here at the moment. He took his boat out yesterday. Peter Carmichael is in berth 112. His boat's called *Voyager*, and Peter Bullock is berth 234 on *Dreamcatcher*.' She passed the paper across to Anna and a map showing the berths. She circled the relevant ones.

'I don't have a detailed description of the man. I just know he's in his thirties and was seen wearing a blue jacket and jeans.'

The woman shrugged. 'Doesn't ring a bell. They nearly all wear jeans and I only see them if there's a problem or when they check in.'

Anna recalled Flora's description. 'If I described him as "wild-eyed" would that jog any memories?'

'Hmm. It could be Peter Bullock. He only arrived two weeks ago and he lives alone on the boat. He's from Essex. I tried to talk to him about it because my sister moved down there, but he wasn't very talkative. He looks like a musician, with long hair, scruffy – a bit like that Bob Geldof. His eyes are like that – unfocused.'

Anna thanked the woman and emerged from the office into the grey. The rain was falling more heavily now. She angled the map so she could see where to head and plodded around the path towards berth 234. Her phone rang and she saw it was Mitz.

'Anna, where are you?' His voice sounded urgent.

'Kings Bromley Marina. I talked to the bus driver and he remembers dropping off the bloke we're after. I've got a name too – Peter Bullock.'

'You aren't there alone, are you?'

Anna didn't respond.

There was urgency in his voice. 'Stay where you are. I'm on my way. You can't go after him alone. He could be dangerous. Call in the name and get some background on him. I won't be long.'

He ended the call. Anna was slightly miffed at his tone. She could manage this on her own. Mitz usually supported her suggestions and encouraged her to follow her instincts. She had the element of surprise here and she was trained. She only wanted to ensure she was on the right trail and would have called it in once she was sure of her facts. If Mitz hadn't raced off in the first place, they'd have been doing this together. The urge to check out the boats was strong, however, in spite of everything, Mitz was right when he said the man could be dangerous. If Peter Bullock was the man who had killed Linda Upton, he was capable of acts of extreme violence. She kicked at a piece of gravel and wandered back towards the squad car to wait for Mitz.

She did as Mitz had instructed and called the station to pass on the name. Robyn had just left so she told David what she had so far. She was searching for information on him on her smartphone when she spotted a figure with shoulder-length hair coming from the facilities block. He was dressed in jeans and a blue coat and hunched forward against the now driving rain. A wisp of blue smoke indicated he had lit a cigarette and was drawing on it. He fitted Bullock's description and was headed in the direction of the car park. He would soon spot her squad car and if it was him, she might lose him. Without any thought to her safety she leapt from the car and marched towards him. With his head down, it was several moments before he saw her. It was only when she said, 'Mr Bullock? Mr Bullock, I wonder if you could answer a few questions for me,' that he looked up, startled. He threw the cigarette to one side, turned and hightailed it in the direction of the towpath. Anna cursed and thundered after him. Although she heard her name being shouted, she continued after the man, who had started running at speed.

Anna pounded the path in her flat, police-issue boots, wishing she were in more appropriate running shoes. However, she had youth and stamina on her side, and soon Bullock began to slow, the adrenalin fight-or-flight rush now over. Boats moored by the canal passed in a blur of gaudy colours as she focused on Bullock and pumped her legs, gaining on him bit by bit.

He turned to face her, hand in the air. 'I give up.' He bent over and wheezed. She slowed to a halt. 'Mr Bullock, I'd like to ask you a few questions.'

No sooner had she spoken than he threw a punch that she dodged. Grateful for her police training, she shot an arm out to grab him, only to receive an elbow in her face. It caught her on the nose, making her drop to her knees, and she let out a yelp of pain as he raced away again. She raised a hand to her throbbing nose and pulled it away. It was wet with blood. *The bastard. He wouldn't get away with this.* She wiped a sleeve across her nose and set off again, more determined than ever to catch him. Her nose throbbed and blood splattered down her shirt, but she ignored it. They were headed away from the marina and deeper into the countryside. Now there were only open fields. They were alone. She could hear the rushing of blood in her ears as she fought to gain on the man. Without warning, he drew to a halt. Only a few metres behind him, she slowed too, reaching for handcuffs and preparing to caution him.

Peter glanced about as if weighing up his options. His tongue flicked across his lips and then he smiled at her. His eyes bored into her and seconds slowed to minutes as she realised her folly. She was in the middle of nowhere with a potential killer. Her brain screamed at her to move but she had become rooted to the spot, transfixed by his blazing eyes. Without warning, he pounced at her, and before she could act he had grabbed her by the arm, tugging at her with a strength that surprised her. He hissed obscenities at her as he kicked out at her feet, trying to knock her off balance. At last her mind unfroze. He was trying to push her into the canal. *And no doubt drown her.* Anna's training came back to her in a rush. They struggled, entwined like two passionate dancers as she ducked and dived and fought back, finally wriggling free of his hold. They stood precariously close to the edge of the water – a brown, sludgy colour and whiffing of damp vegetation. He rummaged in a pocket and she prepared to fight off a knife attack, one arm raised to protect her face.

'Anna!'

Mitz was running towards them, too far away to help her now if this lunatic stabbed her. Peter spotted Mitz too, spun around and raced away again.

She was going to catch the scumbag and, in spite of the pain, she pounded on. The man was only a few feet away and she drove her legs on, launched into the air and felled him. He let out a squeal of protest.

'Mr Bullock, I am taking you in for questioning.'

Peter Bullock squirmed and bucked, knocking her off so she landed on her back, winded. She coughed on the blood now filling her nose and mouth. She couldn't breathe. Her heart beat faster. She had to move or she'd choke to death. Peter Bullock was crawling to his feet. She didn't have long. She pulled herself up and spat out the blood. He was up and ready to run again. She was about to launch herself at his feet and fell him when there was a rush of air and Peter Bullock landed with a whoosh on the towpath.

Mitz Patel grabbed Bullock by his collar and yanked him to his feet. Bullock spat at him but missed his mark. Mitz maintained a quiet dignity as he cautioned the man, 'You do not have to say anything. But it may harm your defence if you do not mention when questioned something which you later rely on in court. Anything you do say may be given in evidence…'

'You okay?' he asked, as Anna, one hand stemming the flow of blood from her nose, joined him. The adrenalin that had kept her going was ebbing and she wanted to sit down, but she was not going to lose face. 'Fine. Let's get this bugger back to the car.'

'You really okay?' asked Mitz quietly, once they had Bullock in Mitz's car and were standing next to it.

'I'm okay. It's almost stopped bleeding.'

'You know you should have waited, don't you?'

She nodded dumbly. It could have gone very badly wrong, especially if Bullock had been carrying a dangerous weapon. She had been foolhardy and she knew it.

'Are you going to report me?' she asked. 'Please don't. I should have known better. I got carried away with it. I really wanted to catch him. You know that feeling, don't you? Please don't tell anyone. I don't want to blot my copybook.'

Mitz shook his head. 'No. I won't tell anyone, even though I ought to. It's partly my fault. I shouldn't have asked you to take over.'

'Thank you. I owe you. I won't do anything like this again. And thanks for jumping on him. I thought he was going to knife me.'

'He had no weapon. You were lucky. It could have been worse. You sure your nose is all right?'

'I don't think it's broken. I inherited my dad's nose. The Shamash family all have good, strong noses. Large but strong.' She gave a half smile. Mitz picked up on her attempt at humour and returned the smile.

Mitz walked around the side of the car and was about to climb in when she asked. 'Mitz – your gran, how is she?'

He shook his head sadly. 'Granny Manju passed away an hour ago.'

'Oh no. I'm so sorry. You should be with your family.'

'I'll see them tonight. I had to return to work. I shouldn't have left you alone on the case. I'm a sergeant now and I have responsibilities here too.'

She wanted to offer a word of comfort, but Mitz slid into the car, shut the door and was already calling the station. Bullock sat passively in the back seat. The fight had gone out of him. She hoped she hadn't made any errors and that they'd got their man.

Back at the station, Mitz organised an interview room. Peter Bullock was now quiet and compliant. When asked to turn out his pockets he acquiesced, placing coins, cigarettes, a lighter and a transparent plastic bag containing white powder on the table.

'What's this?' asked Mitz, lifting it up and examining it in the light.

'What d'ya think it is?' His sharp, south London accent was a sharp contrast to the local accents of Staffordshire. 'It's why you were chasing me, innit? It's Charlie, C, coke, cocaine.' He sat back in his chair, eyes glowing fiercely. 'Shouldn't I have a brief if you're gonna charge me?'

Mitz shook the white powder and replaced it on the table. He took a deep breath. Anna glanced at him and felt her heart sink.

'You ran away from, and assaulted, a police officer, Mr Bullock. That's a serious offence. Why did you do that?'

Bullock sneered. 'I thought you were gonna do me for possession. I was coming back from the toilet block when she stopped me. I don't know why I decided to leg it. I should've stood me ground and heard her through, but it was automatic to run. I grew up on a dodgy estate and we was forever pegging it when we spotted one of yours. I couldn't help meself. I know what you lot can be like.'

He folded his arms and glared at Mitz.

'Mr Bullock, cocaine and assault to one side, we were trying to locate you to help with our enquiries regarding another matter.'

Bullock's face dropped. 'Oh shit. It's nuffin' to do with the drugs?'

Mitz shook his head. 'No. We weren't after you for having drugs. Unless you have a large quantity in your boat that you'd like to tell us about?'

Bullock laughed. 'You're joking. This packet set me back enough. You can go check it out if you don't believe me. I only have enough for me.'

'We're investigating an incident in Kings Bromley and wondered if you'd witnessed anything untoward. Mr Bullock, did you catch a bus from the bus stop at Kings Bromley yesterday morning at about ten fifteen, and get off near the marina at Bromley Hays?'

'Yeah, I did. I'd been visiting me auntie. She lives in Kings Bromley. She's coming up seventy and I thought I'd drop in and see her. I've only been in the area a couple of weeks. Lost me job last year and didn't know what to do wiv meself, so I took me redundancy money, sold me house and bought a boat. Best decision I ever made. I've been all over the country. You meet some nice people on the canals. I'm headed to Nottingham next. I was going to leave last week but it's nice at this marina – really peaceful. Thought I'd hang out here a bit longer than normal and enjoy the nature. I've dropped out of the rat race now. Don't think I'll ever go back. I don't need much money to live on the boat, just enough for essentials.' He shook the packet of cocaine and gave a wry smile.

'I don't suppose you noticed any abnormal activity while you were waiting at the bus stop, did you?'

'What'cha mean "abnormal"?'

'Anyone in a hurry, anyone looking shifty?'

'Nah, it's a really quiet village. I left me auntie's at ten. She made me leave early in case the bus was early. It wasn't early and I stood about like a right prat for fifteen minutes. There was no one else waiting at the stop. There were quite a few lorries going through the place. Shame really, cos they don't half spoil it. All them little thatched cottages and bloomin' big lorries chugging past, belching out fumes. Can't say I saw anything odd. Hang on, there was one bloke who went into the pub car park. He was obviously late for the gym cos he was getting a wriggle on – running like. He was in a sweatshirt and tracksuit bottoms. Adidas, I think, judging by the white logo, or is that Nike? No, that's a white tick. This was like a crown with the name under it. I always get mixed up with the labels. He was carrying one of them big sports bags. He got into a car cos I heard the door bang loudly and the engine start. Next thing, he drove past me and headed towards the A38.'

'Did you get a look at his face?'

'Nah. I wasn't paying any attention to him. I was getting fed up of waiting for the bloody bus. I was thinking about walking it, to be honest.'

'Have you any idea what make the car was, Mr Bullock?'

'Now that I can help you with. It was a silver Fiat 500. It was on a 2014 plate.'

'Can you be sure of that?'

Bullock sat back looking more confident. 'I certainly can. My aunt Jean has one just like it in white.'

CHAPTER THIRTY

Alan Worth was an arrogant man who barely acknowledged Robyn as she was shown into the room by his housekeeper, a delightful Asian lady with shining black hair, clipped back with colourful butterfly slides. His study was a huge space with a polished oak floor, and covered with what she recognised as expensive rugs. Two abstract paintings of coloured geometric shapes hung on the walls. In the corner of the room stood a five-foot bronze sculpture of a naked woman dancing, one knee raised and both arms flung out in front of her. Two other erotic statuettes were on a bookcase that held only a few books and various other ornaments.

She stood in front of a handcrafted mahogany desk that would not have looked out of place in a Victorian headmaster's study or a lawyer's office, and offered her hand.

He shook it once. His handshake was limp and his palm damp. 'How can I help, Detective Inspector Carter?'

'It's regarding Harriet.'

He dropped back into his leather chair and observed her with heavy-lidded eyes. His hooked nose added to the impression of a bird of prey. 'Harriet died four years ago.' He fell silent, waiting for her to speak again.

'I'm investigating a case that may be linked to her death.'

He steepled his fingers together and stared at her. 'In what way?'

'I'm not sure at the moment, but I'd very much appreciate your cooperation.'

A noise, somewhere between a hiss and a sigh, escaped his nostrils. 'What do you want to know?'

'I've read the file on your wife's death. I'd like to know some more details – you were going to sue the Bishtons who owned Bromley Hall, yet you didn't take the case to court. I'd like to know why not and how much you settled for.'

He glared at Robyn, who maintained a steady gaze. 'I don't see how that's any of your business.'

'I appreciate that, Mr Worth, and I can assure you that any disclosure will not become public knowledge. However, I must ask you as it may have a bearing on our case.'

'Again, I can't see how that's any of your business, and unless you explain why you need to know, I shall be showing you out.'

'You'll appreciate that we can't discuss ongoing cases, sir. I am very much banking on your generosity of spirit, especially as it involves someone you know.'

His eyes widened a fraction. 'Who?'

'Linda Upton.'

Alan blinked several times. 'Linda? What's happened to her?'

'She was found dead at her house. There was a piece about it in the *Lichfield Times*.'

'I don't bother with that rag. When did it happen?'

'Yesterday morning.' She studied his reaction to the news. He blinked again, before regaining his superior composure.

'You're suggesting she died in suspicious circumstances, aren't you? I hope you don't consider me a suspect. I was in a meeting all morning with my accountant dealing with tax returns. I have several witnesses too who saw me at lunch at the Olive Tree in Lichfield.'

'As I said, sir, I was simply interested in learning how much the Bishtons paid out as compensation for the death of your wife, Harriet.'

He rose suddenly and stalked to the door. 'If I'm not a suspect, I'll thank you to leave now. I have an appointment in a few minutes and I can't help you any further in your enquiries.'

She stood up and moved towards him. She had only one card left to play, and if Mulholland found out she was not adhering to police protocol in this matter, she would be in deep water. She would try to jolt him into talking to her. 'You'll appreciate, sir, that I am concerned about your safety.'

He paused, hand on the doorknob. 'You think I might be in danger?'

'I don't know. If you could answer my question, I'd be in a better position to make a judgement on that.'

He sighed. 'One and a half million. I was offered one and a half million by the Bishtons. I accepted it on the condition they shut down the spa. I wanted to make their lives difficult. I hoped it would ruin them. I hadn't banked on them building a massive extension to the property afterwards and creating an even bigger spa. If I had, I'd have demanded far more than one and half million. By the time they'd decided to build it, I had no more leverage. After all, I had accepted the money and so I got on with my life.' His head drooped, and for a moment he appeared more vulnerable. Then he pulled himself upright. 'Do you think I'm in danger?'

Robyn cast a look at the man, the haughty sneer back on his face. He had shown no emotion when he had learned Linda Upton was dead and was only concerned about himself. Although she now had the information she required, she knew her handling of the situation had been unethical. 'I shall continue my investigations and certainly ensure you have police protection if I believe you are, sir. Thank you for your time.'

Robyn strode out against the wind and drizzle that was now falling and threw herself into her car, glad to be out of the unwelcoming house. She had two missed calls. She picked up the messages. Both were from Mitz, warning her that Mulholland had asked for updates on the cases and that he and Anna had brought in their suspect only to learn he was not involved in the case. However, the last part of Mitz's message gave Robyn the boost she needed. Their suspect, now turned witness, had identified a vehicle leaving Kings Bromley, and Mitz and Anna were now trying to locate it. She shut her eyes for a moment to visualise her whiteboard. It was beginning to look like they were on the scent of the killer at last. What she needed was to get one step ahead of him. She put her car into gear and gunned the throttle. She would work through the night if she had to. She wasn't letting anyone else get hurt by this Lichfield Leopard.

CHAPTER THIRTY-ONE

'You shouldn't have,' Harriet said. The bunch of brightly coloured flowers filled her arms.

He gave a shy smile. 'They're not from me. They're from Alfie. That's why there are so many yellow flowers. That's his favourite colour.'

She laughed again. Alfie wagged his tail at the sound.

'Do you want me to hold them for you while you exercise? I don't want to stop your routine.'

'It's okay. I could do with a day off. I've been training every day for weeks. I'm doing a fun run on Saturday and I wanted to be fit enough. You've probably done me a favour. My muscles could do with a rest.'

He beamed. 'A fun run? I never thought running was fun.'

Harriet's smile was wide and reached her eyes. He thought he saw his reflection in them and was lost for a moment, until her voice roused him. 'I was hopeless at running when I was younger. Last year, one of my friends got cancer and was terribly ill with the treatment. I wanted to do something to help raise awareness, so I started running and did a half marathon. I raised quite a bit of money, which encouraged me to keep it up, and now I do fun runs regularly.'

'That's inspirational. I expect your friend was very grateful.'

'She was full of energy and spirit. Sadly she passed away all the same. The cancer was too aggressive. I now run in her name, and every penny I get goes towards research to help eradicate this dreadful disease.'

There was such passion in Harriet's voice that he wanted to hold her hand and comfort her, but it was too soon to display such affection. She didn't know him well enough.

'Look, if you aren't going to run today, why don't I take you for that coffee I owe you? Alfie can come too and sit outside the café. It's a decent day so we can join him.'

She turned her attention to the flowers, searching for a polite way to decline. He surreptitiously extracted a dog treat from his trouser pocket and, on cue, Alfie barked for it.

'See, Alfie wants you to come. It's only coffee, and I won't bite. Neither will Alfie.'

Her lips twitched into a half smile. 'Okay. Seeing as you both asked so nicely.'

They trundled to the café in town and he bought her a large latte. He treated Alfie to a piece of shortbread and made a fuss of him. He kept the conversation light and convinced her he was quite the historian, even though he'd got his facts from the Internet only the day before.

'Did you know that Stowe Pool was once a fishery?'

'I had no idea. I thought it was a large pond.'

He laughed. 'It actually used to be a mill pond many years ago. It's been through many hands since then and it was only recently, in 1968, that it was transformed into this recreational area.'

Her eyes widened. 'Wow, you know some facts.'

'I had to look into the history of Lichfield as part of the research for my lecture on cities in England.'

Her eyebrows arched and she gestured with her spoon. 'You're a historian? I always imagine historians to be grey-haired and elderly. I was rubbish at history... and most subjects. I couldn't wait to leave school. I didn't enjoy it much. Now, however, I wish I'd paid more attention.'

He gave her a smile. 'It's not for everyone.'

'Where do you lecture?' she asked.

'Birmingham University, although I'm taking a sabbatical this year to write a book.'

Her eyebrows rose higher still. Her mouth made a perfect-shaped 'o'. 'Even more impressive. What's the book about? Lichfield?'

He gave a half smile. 'If I tell you, you won't laugh, will you?'

She shook her head and rested her forearms on the table, leaning closer to hear his response. He could almost feel her warm breath.

'It's a historical romance set during World War Two.'

Her mouth dropped wide open. 'Really?'

'Yes, but I don't tell many people. I'm writing it under a pen name.'

She licked her spoon, and as he watched her pink tongue dart in and out, he thought he might have a heart attack, such were the palpitations in his chest. Alfie spotted the spoon too and pawed at her. She leant over and patted him. 'He's a very friendly dog.'

'He's a rescue dog. I got him from a dogs' home. I really intended to get a Labrador or something larger. I passed his cage first and stopped. He was a quivering wreck in the corner – just two large frightened eyes. As soon as I saw him, I knew I had to have him.'

She threw him a kindly glance. 'That's lovely.'

'He'd been maltreated. He was so thin you could see his ribcage, and his fur was in clumps – all matted and dirty. He'd been beaten regularly and he was frightened of people.'

Alfie whined and gave her a paw again. Harriet had no idea Alfie was after food. He was always begging at home and Stacey spoilt him rotten. 'He really likes you. He's a good judge of character.'

They chatted aimlessly about Lichfield and interests for a while. As soon as she had finished her drink, he thanked her again for finding Alfie and left her. She waved as he and the dog walked away. Once he was around the corner he permitted himself a grin. His new girlfriend was beautiful, delightful and very gullible.

He drifted back to the present. He had been so lost in memories of his time with Harriet that he almost hadn't heard the doorbell. It rang again – a lengthy peal – the sound of someone exasperated. He let it ring. He couldn't be bothered to answer it. No doubt it was the neighbour wanting to complain about something.

The ringing stopped and he shifted position on the couch, letting the pills work their magic as he drifted back into a semi-conscious state where he could be with his Harriet.

CHAPTER THIRTY-TWO

Robyn strode down the corridor to Mulholland's office first thing Wednesday morning and rapped on the door. Louisa was bent over a document, deep furrows across her forehead, her eyes red-rimmed and moist. She sneezed suddenly several times before reaching for a box of tissues. Her voice was nasal, thick with mucus.

'I understand from Sergeant Higham that you were out chasing a "hot lead" yesterday afternoon. Is that code for *I'm desperately trying to find something so my boss doesn't take my case away from me?*'

Robyn shrugged. 'I actually do have something now. There are definite links between the death of Rory Wallis and Linda Upton. They are both connected to Harriet Worth, who died back in 2012. Here's the old case file.' She had been studying it most of the night and knew exactly what it contained.

'Harriet Worth was at Bromley Hall hotel and spa with her friend Linda Upton, when she slipped and fell into the pool. The incident took place out of hours. The pool area ought to have been locked but it was not, and Harriet, who had been in the Champagne Bar all evening, found her way into the spa, where she undressed in preparation for a swim. At that time there wasn't the security or cameras that there are today in the new extension of the hotel spa. Harriet's body wasn't found until the next morning, by which time she was dead.

'The coroner's report revealed that a blow to Harriet's head, which he believed was caused by a fall, had rendered her unconscious and that she had subsequently fallen into the water and drowned. Forensics discovered blood on the tiled surround of the pool that matched the victim's own, and deduced she had fallen into the pool, hitting her head on the surround as she fell. They also discovered the flooring by the pool was wet from a leaking shower that was due to be fixed that morning, and that a sign warning people of the danger of slipping had been placed in the appropriate place.'

'Where are you going with this, DI Carter?' asked Mulholland, wiping her nose on a tissue. She popped a throat lozenge into her mouth.

'Harriet Worth's death was declared accidental. However, her husband wanted to take the case to court and sue the spa hotel, and the couple who owned it. In the end, he settled out of court for one and a half million pounds, on the condition the spa was closed.'

Robyn paused to make sure Louisa was following her argument. 'It was Linda Upton's suggestion that they took a spa break. The man serving them champagne that night was Rory Wallis. There is a connection. The notes left on both the dead bodies are invoices for a quarter of a million pounds each. If I'm right, we have a killer who is seeking revenge for Harriet's death. Not only that, I think he will kill again, and soon. He is not hanging about.'

'You believe there are possibly four more people on his hit list?'

'I think so, unless Miles Ashbrook was one of those he wanted dead.'

Mulholland's face changed. 'You're not going to worry about that particular angle, are you?'

'No, ma'am. It was merely a thought. I want to interview anyone who was working at Bromley Hall at the time Harriet died. I want to concentrate on the staff at this stage, but I'll also get my team to track down any guests who were there in July 2012.'

'I don't have a problem with that. Go ahead.'

'Thank you, ma'am. So, I'm still in charge of this case?'

'Yes,' replied Mulholland. 'You've got enough to be going on with. I hear you might even have another lead.'

'Mitz and Anna interviewed a witness who spotted a vehicle leaving Kings Bromley the morning Linda Upton was murdered. At the moment we don't have much. They're searching databases for a 2014 silver Fiat 500.'

'Okay. That's good. Can I remind you that unorthodox methods of investigating won't be tolerated on this occasion, DI Carter? I know in the past I have turned a blind eye to you and your team's methods, but I can't afford to this time. You need to be seen to be adhering to protocol. Clear?'

'Excuse me, ma'am, I know I have had to take the odd liberty to get results, but I have always got those results. We have a killer to catch, and if I have to follow my instincts to do so, then surely that should be acceptable.'

'No, DI Carter, it is not. Not this time, and if I hear you have, I'll have no option but to replace you. Robyn, I only have your best interests at heart.'

'Is this because of Shearer? Has he threatened to report you if you don't keep me reined in?'

The moment of silence that followed was all the confirmation she needed. Robyn stared hard at her superior. 'I won't be bullied or intimidated by that man. Nor should you.'

'It's not a question of bullying. It is for your own good. You don't want to be a DI forever, do you?'

'At the moment, I don't care. I just want to do my job, and my job is to find whoever is responsible for killing Linda Upton and Rory Wallis.'

Mulholland paused as if she wanted to say something else, and Robyn waited for her to speak. The moment passed and she found herself dismissed.

She had no sooner entered her office than her mobile rang. It was Ross.

'Hi, cuz. Got a few interesting bits and pieces for you.'

'Hi, Ross. Your timing is perfect. I was about to call you. There's been a breakthrough here and I have a possible link to Bromley Hall.'

'Okay, I'll keep it brief. I can't access the CCTV footage. There's an outside control box on the sauna wall which can be operated with a key. The temperature of the sauna can be overridden by this box, so someone could raise the temperature without anyone inside the sauna being any the wiser. The in-house handyman and the gym manager hold the keys to the box. It is therefore possible that Miles Ashbrook was unaware of how hot it was in the sauna, which would explain how he got so cooked overnight.

'Miles Ashbrook was disliked by several members of staff. He'd recently begun firing individuals and there was a fair amount of bad feeling towards him. There's speculation that Jakub Woźniak, who is in charge of cleaning the spa and pool areas, threatened to kill Miles, although that has yet to be confirmed. He challenged a decision to fire his wife Emily, and was overheard arguing with and threatening Miles. I haven't interviewed Jakub or the person who heard the conversation yet, although we have a name of a guest who can help with that – Fiona Maggiore. It might be better if you conduct that interview on a more official basis.

'I've been unable to talk to Scott Dawson. Sorry. He was in meetings or taking classes every time I tried to speak to him. We're checking out in the next hour. I'll type all my findings up for you and send them over as soon as I get back to the office. I've drawn some layout sketches of the spa that I'll scan and send too.'

'Thanks, Ross. I'll talk to Jakub and Fiona. Don't forget to bill me for your time.'

'I'm happy to give you that information for free. You paid for our spa break. Besides, I enjoyed snooping about. Although it isn't case-related, this place is full of secrets. The old spa area was dug up and the pool filled in after a guest drowned in it. You can't get anyone here to talk about it, although one of the guests was more obliging. I'll tell you when I see you.' He could picture Robyn's face, cheeks sucked in as she digested his words.

'That's very interesting. I think I might already have that information though. It was Harriet Worth who drowned. I've got to have a quick meeting with my team and then I'm coming over to Bromley Hall. I'll see you at reception about two o'clock when you check out.'

Sleep-deprived faces etched with lines rose when she spoke. The cases were beginning to take their toll on her team. Even Mitz, who was always immaculately turned out, had stubble on his chin and deep purple bruises under his eyes. 'Mitz, you're with me. Matt, find out what you can about Harriet Worth – track down old girlfriends and see if you can get any more information surrounding her death. David, are you okay with searching for the silver Fiat?' He gave a mock salute.

'Anna, you still have that CCTV footage from the night Miles Ashbrook died, don't you?'

'Yes, boss.'

'Please go through the entire night carefully. I still can't shake the fact that Ashbrook's death is somehow related to all of this. Look for anything suspicious. Check the timings for when you see Miles appear and any other strange activity in or around the sauna.' Matt threw her a look that she ignored. She was not going to be browbeaten on this, and she didn't care if Shearer reported her or caused trouble. She was going to try and establish, once and for all, that Miles Ashbrook's death was not an accident.

CHAPTER THIRTY-THREE

Jakub breathed in the cold afternoon air and pedalled harder. His face was again wet from the persistent drizzle and he shivered. It had turned dark earlier than usual thanks to the heavy black clouds and he wanted nothing more than to get home and see Emily and his son, Adam. Whenever he was on an early shift he would ensure he got home in time to play hide and seek with the boy. It was his son's favourite game, and always resulted in him being found and tickled until he cried with laughter. Soon Adam would be too old for such high jinks, but, in time, the new baby would also enjoy the game. If they had another boy they had decided to call him Tobias, after Jakub's father. His father would be very proud.

In spite of the bad weather, Jakub felt satisfied with his lot. He had a fine family, and although they struggled at times, he was lucky to have them. Emily had sent a text that afternoon to say she had an interview for a new job. Suddenly the pressure was easing off. He only needed to get the wretched car fixed and all would be fine. The garage had promised he could collect it the following day. He'd be glad to get it back. He was fed up with riding the bike morning and night in all manner of weather conditions.

He looked forward to some warmth, a cooked meal and sitting in front of the television, watching football once Adam was in bed. He freewheeled down the stretch that passed a disused glider field. Only the year before, he had watched the white planes as they passed overhead soundlessly, and wondered what it would be like to be in the cockpit of one. He imagined it would be akin to being a bird in flight, swooping and diving, catching the thermals and gliding high above the fields and the Hall. The gliding school had since shut down and now the land was for sale.

He passed the crossroads, changed gear and was preparing to pedal up the slope when he lost control of the bike. It skidded on the incline and, catching it in time before it toppled over, Jakub dismounted and swore loudly. His front tyre was as flat as could be. How had that happened? He'd only checked the bike that morning. He must have ridden over something sharp. He pulled out his mobile to alert Emily and get assistance when he spotted headlights approaching from the direction of the Hall. Thinking he might be able to catch a lift or some assistance, he stood in the road and waved his hands. The car was travelling very slowly, almost too slowly. In his high-visibility jacket, the driver would be sure to spot him. Jakub smiled to himself as the vehicle approached. He recognised the car and knew the driver. He wouldn't have to walk home after all. He waved again to make sure he'd been seen and waited for the car to halt beside him. The car, however, did not stop. Jakub's smile faded as the car suddenly accelerated and headed towards him at speed. He knew he should dive out of the way yet he was frozen to the spot, helpless, unable to move and, although his brain screamed at him, he stood, arms dangling by his side, mouth open in surprise as the car drove at him. He felt absolutely nothing as he rose high into the air, fields spinning below him as he soared. His felt like a bird flying. At last he understood the sensation of weightlessness and freedom that birds experienced.

He dropped back on the tarmac, broken and unconscious. The driver checked his rear-view mirror before reversing the car. He got out and bent over Jakub's prone form, kicking it lightly. When it made no noise, he pushed a rolled-up piece of paper into Jakub's trouser pocket, before returning to the car and speeding off down the road.

CHAPTER THIRTY-FOUR

The rain was falling steadily as Robyn drove out of Stafford. Traffic was incessant, and the oncoming vehicles cast gloomy yellow lights on the large puddles forming in the roads. She cursed as they were held up at yet another set of traffic lights and crawled slowly to the junction.

Mitz had been quiet since they'd left the station and she had initially believed that he too was feeling the weight of the case. She had jollied him along, asking about his latest blind date; Mitz had an endless stream of blind dates that invariably ended disastrously. He smirked for a moment.

'I went on one last Friday. I thought I'd cracked this one. She was very beautiful. It went well, or so I thought until the end, when we parted. I went in for the kill and she patted me on the shoulder. Patted! I ask you,' he joked. For a moment some sparkle had returned to his eyes.

Robyn had a great deal of respect for the young man. He had worked tirelessly and had recently been promoted to sergeant. Silence fell as she navigated the cluttered roundabouts of Stafford, now filled with anxious shoppers getting their early Christmas bargains. It seemed to start earlier every year. That reminded her, she had to buy Amélie a gift, and she still had their day out to arrange. She finally gathered some speed on the road past Cannock Chase. Brown bracken and the soggy branches of trees added to the gloomy picture.

She glanced at Mitz, whose mind seemed elsewhere. 'Everything okay?'

Mitz shook his head slowly. 'Not really. My super Granny Manju passed away yesterday afternoon.'

'I'm so sorry.' Robyn was deeply saddened by the news. Not only was Manju a truly unique lady who was incredibly proud of her grandson, but she knew how close Mitz was to her. This would have shaken him badly. 'You should take some time off.'

He shook his head. 'No, boss. Granny Manju taught me many things and was proud of what I had achieved. She was so happy when I made sergeant this year. She would want me to find this killer, not mope about at home.'

'The funeral will be next Tuesday. The Indian ceremony will be at one o'clock, and the cremation at two. Just like my gran's home, everyone is welcome, so if you have a chance…'

'I'll be there. She was a wonderful lady.'

There was silence again. Eventually Mitz spoke. 'Boss, I left the scene of an investigation yesterday. I left my junior officer in charge. It was most unprofessional of me. I was going to remain quiet about it, then I thought that was wrong too.'

'What happened?'

'I got the call from my mother saying Granny Manju was dying and I rushed off to see her for the last time. I phoned Anna and she took over. I'd been waiting to interview a bus driver. He had information on the man spotted at the bus stop. Instead, Anna got the information and acted on it. I should have been there. It could have gone horribly wrong and Anna could have been hurt worse than she was.'

'You assisted with the man's capture, didn't you?'

'I did. When I got to the house, Manju had slipped away. I'd missed my chance. I paid my respects and had a few words with my parents, after which I immediately rejoined Anna.'

'There were extenuating circumstances for your departure and you did absolutely the right thing by returning. That shows dedication. Is Anna okay?'

'She got thumped in the nose, but she's all right. The medical officer checked her over. I insisted. Anna knows she shouldn't have gone off after a suspect like that. I didn't want her disciplined. She's a bright officer. With hindsight, I ought to have reported it. I feel bad about the whole episode, and I don't like covering up stuff.'

Mitz looked deflated and miserable. Robyn threw him a kindly smile. 'I wouldn't give it a second thought. I'm quite satisfied you behaved appropriately. Now forget all about it.'

'But what if I had stayed at the house longer? Anna could have been seriously injured.'

'There are no "what ifs". All is well. You apprehended a potential suspect and obtained information that will prove useful. We are a step closer thanks to your actions. Now drop it or I'll be forced to play you my collection of eighties dance music.'

They left the main road and sped down wide lanes towards their destination, unimpeded by traffic, and fifteen minutes later, at two thirty, drew up outside Bromley Hall. Virginia creeper covered the façade. In autumn its leaves turned flame-red, setting the Hall on fire, but it was in its winter state now, a huge network of dark veins that spidered up the brickwork to the very top of the building. She turned to face her colleague, an elbow on the wheel. 'Come on, Sergeant Patel, let's see if we can make some headway.'

A serious-faced young man in a porter's outfit stood by reception, waiting to assist any guests. He saw Robyn and Mitz enter, and scooted forward. Ross intercepted him.

'It's okay, Dan. They're with me.'

The man bowed his head with a deep-throated, 'No problem, sir.' Robyn tried not to stare at the young man's right ear, which was rather large and stuck out, and instead gave him a tight smile. He nodded at her.

'Dan!' A young woman on reception beckoned to him and he darted off.

'He's a porter-come-dogsbody,' said Ross, when Dan was out of earshot. 'He's bit of an oddball. Doesn't like chatting and spends most of the day staring into space. He's the first young man I've ever met who isn't always on his smartphone. Inoffensive though.'

They moved into the Long Galley with its plush furnishing and thick embroidered curtains, and found a quiet corner near a cabinet of china. They dropped down onto the elegant sofas and chatted in low voices as Ross imparted all the information he had uncovered. Mitz made notes while Robyn sat forward, listening intently to Ross's every word.

'This place used to be owned by a wealthy family – the Bishtons – who sold out in 2013. They kept the large mansion near the Hall and still spend time here, although they spend the greater part of the year travelling and have a place in Thailand. No one is in the house at the moment, so I couldn't talk to either Lord or Lady Bishton. However, I learned Lord Bishton is returning for an annual hunt ball that takes place this coming Sunday. He's rarely around, so if you want to interview him, you'll need to get an appointment with his secretary. He's due home Friday morning but is only staying until Tuesday.'

Mitz scribbled in his pad.

'Scott Dawson has been impossible to pin down. I can't work out if he's incredibly busy or is trying to hide from everyone. Maybe the responsibility of being manager for the moment is proving too great for him. He also has family pressures. Jeanette found out via the grapevine that he and his wife are going through a rocky patch at the moment. He's been at Bromley Hall since the place opened, and was promoted to gym manager in 2010, so he will have been here when Harriet drowned.'

'I'll talk to him first. Is he here at the moment?'

'He disappeared earlier. Donna on reception said he nipped home for a while. He's due back to take an early evening class, so you'll be able to talk to him after that. He should be around at about five.'

'And Jakub?'

'He was on an early shift so I think he'll be off duty soon. You might have to wait until tomorrow to speak to him.'

Robyn shifted in her seat. 'Regarding the other matter, who do you think I should speak to?'

'Start with Bruno Miguel. He's a commis chef and he's involved in a long-term affair with one of the guests, Fiona Maggiore. They've been keeping it very hush-hush, for obvious reasons. The lady in question became loose-tongued after several glasses of champagne with Jeanette. It transpires she's been seeing Bruno since she started coming here. Initially it was a one-night stand, then, each trip she made, their relationship became more serious. She's considering leaving her husband for Bruno but they're not making it common knowledge yet.'

'Bruno? That's a Spanish or Italian name, isn't it?'

'Actually, it's a German name. However, this Bruno is Portuguese, although he's lived in the UK from a very early age so he speaks English fluently. He told Fiona he was thinking of quitting his job here. He thought the new management company would make the place even bigger and better, but instead they've lost their way and introduced stringent cost-cutting measures and staff reductions. The kitchen is under enormous strain. He wanted to talk to Miles Ashbrook about it, but on reaching his office he heard raised voices. He left, imagining he would talk to Miles in the morning.

Of course by then it was too late. Now this is all hearsay from the lady he's been seeing, so you'll need to confirm that.'

'That's very helpful, Ross.'

'Not a problem. As I told you on the phone, I think it's feasible that somebody with a key could have interfered with the heat regulator attached to the sauna. A person may think they are sitting in seventy or eighty degrees when in fact it could be much hotter than they think. If the temperature rises to 110 degrees, it is quite possible for skin to burn. I checked the CCTV camera and observed its movements, and it doesn't appear to cover that part of the spa. You'd be incredibly fortunate to get a shot of anyone by the box. I've written down the length of time the camera spends surveying each area and in which direction it travels. You should be able to check the timings on the CCTV footage for accuracy and spot if anyone has interfered with it.'

Mitz lifted his pen like a schoolboy trying to grab attention in class. 'Do you suspect someone turned up the heat in the sauna, guv? Surely DI Shearer would have found that out.'

'This is between us, okay? I'm going out on a limb here, which is why I asked Ross to look at the possibility. There's probably nothing in it, although I wanted to check it out all the same. Leave no stone unturned, so to speak.'

'For what it's worth, I think it's most unlikely anyone fiddled with the box. There was no reason for them to. Ashbrook had a dodgy ticker. He had a heart attack. He went into a hot sauna.' Ross made a starfish shape with his fingers – poof, a magician's gesture.

'I still can't get it out of my head. He knew he had a heart condition. It doesn't make sense.'

Ross let it lie. Robyn could be very dogmatic and wouldn't listen to reason at times. That was one of her failings, and her strengths. He tried to catch her eye but she avoided his gaze. She was haggard, high cheekbones pronounced, eyes red-rimmed with tiredness, and more emaciated than ever. She was in danger of working herself into an early grave. Maybe that was her plan. She was still struggling with losing Davies, even after this length of time. Maybe she was going to push herself to the limit until something gave.

She dropped the subject of Ashbrook's death and instead continued questioning Ross about various members of staff and the layout of the Hall. Before long they were joined by Jeanette, dressed in twinset and pearls with matching tweed skirt. She greeted them all before tugging at Ross's arm. 'It's after three, Ross, and time to leave these officers to their investigations. Robyn, thank you. It was a lovely break and I think Ross benefited from the rest.'

'Pleasure. Did you take a photo of him in his Speedos?'

Jeanette laughed. 'I most certainly did not. I took one instead of him in his fluffy gown, fast asleep on a lounger, which I'll keep to remind him he needs to look after himself.'

Ross gave her a sheepish look, shaggy eyebrows lifted. 'You didn't?'

'You bet I did,' she replied, and putting her arm through his, they left.

Robyn stirred into action. 'I'm going to talk to Jakub Woźniak, if he hasn't left, and then have a word with Bruno Miguel about what he overheard the night Miles Ashbrook died. Use your charm on the receptionist and find out how many of the current staff were employed at the Hall in 2012 when Harriet died. Interview any of them that are on the premises. As soon as Scott Dawson turns up for class, we'll talk to him. Meet me at the gym at half four. I don't want to wait until after his class, in case he goes off again.'

Mitz spoke quietly. 'You're intent on following up on Ashbrook's death, aren't you?'

'Have you got a problem with that?'

Mitz chewed on his lip before answering. 'I'll be honest, I'm not comfortable with it, but I shan't say anything. I just hope this doesn't get back to the station.'

CHAPTER THIRTY-FIVE

His mind was fevered. The thrill of the kill was a high he had never experienced before. Apart from the odd rabbit he had shot with an air rifle and a few neighbourhood cats that he had practised his neck-snapping technique on, he had not killed before this big mission. It had been so easy and electrifying. He replayed the sound of Jakub's body hitting his car bonnet over and over again in his head, and when he closed his eyes he could see the man's look of utter surprise as he flew into the dark sky.

It had been perfectly set up: a drawing pin in Jakub's bike tyre that caused air to escape little by little. The tyre wouldn't fully deflate until extra weight was placed on the bike. His calculations were perfect, and Jakub fell by the side of the winding lane, just as he had hoped. It couldn't have gone better. He mustn't get too agitated or excited about it. He had to maintain his act. There would be time to celebrate later.

He opened his wallet and gazed at the photograph of Harriet he kept there, then blew it a kiss. He whispered her name over and over again as he let his memory travel back in time.

He played it cool over the next few days. He didn't want to frighten Harriet off. Every time she ran around Stowe Pool he'd be on the playing fields with Alfie, throwing a Frisbee or Alfie's squeaky ball and pretending to be enjoying every minute of it. Whenever she exercised on the outside equipment he would be showering Alfie with affection and throwing dog treats for him. He would only raise a hand in greeting and smile in her direction or say hello. This was the way to win her over. She wouldn't want to know that while she was showering after her run he was walking past her road, and that he now knew a lot about her.

His sister Stacey, on the other hand, was growing increasingly suspicious of his actions. She couldn't understand why he'd go out of his way to take Alfie out every day. He had fobbed her off on several occasions.

'He's good for my health. The doctor told me I needed fresh air, and taking Alfie for a walk encourages me to go out.' That might have washed with her if she hadn't caught him kicking the dog in the backyard. He didn't know she had come home early while he was enjoying a sneaky ciggy out there – Stacey created blue murder when he smoked in the house. Alfie had come outside with his squeaky ball and insisted on squeaking it incessantly. The noise got to him and he'd lashed out with his foot, giving Alfie a good kick in the nuts. The animal had howled in agony, and Stacey had seen the whole thing from the kitchen window.

She folded her huge arms over her chest and regarded him with cold, unblinking eyes. 'You'll have to find somewhere else to live. You can't stay here any more. It was only ever supposed to be temporary. You've been here five months. You'll have to go. I need my space.'

He pleaded with her, knowing he usually wormed his way back into her affections. 'Sis, it was an accident.' Stacey gave him that same wary look she had given him when they were younger. She knew what he really was. And she knew he couldn't be trusted. She blocked the kitchen door like a sumo wrestler and shook her head. He'd run out of luck.

This changed his plans, and instead of engaging Harriet in banter or impressing her with passages from his novel – which he had actually copied from the Internet – he had to conjure up an alternative plan. He put it into action immediately and headed towards Stowe Pool at his usual time. He couldn't help himself. The urge to see her was too great.

It felt strange not having the dog with him. Listening to the ten o'clock chiming of St Chad's church bells, he rubbed his eyes hard until they hurt, and, arching backwards, he filled them with eye drops stolen from his sister's cabinet. He wandered onto the path around the reservoir, head bowed. By the time he'd reached the playing fields he heard her calling him. He ignored her voice. Curiosity would lead her to him. Sure enough, he soon heard her breathless voice as she ran up to him, 'Hey. What's happened? Where's Alfie?'

He swiped the pad of his thumb under his eye before blowing his nose on a tissue. His bloodshot eyes and heaving dry sobs told her everything she needed to know.

'Hey,' Harriet repeated and put an arm around his shoulder, pulling him towards her. He hoped she couldn't hear his hammering heart. He sniffed and gulped back imaginary tears. The eye drops streamed down his face.

'Alfie got hit by a lorry.'

'Oh no!' Her hands flew to her mouth. 'Is he——?'

'He died in my arms. It was the postman's fault. He hadn't fastened the gate properly, and when Alfie bounded out to do his business he spotted something on the far side of the road and raced after it. I heard the squeal of tyres and I knew. My poor little dog.' He sniffed again and wiped his eyes.

'I'm so sorry. I don't know what to say.'

His body shook, mostly due to her proximity, although she misinterpreted it as shock.

'When did this happen?'

'First thing this morning. I couldn't bear to stay in the house. I had to get out. I haven't buried him yet. I've left him in his bed with a blanket over him. It's like he's dozing, and any minute he'll leap up to come for a walk. Does that sound stupid?'

'Not at all. You need a while to adjust. Hey, why don't you and I go for a cup of tea, and after that you might feel more able to bury him when you get home?'

He gave her what he hoped was a look of gratitude mixed with sadness. He took her hand. 'You're very kind. I can't trouble you. I'm just some bloke who's lost his dog for good. You've got your training, and I've taken up enough of your time the last few days.'

'I insist. You can tell me about your book. Take your mind off the terrible shock.'

He nodded miserably. 'You're probably right. Thank you. Let me pay for it.'

'I wouldn't dream of it. I'll pay. After all, Alfie bought me such beautiful flowers.'

He blew his nose again and wiped his eyes. 'Only if you're sure. That'd be really kind.'

She chose a quaint café, down from the church, which was empty bar the two of them, and insisted on getting him a slice of cake as well as a pot of tea. The café walls were painted in white and decorated with large black and white photographs of street scenes from the 1950s. The tablecloths were red checked, and on each table sat a small vase of flowers.

He kept up his act: a man distraught and confused. 'I can't thank you enough for your kindness.'

'It's nothing. Tell me, have you written any more of your novel?'

He pulled at the serviette, plucking the edges. 'Actually, I have.'

She watched him as he picked up his cup, hand trembling. 'Next time, you'll have to read some of it to me.'

She chatted for a while about books she had read, and they got onto films. Fortunately, he could talk about those she professed to enjoy as he had been subjected to them while living at Stacey's house. She was a chick-flick addict. He had spent many a dull evening watching that nonsense, and dreaming up ways to kill his sibling while she chewed her way through her own body weight in chocolates and laughed and cried at the antics on the screen. He had a sudden vision of strangling his sister and smiled. Harriet thought he was smiling about the film she was describing, and touched his hand in her enthusiasm. The jolt that ran up his arm was intense. He suddenly felt his stomach tighten. He wouldn't be able to keep up this act for too much longer. He wanted Harriet with every fibre in his body.

He drained his cup and thanked her. 'I feel better now. I'd better go and face up to the dreadful task while I feel stronger. Thank you, Harriet. I really would have crumbled if I hadn't bumped into you. I know he may only have been a dog, but he was the world to me.'

She stood with him and placed a gentle kiss on his cheek.

'Good luck.'

She was almost his. It took all his willpower not to leave the café and cheer. Instead, he plodded out, head down, every inch the broken man.

CHAPTER THIRTY-SIX

The kitchen at Bromley Hall was surprisingly well organised and calm, and not full of chefs barking instructions or clattering pans, as Robyn had expected. A couple of younger chefs were preparing vegetables and sauces for dinner and she detected a delicious aroma of basil coming from something cooking in the oven. She found Bruno Miguel, immaculately attired in his uniform, sitting on a stool and sipping herbal tea. His chef's hat stood to attention and his shoes shone. He was dressed for a chef's parade rather than for a day of cooking.

'Been sorting out a huge meat delivery and need a rest,' he explained. 'The suppliers delivered everything late, so it's been manic. This is the calm before the evening storm, although I don't think we have many diners in today. There are only a few guests. Head chef has taken the day off to go Christmas shopping, so I'm working with the sous-chef. He's outside having a fag break. If he doesn't get his regular dose of nicotine, he's a nervous wreck by end of service.'

'I had a look at the menu, and it all looks very appetising.'

'And disgustingly healthy,' he added.

'I'm keen on healthy living and eating.'

'Then you should try a dish or two. You don't have to be a guest to eat here at the Hall, and we make the best carrot cake, with carrot sorbet and pumpkin seeds, you've ever tasted.'

'Sounds delicious.'

'It is. It's one of our "eat without guilt" dishes we pride ourselves on.'

'Have you got a minute to talk?'

'Sure. What's it about?'

'I understand you overheard someone threatening to kill Miles Ashbrook.'

Bruno's face changed. His relaxed pose disappeared. He leant towards her and hissed, 'You heard wrong.'

Robyn persisted, unperturbed by his change in attitude. 'I have reason to believe you overheard a conversation between Jakub Woźniak and Miles Ashbrook, during which Mr Woźniak threatened to kill Mr Ashbrook.'

'You're mistaken. Now, if you'll excuse me, I have to get ready to cook.'

'Thank you for your time, Mr Miguel. It's a pity you didn't hear anything. I shall now have to interview Mrs Maggiore about it.'

He slammed down his mug of tea. 'Leave her out of this.'

She lifted an eyebrow. 'I wish I could. I have to follow this up.'

'Okay, but don't bring Fiona into this. We're trying not to draw attention to ourselves. Yes, I overheard a conversation between the pair of them. Jakub was really cheesed off about his wife being made redundant. She was earning more than Jakub and they needed the income. It wasn't just the fact she was laid off, it was the way Ashbrook did it. He called the women into the office, one by one, and fired them there and then. Jakub was furious about it. You didn't need to ask him to know he was angry. He cursed and carried on all day after it happened. I was brassed off too. Ashbrook had been having a right old sacking session. I've been here since 2010 and I've never seen such low morale. It's hard enough with all the personality clashes here, and harder still when you can't keep hold of any member of the team for longer than six months. Part of my duties is to keep the kitchen team motivated and organised. It's been hell the last few months. We've been losing kitchen porters and chefs like there's no tomorrow, and the workload keeps falling on the shoulders of us poor buggers left behind.'

'So what did you hear exactly?' Robyn asked, trying to get him back on track.

'Jakub was shouting. He has a distinctive way of speaking so I knew it was him. He told Ashbrook that he'd handled the sacking badly and he was going to challenge it. Ashbrook said it was out of his hands. He was only following instructions, and he personally hadn't wanted to fire the women that way. Jakub called Ashbrook a coward and said that a proper man would stand up to the management's decision. Ashbrook told him to get out of the office or he'd "find himself joining the dole queue". Jakub growled something I couldn't hear and I think he threw something, or thumped the table. There was a clattering and Ashbrook yelled, "Get out before I make life so difficult for you, you'll have to go back to Poland." To which Jakub responded, "You'd better watch your back. Where I come from we have ways of dealing with people like you." Ashbrook shouted, "Are you threatening me?" Jakub replied, "Yes." That's it. I left before Jakub came out of the office.'

'How much did you all know about Miles Ashbrook?'

'No one really knew him well. Other than meetings and work-related conversations, we had little contact with him. We're too busy down here to bother with the Hall minions. As long as they don't interfere with what we're doing, we all get along. It's like there are four separate parts to this place. We're the kitchen team, and there's also the beauty department team, the gym staff and the Hall staff. We don't tend to fraternise with each other. Many of the employees are part-time, and so we don't see them very often, what with shift patterns varying and so on.'

She noticed the back door was open. The sous-chef was returning, and work would begin. She couldn't keep Bruno for much longer.

'I imagine times were different when the Hall was owned by the Bishtons.'

'Totally different. We were like one big family. It's diluted now. I don't know many of the staff who now work in the Hall, apart from Charlie the porter.'

'Did you know Rory Wallis?'

Bruno sighed. 'Yes, I knew Rory. I heard he'd died. He was murdered, wasn't he? What a horrible thing to happen. Poor bugger.' Bruno shook his head.

'I understand he worked here a few years ago.'

'He managed the Champagne Bar. He was an ace cocktail maker. He left to run a pub. I haven't spoken to him in years. Why do you ask?'

'We're currently investigating his murder and would appreciate any help you can give us.'

Bruno continued to shake his head. 'I can't be of much help. He left here early in July 2013 about the same time the Bishtons decided to revamp the place. I guess he saw the writing on the wall before the rest of us did.' He stared into space for a second. 'Rory was okay really. Kept himself to himself, but he was a decent guy.'

Robyn gave him an understanding smile. 'I heard the Bishtons decided to improve the place and sell it after the unfortunate incident with Harriet Worth.'

Bruno let out a long sigh. 'That's right. I didn't get to hear all the ins and outs of it. Harriet was one of our guests who accidentally drowned in the old spa pool. The place was shut for over a month while they hammered out the implications and legalities, and we closed again a few months later so the pool could be drained and the spa closed down. We were assured our jobs were safe and we kept the restaurant and Hall open, but we lost many of our regular customers. They didn't like the disruption and found other places that offered similar facilities.

'The new extension was finished quickly and it all looked promising. The Bishtons sold up almost immediately after it opened. The new owners live in Hong Kong. We're part of their global empire. Periodically, one of the bosses turns up and we put on a spread for them. Ashbrook was merely their puppet.'

'Did you have any contact with Harriet when she stayed here?'

'No. I had a week off and was travelling around Turkey.'

The sous-chef, a grouchy-looking individual, called out and signalled for Bruno to get back to work. Bruno stood up. 'Is that everything?'

'For now.'

'You won't need to talk to a certain guest?'

'No. I think I have everything I need, Mr Miguel.'

There was more activity in the kitchen now, an orchestrated dance that they clearly practised on a daily basis. She wouldn't be able to find out any more from Bruno Miguel. Besides, it was half past four, almost time to meet up with Mitz and interview Scott Dawson. Dawson ought to be returning soon if he had a class at five.

She wandered along the dark corridors, trying to imagine what the Hall was like in its heyday. At the moment it was a mishmash of old and contemporary and had lost its way. She didn't hold out much hope for its future.

Upstairs again, she reached for her mobile. She had a message from David Marker. Peter Bullock had had a pang of conscience, probably hoping Anna wouldn't press charges against him. He had phoned the station with some new information. He remembered seeing a small sign in the back window of the Fiat 500 that read 'I Love Westies'.

CHAPTER THIRTY-SEVEN

The alarm on his mobile beeped loudly. It took three attempts to locate it with the palm of his hand. He wanted nothing more than to turn over on the settee and go back to her. He groaned. He'd been dozing for an hour but now he had to get up. There was yet another debt to settle. He wriggled his toes, numb from being cramped up against the arm of the settee, and tried to recall some of his dream.

He had been sitting with her in front of a log fire. She had fitted snugly into his lap and he had an arm curled around her. He could smell lilies as he pushed his nose into her hair to kiss her on the back of her neck. She closed her eyes and murmured pleasurably.

His feet were still cold and his body was awakening. The dream receded, and in its place he felt anger – anger that the scene could never take place. It had been snatched from him.

He dragged back the curtains and surveyed the ring road, empty of traffic for once. November was drawing to a close and December would be arriving with all its glitz, glamour and commercialism. In a few hours, the road would be jammed again as people, eager to purchase Christmas paraphernalia, flooded into the city.

A few days earlier he had crossed the road, via the passageway, to buy some cigarettes and booze, and found the Intu shopping centre brimming with people. There were crowds of shoppers wherever he turned, milling about, knocking into him with plastic bags filled with purchases. It had all been too much for him and he had jostled his way back home, stopping at the petrol station near his flat instead, his eyes stinging from the bright Christmas lights and a whopper of a headache.

He hated this time of year. What was there to celebrate when you lived alone? Most of his Christmases had been miserable. He and Stacey had been passed from one foster family to another. Stacey had fared better and settled with a couple in Nottingham, but he had been a sullen, ugly child and an even more sullen teenager, who had got into trouble more often than not. He had one or two pleasant memories of Christmas. When he was ten years old, his foster parents at the time, Mr and Mrs Dobson, had tried to give him and the other foster children they were looking after a happy Christmas. There had been a large real pine tree decorated with glittering handcrafted balls and a large gold star on the top. Underneath were neatly wrapped presents for all four of them. The house had been infused with delicious smells. Mr Dobson played the piano and they all sang Christmas carols.

He had been given a Game Boy. It was the best present he'd ever had. They'd had turkey and a Christmas pudding, which they'd set alight. It had all been fun until Gregory, an older boy, had tried to steal his Game Boy and they'd got into a fight. Gregory was much bigger and stronger than him, but he was the more streetwise, and knew how to fight dirty. He'd yanked on Gregory's hair and bitten his earlobe hard. Gregory had screamed like a terrified pig. Deaf to the noise, he'd held fast. It was only after Mr Dobson had separated the pair of them that they'd discovered part of Gregory's ear still in his mouth. He had bitten it clean through it. He spat the flesh out on the carpet and wiped blood smugly from his mouth; Gregory would never steal from him again. That turned out to be true: he was sent back to the home in the New Year.

He checked his calendar. The large X was only four days away. He lit another cigarette and dropped down onto the couch. He didn't fancy any breakfast. He'd smoke this and get off. He allowed himself five minutes to think about the last time he had seen her. It would help prepare him. He was going to kill again...

He had been waiting for Harriet all morning again. This was the fourth day on the trot she had not appeared at her usual time. He had walked past her road and her car had been on the drive so he knew she was around. She must have had other business to attend to and had to change her routine. He hoped fervently that she was not ill, injured or had given up running. If Harriet did not appear today, he would have to knock on her door. The anxiety was making him very twitchy. He hadn't slept the night before. It had been noisy at the sheltered accommodation and a drunk had come in late at night, waking him. The man had snored so loudly he'd kept him awake for the rest of the night.

He had planned this day so well and now it was going wrong. This was his fourth attempt and he was fast losing patience. A drumming began in his head. He had spent a great deal of time copying out the perfect passage to read to her. He'd taken it from an online writing forum and copied it word for word into his notepad. Writing wasn't his forte, so it had taken him several exasperating attempts to get it right. Now he was wondering if he'd ever get to read it to her.

It was two o'clock when he finally spotted her. By which time he had spent most of the day walking from one entrance at the end of the reservoir to town and back, and was feeling hugely irritated. She was using the leg press machine, oblivious to everything except counting repetitions as her legs pushed and her thigh muscles tightened. Her mouth opened in a small 'o' as his shadow loomed over her.

'Hello, Harriet. I didn't expect to see you here at this time of the day.'

She gave a tight smile. 'I had to wait in for a parcel earlier.'

'I've been at the café writing. It's such a beautiful day. I got quite a lot done.'

'It is a super day. I'm glad you're feeling better.'

'I miss Alfie. It's worse when I get up in the morning and he's not there to greet me. The house feels empty.'

'Maybe you should get another dog.'

'In time. I can't face it at the moment. I don't suppose you could do me a favour? Could you listen to a little of what I've written to see if it sounds okay? I'm not sure I've got the romantic element right, being a bloke and all,' he laughed. She shifted uncomfortably on the seat. 'Would you like to hear some of what I've written? It won't take long.'

She hesitated too long for his liking and he could feel heat rising in his veins. Her eyes darted around the field and, spotting several other people, her shoulders relaxed. 'Okay. Why not?'

She wiped down the handles of the equipment she'd been using with a facecloth, tucked it into her tracksuit pocket and followed him to a bench near the outside gym. The afternoon sunshine afforded them some warmth and cast sparkles across the reservoir. He heaved a sigh. The red mist that was threatening to descend had lifted.

He opened his notebook and began reading, 'John searched her large blue eyes and felt a powerful surge. Tessa was everything he could ever desire; her honey-coloured hair, soft and feminine, was pinned on top of her head and perfectly coiffed in small curls that shone in the sunlight. She wore a green spotted dress with a nipped-in waist, an A-line skirt to the knee and a white collar that showed off her swan-like neck. The guard blew his whistle and in that instant his world sped up. "I love you. Will you marry me?" His heart stopped as he waited for her response. She threw her arms around his neck. "Yes, yes, yes. Of course I will."

'They had little time to embrace. He felt her warm soft mouth on his and for the longest minute, he held her to him. The train let out an angry belch of steam, and reluctantly he hauled his kitbag from the platform and hurled it into the train, leaping up to join it as it *pulled away. He waved at her. She kept pace with the train, shouting that she loved him. He blew her a kiss. The train picked up speed and he watched the small figure on the platform, waving madly, recede. He collected his bag and shuffled into the compartment. Now he had a reason to fight and a reason to live.'*

He stopped reading. 'Well, what do you think?'

'It's lovely. I think I'd want to read the whole book.'

'You don't think it's too soppy?'

'Not at all.'

The ducks on the reservoir swam contentedly in the water, occasionally bobbing for food. Two swans glided up to the edge of the water and hesitated in front of the bench. He felt like part of a couple. He wanted to stay with her like this forever. He caught the scent of honeysuckle perfume and decided to be bold.

'You are Tessa in the book. Whenever I write about Tessa, I see you. You're the inspiration.'

'Well, that's very nice and flattering. Thank you.' She shifted on the bench.

'How's the training going?'

'Okay, thanks. I'm running the Race for Life tomorrow, and afterwards I'm going to relax – take a few days off exercising. I've been invited on a posh spa break.' She bit her lip. She ought not to be sharing any personal information with this strange man, yet she was burbling, saying anything that came to mind and all the while, thinking of ways to escape from him. The words tumbled out. 'My friend Linda suggested it. She got a special deal or we'd never have been able to afford it. Linda's my running partner. I do longer runs with her. I just do little warm-ups here to work my muscles. I usually run on an evening or weekends with her. We try and complete ten miles.'

'That's a fair distance.'

'You get used to it.'

'Is that Linda Cheshire? She's a runner. I know her husband.' He wanted to sound as normal as possible. Harriet had seemed skittish today and he worried she might be going off him.

She shook her head. 'No, she's Linda Upton. I don't know anyone called Linda Cheshire.'

His mouth turned downwards and he shrugged. 'Oh well, I'm sure there are lots of ladies who are called Linda who run.' He was rambling nervously. She clearly wanted to get off and he didn't want her to leave him. Sure enough her next words were, 'I have to go now. I'll no doubt see you around.'

He felt sick. It might be ages before they had another moment like this. 'I'll keep you up to date with my book.'

'Yes. Super.'

'Enjoy the spa break with Linda and good luck for the run.'

'Cheers. I'm looking forward to it.'

They both rose. He suddenly panicked. He wouldn't see her for a few days. Worse still, after her spa break and with no more fun runs planned, she might not keep to her running schedule and he wouldn't see her again, ever. He wanted more than just a few minutes on the bench with her. As she moved away words tumbled from his mouth. 'Harriet, you know I've based the character of Tessa on you? Well, I'm John.'

She stopped in her tracks.

He carried on, emboldened. He had to tell her. 'I'm John in the book. And… and I love you. Harriet, I love you.'

Her face turned red and she looked at her feet. 'Oh, okay,' was all she could say.

'I know it's all sudden, yet I've known from the first time I set eyes on you. You don't need to say anything. I just wanted to tell you.' He grabbed her hands and clumsily enveloped them in his own, feeling the soft skin and delicate bones of her slim fingers as he tightened his grip, knowing they could be crushed too easily.

Confusion and surprise flickered across her face – that, and something else he didn't recognise. Harriet nodded. 'Okay. Well, it's a bit of a surprise—'

He shushed her. 'Don't say anything. Don't spoil it. Tell me you feel the same way when you're ready to.'

A man on a bicycle rode towards them and dinged his bell for them to move off the pathway around the pool. Still he held her hands and gazed into her eyes, willing her to see the love in them. The bicycle bell rang several times. 'Out of the way, please,' shouted the man. Harriet broke contact with him and pulled her hands away, moving off the path. The mist descended. The man had ruined the moment. He stood his ground. The man on the bike yelled at him to move, but he stayed firm and the man was forced to jam on his brakes at the last minute. He skidded and fell off onto the grassed area.

'You bloody idiot,' he shouted, trying to untangle himself from his bike. 'You could have killed me.'

'Yes, I could,' he replied, eyes glittering dangerously. He was so tempted to squeeze the very life out of this stranger who had interrupted his love declaration and ruined the special moment. He turned to speak to Harriet again. It was too late. She had disappeared.

He opened his eyes. He had never seen Harriet again. And he knew who to blame for that. Today, someone else would pay their due debt.

CHAPTER THIRTY-EIGHT

'The list of people who own silver Fiat 500s is ridiculously long. I hadn't realised it was such a popular car.' David Marker scrolled through the list, brow furrowed, and complained, 'It could take forever.'

Robyn made a noise in the back of her throat: no. She would get the breakthrough they needed. 'Stick at it, David. We've got to try and locate it.'

'At least we can narrow it down to a car purchased in 2014.'

'Keep at it until we find it.'

She'd called the office from the Hall, to see if there was any more news. With Bullock's latest recollection, they had something to go on. Mitz was standing by the gym entrance. Inside the gym, someone was working out on the indoor rowing machine, exhaling noisily with every pull.

'I have a list,' said Mitz. 'There are quite a few names on it – seventeen, to be exact – and that includes Bruno Miguel, Scott Dawson, Lorna Davidson who's in charge of the beauty side of things, and Else Goodman who deals with all the bookings and the guests.'

'We can rule out Bruno Miguel. He was on holiday at the time of Harriet Worth's accident. Jakub Woźniak clocked off earlier so I couldn't speak to him.'

She turned at the sound of soft voices. Scott Dawson in conversation with a tall, bald-headed man. He spotted Robyn and Mitz and said something to the man who disappeared towards the changing rooms, leaving Scott looking perplexed.

'DI Carter, I wasn't expecting you. I have a class at five.' He checked his watch as if to make the point.

'Sorry. We didn't have time to make an appointment and it is important we talk to you.'

Scott could barely stand still; a nervous energy pulsated through his body and his hands and wrists jiggled while he talked. The drama of the last week and his new responsibilities were taking their toll, and, if Ross was correct, so too were marriage difficulties. Scott led them to his office, where he propped himself against the desk.

'Is it about Miles?'

Robyn shook her head. 'Harriet Worth.'

Scott slumped a little. 'Mrs Worth died in 2012. The police came. It was an accident.'

'So I understand. Tell me what you know about that night.'

'I don't know a lot. I'd recently been promoted to gym manager so I was more concerned with making sure our clients were satisfied with the gym and the training programmes we were offering. Harriet dropped by to check out the gym. I remember her and her friend coming in. Both were into running, as I recall. We had a chat about the forthcoming Olympic Games in London. She was really excited because she'd got tickets to watch some track event. She complimented me on my trainers that day. They were brand new and had cost me a fortune. I'd bought them to celebrate being promoted to gym manager. That's pretty much why I remember her.'

'Okay. And were you in the building when she died?'

He sighed. 'I wasn't. I'd gone home at about seven thirty. It was my mother-in-law's birthday and I was in charge of doing a surprise barbecue for the family.'

'The verdict was accidental death. Who was responsible for the spa area at the time?'

'The spa was a shared responsibility between the gym and the cleaning staff. We made sure used towels were collected regularly and floors were kept clean, the pool levels were correct and so on.'

'The night Harriet died, there was water on the floor.'

'That's right. The shower next to the pool was leaking. It was discovered late in the day, too late to get an outside plumber to fix it. Jakub Woźniak was quite handy at that sort of thing so I asked him to take a look at it.'

Scott tugged uncomfortably at the collar of his polo shirt. Robyn studied him for a moment before asking, 'Who had responsibility for locking up the spa?'

He gave a dry cough. 'All the managers took it in turns to be duty manager and check all the doors to the beauty salon, gym and spa were locked and secure.'

'And who was duty manager that night?'

'Me. I was duty manager. I failed to lock the door. Jakub spent an hour trying to fix the shower and I'd been busy with a client. The client wanted me to go through a written personal programme afterwards, and consequently, I was running late. My missus called me to say her parents had arrived and asked where the heck I was. I wanted to lock up and asked Jakub to get a move on but he needed another ten minutes and said he'd lock up. I don't know if there was a miscommunication or what. Anyway, he didn't lock the door.

'I admitted all this to the police at the time and to Lord Bishton. He told me not to worry and he'd handle it, and I was never charged. Am I being charged now?'

She responded with a shake of her head. She had no more questions regarding Harriet. She was now concerned that Scott might be targeted by a killer intent on revenge. She would have to make sure he was out of harm's way. She'd clear it with Mulholland first. She had to talk to Jakub Woźniak.

'Do you have Jakub Woźniak's number?'

'Sure. He'll tell you the same story. We didn't hide anything.' He pulled out his mobile, scrolled through his contacts. Robyn copied Jakub's number into her mobile.

'I'm sure you didn't. Look, when you finish your class, don't leave the premises without telling Sergeant Patel.'

'I don't understand.'

'I'll explain later. First, I have to talk to Mr Woźniak.' She moved away from the gym entrance and dialled the number. It rang four times and a woman's voice answered.

'Hello, can I speak to Mr Jakub Woźniak please?'

'I'm sorry, who is this?'

'It's DI Carter from Staffordshire Police. Can I speak to Mr Woźniak? It's very important.'

The woman at the end of the phone spoke so quietly Robyn could hardly hear her. 'DI Carter, this is PC Fallows from Burton-upon-Trent. We have an incident here. Mr Woźniak has been killed. We're at the scene now.'

'Where are you?'

'Near Bromley Hall. We're two miles along Branston Lane in the direction of Burton, just after the crossroads. Do you need GPS coordinates?'

'I'm at the Hall. I'll be with you in a few minutes.'

She pulled Mitz to one side and indicated Scott Dawson. 'Keep him in your sights. Jakub's been killed. I'm going to find out what's happened.'

CHAPTER THIRTY-NINE

She spotted the flashing lights almost as soon as she turned into the lane and passed the church. An ambulance was parked on the verge along with several other cars, and, in spite of the rain, there was a flurry of activity. A squad car blocked the road at the crossroads. She wound down her window and spoke to the officer standing in the road. He was drenched.

'DI Carter. You have a hit-and-run victim.'

'Yes, ma'am. Over there.' He pointed towards a line of bushes and groups of individuals huddled in plastic ponchos. A tent had been erected over the body.

She guided the Golf into a space between a Volvo and a squad car and got out. The rain was easing a little. She stood for a moment and surveyed the scene. If it weren't for the squad car lights and torches, the area would be pitch black.

She flashed her warrant card at a female PC with a neat bob.

'I just spoke to you on the phone, ma'am. I'm Karen Hall, the family liaison officer on this case. I'm just about to inform Mrs Woźniak of the sad news. Her husband was found by the side of the road. Whoever hit him did a runner. There are no witnesses, other than the Tesco van driver who happened upon the body and called us. We took a statement from him. He had to leave on account of his deliveries.'

'The driver wasn't involved?'

No, ma'am. All deliveries and delivery times are monitored by the company, so we were able to track his route. The pathologist thinks Mr Woźniak has been dead for two or three hours. The van driver was loading up at the depot at that time. DI Young is the officer in charge. He's with the pathologist.' She pointed out three men huddled under a large blue umbrella. 'The man in the anorak is the forensic photographer. He's been here for a while. I think he's about to leave.'

Robyn recognised the familiar green anorak. It was Sam Gooch. He spotted her and lifted a hand, leaving the officer and heading in her direction.

'Nice evening,' he commented. 'I was happily playing bridge with my dear wife when I got dragged out into this filthy weather. Now, what are you doing here? Other than the obvious. I thought you were occupied with another case in Lichfield.'

'I think this could be related.'

He chuckled. 'Haven't you already got enough dead bodies? You're getting greedy, Robyn. There was a note in the victim's trouser pocket similar to the one you found on Rory Wallis's body. I'm pretty certain you'll find they're linked. Anyway, I'll let you get on with it.'

The rain tapped on Sam's umbrella like keys on a typewriter. He gave Robyn a small smile. 'I've seen enough death. It's time to see some life. I'm having a leaving party at my house next month, once Christmas is over. I'll send you an invite. Bring a friend.'

'I'll bring Ross. He'll want to wish you well.'

'Lovely. We've seen some things, the three of us in our time, haven't we?' With those words and a cheery wave, he scuttled away to the Volvo.

Robyn walked towards the tent and Chris Young, the officer in charge. He was taking photographs and recording a video of the scene on his phone, and cast a cursory glance in her direction. Droplets of rain splashed onto his head and trickled down his face, leaving silvery lines: *snail trails*, she thought. Satisfied he had captured sufficient detail, he tucked his phone into his pocket and turned his attention to her.

'Ah, the infamous DI Carter. Chased any blind men recently?' He laughed at his own joke. Robyn smiled as pleasantly as she could.

'It wasn't my finest moment.'

'We all make mistakes. I have to admit that was a cracker. I'm Chris Young.' He had a soft drawl she couldn't place and a lazy smile. 'I'm afraid I'm one of Tom Shearer's mates. We have met, although it was a while ago. You were assigned to the Buxton Barber case at the time and I was a mere junior aspiring to greater things.'

She vaguely recalled a fresh-faced PC with sandy hair who had followed her about with the air of an eager puppy. 'I remember you now. You wrote everything down in shorthand.'

'A skill I picked up from my mum, who assured me it would be useful. It's helped me on many a case. No long-winded sentences. No one can read what I've written, though, so I still have to copy stuff out.'

'You're friends with Tom?'

'We live near each other. I bump into him from time to time at the local pub. He's the one who told me about the gaffe with the blind man.'

'That explains it. Are you the SOCO on this?'

'I am. Hit and run. Name of Jakub Woźniak.'

'I reckon I know who this man is. He worked at Bromley Hall. He came off shift about three hours ago.'

'That accounts for why he was cycling down this lane on a shitty November afternoon.'

'I wondered if this accident might be connected to a case I'm working on. If you don't mind, I'd like to take a look.'

'Sure, be my guest.'

He led the way past an abandoned bike that lay on the verge. 'Any clear idea of what happened?'

'It looks like he wasn't actually riding the bike when he was hit. The front tyre is flat. My initial thoughts were that it had deflated after the accident, but there was no damage at all to the bike, and I discovered a drawing pin in the tyre. He'd picked it up from somewhere else and got a slow puncture. That seems to be borne out by the fact we can't find any tyre tracks, no rubber left from a vehicle skidding to a halt, or weaving to avoid him. In nearly all cases there is some evidence, especially when a person is spotted at the last moment and the driver swerves to avoid a collision. It's as if the driver didn't see him at all, whacked into him and carried on driving.

'There's significant trauma consistent with being struck by a vehicle while standing or walking. Forensics took samples from his clothing to help determine how the damage was caused. The pathologist confirmed Woźniak has several broken bones, ribs and other injuries, that were most likely caused by a frontal collision, and he'll be able to tell us more when he's conducted a full examination of the body.'

'Sam said you found a note in his trouser pocket.'

'Yes, I didn't understand its relevance. As you know, you have to look at every angle, and he may have had the note on him before he was hit.'

He lifted the tent opening and she entered. Temporary lights had been set up and shone on the victim's ruined face, which was covered with blood the colour of black tar. His right leg was twisted at an awkward angle and his foot was facing in the wrong direction. The shoe had come off. The sock bore the words 'Best Dad'. She didn't need to look at him for long. She heaved a sigh and moved away. Chris lifted the tent flap and signalled for the undertaker, who had been waiting in his van, to remove the body. She stared at the sheet covering the man she had hoped to interview. It was too late to find out what he had known about the night Harriet had died.

She couldn't be sure whether Jakub had met an untimely end unconnected to her cases, but the note in his pocket would surely be the clue she needed.

'Where's the note?' she asked.

Chris extracted three evidence bags from a box by the tent flap and handed one to her. Her mouth went dry. She held the transparent bag up to the beam from one of the lights and recognised it to be an invoice like those she had found on the bodies of Rory Wallis and Linda Upton.

'Chris, can you give me everything you get or have on this? It's definitely connected to my investigations.'

Chris gave her a genial smile. 'I'm glad about that. It's Chelsea versus Spurs in the Premier League this weekend and I promised my lad I'd take him. Thanks – now I won't have to miss out.'

Robyn phoned Mitz to fill him in on the latest development.

'Stay with Dawson until I can get someone to keep a proper watch on him, or get him into protection. I'm going to talk to Mulholland as soon as I can. Make sure he stays at the Hall until we arrange everything.'

She now had three invoices. So far, they totalled three quarters of a million pounds. That still left a shortfall of the same amount. If the killer was keeping the value at £250,000 per invoice, there could be three more victims in his sights. She had to ensure he didn't get to them. The trouble was, the killer was one step ahead of them and they had no idea who he was.

CHAPTER FORTY

Tricia turned over the USB stick in her hand for the umpteenth time. It wasn't for her to nosy at it even if the stick contained information that would be useful in determining how Miles Ashbrook had died. More importantly, the receipt she held in her hand was evidence that Miles had kept secrets, and secrets were, as Tricia knew, never a good thing.

She swiped her contact list, tapped a number and was transferred to Robyn's answering service. 'It's Tricia. I've found a USB stick among Miles's personal effects and a receipt from a hotel in London – the Hideaway – for a night's stay in a double room with dinner and breakfast for two people. No one, not even his mother, was aware Miles was involved with anyone. He's been keeping this quiet. I don't know if it's significant, but wondered if it might be a clue or, oh I don't know…' She rubbed her stiff neck, pressing on a muscle for a minute, easing the tension there.

'I hoped it might lead to something. Also, we found a pay-as-you-go mobile phone in a jacket pocket. It isn't his usual phone. I can't get it to work – the battery's dead and my charger won't fit it. I could take it to a phone shop, but then I thought I'd tell you first before taking any action. Anyway, call me when you get this. I want to hand it all over to you.'

Robyn took another look at her Post-it notes scattered on her desk. She needed to put together a cohesive argument for Louisa

Mulholland. It was nearly nine o'clock on Thursday morning, and she'd barely slept. Her head had swum with images of the killer's victims – Rory, Linda and Jakub. She owed it to them and their families to find their murderer.

Mulholland's door was ajar. She tapped lightly on it and was called in. An untouched mug of coffee was on her desk. She motioned for Robyn to sit while she finished a phone call. No sooner had she finished her conversation than Robyn got straight to the point.

'There was another murder yesterday afternoon – Jakub Woźniak. Like the other victims, he had an invoice on his body. I now have reason to believe there's a tie between the victims and Harriet Worth, the woman who fell into the pool at Bromley Hall in 2012 and drowned. Jakub was at Bromley Hall the evening Harriet Worth died. He was asked to repair a shower. He didn't have the part to fix it and it continued to leak. Harriet slipped in the water that leaked from the shower.' Robyn paused for a second. 'The spa door should have been locked but Scott Dawson, who was the duty manager, left early that night in the belief Jakub would lock up. Jakub either didn't hear or understand, or forgot, and the door remained unlocked. As a consequence, Harriet was able to enter the spa and pool area. I'm now convinced certain members of staff who were at Bromley Hall in July 2012 are in danger. I think our killer believes they were in some way responsible for the death of Harriet Worth. And I think he'll try to kill Scott Dawson. As duty manager that night, it was Scott's responsibility to lock that spa. I want to arrange protection for him.'

Louisa Mulholland had a coughing fit that prevented her from speaking. After a few minutes, she wiped at her watering eyes. Her voice was croaky. 'This is dangerously close to getting out of hand. I understand why you want to protect these people, but how many are we talking about? I can't spare officers to babysit members of the public when they have other duties to perform. Have you a list of people you think are likely to become targets?'

'We're trying to narrow it down. There are seventeen on our list. We've already eliminated one of them. We'll have the numbers down to a more manageable size soon. Most of them were chambermaids or beauticians. I doubt they played any part in Harriet Worth's death or even met her.'

Louisa shook her head. 'Sorry. No. You'll have to use your team to cover those you feel are in imminent danger. We can't use any other officers. Most are currently working on the spate of gang wars we seem to be having. Tom Shearer is heading a team and they are currently deployed throughout East Staffordshire, in Burton-on-Trent, Uttoxeter and Branston, where we're experiencing the most trouble. I can't drag them away from their duties.'

Robyn felt aggrieved. She could do with some support from her superior.

'Yes, ma'am. I'll use my officers, but if someone else gets murdered because we couldn't provide adequate protection, I want it noted that I saw you and requested extra assistance.'

Louisa pulled at a tissue from a box on her table and blew her nose. 'Duly noted, Robyn. I'm sorry I can't give you what you want, but you're resourceful.'

The hairs on Robyn's arm rose. She wanted to protest, but respect for her superior won the argument and she bit her lip.

'Have you dealt with that journalist, Amy Walters?'

Robyn cursed herself mentally. She'd got so involved with the case she'd forgotten about troublesome Amy. Honesty was the best policy, so she shook her head. 'I didn't wish to engage in verbal fisticuffs with her. She's got a reputation for being keen, and anything that is said gets put into that newspaper. She only joined the paper eight months ago and already she's been promoted to senior correspondent.'

Louisa pondered Robyn's words. 'Probably best to ignore her. I'm concerned this moniker might catch on – the Lichfield Leopard. I'll talk to the media team and see how best to handle her and any others, especially now there's a third murder.'

The phone rang shrilly. Robyn rose from her chair and left her superior to answer it. She found Anna glued to her computer screen watching the CCTV footage from the spa.

'I'm going to have to take you off this case, Anna.'

Anna was too distracted to listen. She pointed at the screen. 'I think I might have something here,' she replied.

Robyn slid onto the chair next to Anna. 'Show me.'

'I've been through it several times now. I was watching this section where Miles takes a shower before going into the sauna, and when I rewound it, frame by frame, I spotted something I hadn't noticed before.' She pressed a key on her pad and the screen came to life. At first there appeared to be nothing of note; the camera recorded an empty pool, an empty spa and empty loungers. It rotated towards the shower in front of the sauna. It too was empty. Without warning, a shadow flitted across the screen.

'Whoa!' said Robyn.

Anna rewound it again, this time slowing the recording to run the film frame by frame. The shadow appeared again. Robyn copied the outline onto a piece of paper and examined it.

'Have you ever seen those silhouettes that artists draw at the seaside?' she asked. 'This almost looks like one of those – like someone's head. Although this is more like an alien's head.' She studied the domed cranium. 'Got anything else?'

'No, I've been through this so many times, I'm beginning to imagine people.' She pointed at a sketch of the spa layout that Ross had sent. 'I've calculated that the shadow was cast by light coming from here,' she said, stabbing at the ice room. 'According to Ross, there's a light above it.'

'So where do you think the person was standing at the time?'

Anna scrutinised Ross's plan and drew pencil lines across it. She shrugged her shoulders. 'I can't be sure. If Ross's information is correct, it appears somebody was standing outside the sauna, here.'

Robyn tapped the plan with one finger. 'The control box is on that side of the sauna. What time was this recorded?'

'Time shown is seven thirty. Spa was closed at seven.'

'What was Miles doing at seven thirty? Do we have a record of his movements that night?'

Anna found the information on her screen. 'He was in his office. He went to the dining room at six thirty and had a meal. After that, he returned to his office. He was seen by several people.'

'Therefore it's unlikely to be him at that time. Anna, I think we've got a glimpse of a murderer.' Robyn slapped the palm of her hand on the table. 'Come on, we're going back to Bromley Hall.'

En route, Robyn called Matt. 'Any joy with finding Harriet's friends?'

'I've located four who used be members of the same running club. I've contacted two of them already. Neither could tell me much more about her than we already know. She appeared to be content with her life. There didn't seem to be any boyfriend or part-time lover. She worked part-time as a secretary at a legal firm in Lichfield. I've got an appointment later today to speak to the solicitor she worked for – Joyce Garner. I'm on my way to see Diane Roper, who was one of her closer friends and who also works in Lichfield, to double-check if there was anyone else in her life other than her husband.'

'That's great. Keep me informed.'

She ended her call. She was sure the murderer was working out a vendetta. So far he had murdered three people who were somehow connected to Harriet's death. If he were targeting individuals who were working at the Hall at the time Harriet died, then there were several people he might blame for her death. How could she be sure any of them were safe? So far, he had killed the barman who had served Harriet drinks that night, the cleaner who had not locked the spa or ensured the floor was dry, and the woman who had accompanied her friend that day. She sat up with a jolt. She was forgetting someone – Alan Worth. She called David, who was still at the station.

'David, can you contact Alan Worth for me? Check he's okay. Mulholland can't spare any officers, so would you mind watching over him for a while until I can convince Mulholland we really need assistance on this? Ask him to stay in his house for the time being.'

David sounded as tired as she felt. 'Sure. Will do.'

She was about to make her next call when she spotted the answerphone symbol. She dialled and listened to Tricia's message. She punched out Tricia's number and spoke to her.

'I'm investigating Miles's death. I'm sending someone around to look at the USB and receipt and see if they offer us anything to go on.'

'Thank goodness. I can't bear not knowing exactly what happened to him. His mum is like a zombie at the moment. I'm round her house every spare minute. I'm worried about her. She's not eating.'

'Give her time. It's a horrendous shock and he was her only child. She'll really be glad you're there, Tricia.'

'I won't leave her. I haven't even been to the gym this week. I guess you haven't either.'

'No. There's not been a second to spare. I've got to call Ross. He'll be the guy coming to check out the USB, receipt and phone. He's an expert in all of this. He's a private investigator, so he'll hopefully find out who Miles was seeing and determine if that person had anything to do with his death.'

'Thanks, Robyn. This means a lot to me.'

She rang her cousin and asked him to drop by Tricia's house.

'I can't spare anyone here, Ross. You'd be doing me a big favour.'

'I'll get back to you as soon as I have something.'

'I need it quickly, Ross.'

'I'll work fast, don't fret. Did you speak to that cleaner fellow?'

'Couldn't. He got run over on the way home from work.'

Ross knew better than to discuss cases, especially over a mobile.

'Crikey. That scuppered things a bit.'

'It certainly did. Okay, talk later. Someone's trying to get through.'

David Marker was on the phone. 'Can't reach Alan on his mobile or his landline. Want me to head down?'

'Hang fire for the moment, David. I'll send Matt because he's closer to Knowle.'

She called Matt and explained the change in plans before turning her attention back to the CCTV footage. The cases had to be entwined in some way. Her intuition was rarely wrong, although she was reminded of the fiasco the week before when she had identified Nick Jackson by his luminous green bag; sometimes her instincts failed her. She was sure the net was tightening on their killer, but she really didn't want a high body count before they finally uncovered him. She chewed the inside of her cheek while her mind churned the possibilities around. Robyn was sure of only one thing – if he hadn't already, the killer was going to strike again, and judging by how quickly he was acting, it would be soon.

CHAPTER FORTY-ONE

The black Bentley Continental pulled into the drive. Alan Worth yawned loudly as he aimed his key fob and waited for the door of the four-bay garage to lift automatically.

It had been a very successful night. They had bagged a table overlooking the canal and watched the boaters as they trundled past. Alan could still savour the scallops he had eaten, along with a bottle of Châteauneuf-du-Pape Blanc, which had washed them down perfectly. He and a friend, Francis Hamilton, who usually partnered him at golf, had taken a taxi into Birmingham where they had gone to the theatre, finally rounding off the night at the roulette tables at Grosvenor Casino on Broad Street. They'd both struck lucky, although Francis had bet all his winnings, and more, on the tables, and turned the night into morning trying to win back what he had lost. They had tumbled out of the casino at five o'clock, Francis claiming as usual that he would never gamble again. Unlike his friend, Alan had cashed in his chips and collected his thousand pounds in winnings. The notes were currently filling his wallet nicely.

The garage door was now fully open, the lights inside had come on and he manoeuvred the Bentley into place and yawned again. The effects of the wine had worn off and had left him feeling lethargic. He was getting old. There was a time when he could have stayed out all night drinking; nowadays anything after one o'clock was pushing it. He wished Francis had not kept him out all night. It was seven in the morning. He should be getting up at this time, not going to bed. Alan swung one leg out of the car and halted. A movement had caught his eye. There was an animal in the garage. It was most likely a cat or a fox that had followed him in. He hoped it hadn't decided to hide behind the boxes and clutter at the far end of the garage or he'd have a devil of a job coaxing it out, and he really wanted nothing more than to go to bed.

He moved quietly to the rear of the garage, head down, scanning for further movement. He couldn't see the creature. Maybe it was a rat. That would be worse. He'd have to call in the pest controllers. He decided to let it be and deal with it later after he'd had some sleep. He moved towards the side door when, without warning, he felt an arm tighten around his neck, crushing his windpipe so he couldn't speak. He was being pulled backwards and was powerless to break away from his attacker. He reached up with both hands and tried to prise the arm away, yet was unable to move it. It was like a gigantic python, wrapping itself around his neck and slowly crushing his windpipe. He couldn't catch a breath and began to panic. His assailant was squeezing the life out of him. The automatic lighting system in the garage flicked off, leaving the pair in complete darkness. Alan felt a rush of desperation and kicked backwards, catching his attacker on the shin. His assailant cursed and loosened his hold enough for Alan to yank the man's forearm away and bite it hard. He was released immediately and fumbled towards the side door. He knew his way around in the dark. He hoped the man intent on killing him did not.

Alan put out his hand, felt for the wall, groping his way, heart thudding wildly. He was sure it was only a few paces to the door. He only had to get to it and he could escape this madman. He couldn't hear his attacker, and that panicked him further. What if the man were already in front of him? Fear spurred him on and he moved faster, desperate to escape. Then his foot caught something that clattered in front of him and he stumbled over it, falling heavily on the floor. He had forgotten about his golf bag standing near the door. He had intended moving it earlier, but had been running late for his night out and had left it out rather than put it back in its usual place. The clubs had spilled out onto the floor, and as Alan pushed himself up, he knew he had made a monumental error.

The intruder tugged him to his feet. In the darkness, Alan could feel the man's anger radiating from him and knew he didn't stand a prayer.

CHAPTER FORTY-TWO

'Just one moment, please.' Ross waited while Frieda tapped away at her computer keyboard. He could picture her now: tall, blonde and blue-eyed. She had sounded uber-efficient when he rang the Hideaway Hotel.

'Certainly, Mr Cunningham, let me assist you with that.' She had a charming accent that made Ross think of mountains and the midnight sun. He'd conducted a quick search on the hotel and found its website. It was a delightful boutique hotel, which appeared, at first sight, to be a smart, private residence. The receptionist was certainly polite and attentive. The typing stopped and she spoke again, 'I see Mr Ashbrook made the reservation.'

'Can you tell me who he was with that evening? Did they both sign the register?'

Frieda sounded less helpful. 'I'm sorry, Mr Cunningham, I'm not able to discuss such matters without some proof of your identity. I'm sure you understand.'

Ross sighed. 'Yes, Frieda, I understand. Can you just confirm that if I make the journey all the way to London and hand you my investigative licence, you will be able to tell me who Mr Ashbrook was with that night?'

There was a silence as Frieda struggled to be polite and helpful at the same time. Eventually she answered, 'Yes. I will be able to give you a name, and if you have a photograph of the gentleman you are looking for, I might be able to identify him for you too.'

'In that case, I shall see you as soon as I can. Thank you, Frieda.'

Frustrated by the call, Ross checked the pay-as-you-go mobile to see if it had powered up sufficiently to turn it on and, seeing it had, went straight to the contact list and felt a frisson of excitement. There was only one contact – with the initials 'JJ'. Tricia was correct when she said Miles was keeping secrets. He clearly didn't want anyone to know about this person. He thumbed the screen until the display revealed the messages. There were only two messages in the inbox, both from JJ, and both were sent the night Miles Ashbrook died. The first read:

Ten minutes. That's all I ask.

The second, sent at eight ten, stated:

You know where to find me. Meet me there.

He checked the sent messages, where he found one word in reply to the messages:

Okay.

There was nothing else on the mobile, and Ross put it to one side. He slid the USB stick into his laptop and scratched at his stubble. The USB contained one document sent from Bromley Hall's head office in Hong Kong. It was a list of names of the people who were to be dismissed from Bromley Hall, all of them before the end of November. It seemed peculiar that Miles had kept only one document on the USB. He clearly didn't want the list to fall into the hands of anybody at the Hall. It all seemed a little cloak-and-dagger, unless Miles had a good reason to keep the list secret.

Ross spun around in his swivel chair and rang Robyn, leaving a message for her. He admired her nerve. Once she got her teeth into something, she wouldn't let go. That cousin of his was a tough cookie, and she'd need to be. Tom Shearer was guaranteed to give her grief for some time once he got wind of this.

The rain had stopped and given way to grey clouds, occasionally broken by rays of weak sunshine. Matt Higham pulled off the M42 and drove the leafy roads to Knowle, an affluent district of Solihull. Matt wished he could afford one of the places on this route, with its wide roads and green hedgerows. Alan Worth's house was not far from the town centre. Within a few minutes, Matt had pulled onto the drive and was knocking at the door. No one was at home. Matt peered through the front window into a study, sparsely furnished with iron statues of nude women. He rang the doorbell again, stood back and checked for any movement or indication someone was inside. There was nothing. He walked around the back of the house, cupped his hands over his eyes and peered through the conservatory window, finding only wickerwork chairs and several tall yucca plants. Worth was not at home.

He was wandering back to his car, admiring the huge buxus hedges that had been expertly shaped into balls, when a faint sound caught his attention. It was a low, purring noise. He walked back to the house, head turning this way and that to trace its origin. It was coming from the garage – a large wooden structure resembling a Swiss chalet, with painted wooden slats and a tiled green roof. As he got closer, the noise became clearer. It was the hum of a car engine. The sound galvanised him into action and he tugged at the door handle, but the up-and-over door was clearly locked. The engine continued to rumble. Matt banged on the door and shouted – nothing.

The thought hit him quickly – Worth was in trouble. The killer had already got to him. Matt hammered on the door one last time, got no response and raced around the building, searching for another means of entry. He found a side door that was also locked. He heaved his shoulder against it and felt it give. He whacked against it again, and then a third time before it finally gave way. He booted it open. He held his breath and rushed inside, almost colliding with a golf bag on its side, its clubs strewn about the floor. Alan Worth was lying close to the door, head turned towards him, eyes shut. His feet and hands were bound with tape and Matt's eyes widened in surprise when he saw what was in his mouth – someone had stuffed it with fifty-pound notes. There must be a few hundred pounds sticking out between his lips. As he stared at the sight, Matt noticed a faint movement in Alan's eyelids. The man was still alive.

Matt checked him over for injuries before lifting him gently. He carried the man clear of the garage and, pausing for a moment, took a breath of fresh air. He'd ingested some of the fumes, but hopefully not enough to do any serious damage. Carbon monoxide was a killer, and heaven knows how long Alan Worth had been exposed to the fumes in his garage. Matt knelt beside the man and checked for breathing, relieved when he felt the faintest of pulses in the man's neck. He rang the emergency services. If only Alan could stay alive and speak to them, they might be able to trace whoever had done this.

He left the door open to clear the garage of fumes, ingested as much fresh air as he could and, holding his breath, sprinted back inside to shut off the car engine. The garage not only had ample space for the large vehicle but also housed gardening tools, a lawnmower and various storage containers. Standing inside he understood how Alan Worth had cheated death – several wooden slates had warped, and light filtered through the gaps into the garage. Some of the toxic fumes had escaped. One large gap was behind a low shelf containing walking boots, where Alan had been lying. He had discovered it and placed his head near it to breathe in cleaner air. The killer had been sloppy. This was not an efficient way to murder. Matt wondered why he had not been more thorough in despatching his victim. Was he becoming complacent? Matt would voice his opinions to Robyn. There was no way of knowing how much damage had been caused to his lungs, heart or brain, but for now Alan Worth was alive. Only time would tell how fortunate he had been.

As a PC in the south of England, Matt had once before come across a suicide victim who had killed himself with carbon monoxide using the hose method of attaching one end to his car exhaust, the other through the car window. Matt would never forget the sight. The capillaries in the young man's face had burst, his eyeballs had popped and his tongue had swollen to twice its normal size. He shuddered at the memory. At least Alan Worth did not look like that.

The driver's door to the Bentley was open wide. Matt donned plastic gloves, bent in and turned off the engine. Whoever had tried to kill Alan by carbon monoxide poisoning had not done their research. It was largely older cars that emitted sufficient amounts of the odourless gas that could kill quickly. This car had a catalytic converter and produced lower amounts of carbon monoxide than many other vehicles. That, combined with the fact that Alan's garage was not airtight, had probably saved his life. Matt couldn't work out how long the man had been in the garage. It was just after nine thirty now. He couldn't have been in there all night or he'd have been dead.

The paramedics were on their way, sirens blaring. Matt was about to vacate the garage when his eye caught a flash of white under the car. He knelt down, lifted the piece of paper by one corner and read it. His pulse quickened. He had to call Robyn immediately.

CHAPTER FORTY-THREE

He stood in the shower for the longest time, water cascading over his shoulders, easing the tension in them. He wanted to look his best for her. There were hardly any obstacles between her and him now. Soon they'd be together forever.

He'd waited hours for the scumbag to get in from a night out. Hours and hours in the cold, getting angrier and angrier until he could barely think straight. The drumming in his head had been so overwhelming he almost hadn't been able to carry out his plan. He smiled at the memory of Alan Worth's terrified face. He'd disposed of her husband, the dirty rotten lowlife who had benefited from her death. If *he* had been her husband, he would have fought the owners of Bromley Hall. He would have gone to court and ruined the Bishtons once and for all. Her death had been glossed over – a mere accident – and no one had accepted the consequences. He knew all about consequences; he'd paid his dues for his own misdemeanours.

His mind flipped a couple of decades and he was once again the boy under the bridge where he lived, having run away from his latest set of foster parents…

The large bloke with the neck tattoo gave him a sharp kick. He curled into a tighter ball.

'You fucking shit. What'ya done with my gear?'

He forced back the tears that threatened to spill from his eyes. The fresh pain in his groin made him want to scream out, but he knew better than to show a bully any sign of weakness. He braved it out.

'I haven't got it. I never touched your gear.'

The ugly brute bent over him, showering him with spittle and bad breath. 'You lying, cheating, fucking...' He kicked him hard again and again in his chest, his legs and his head. Each blow from the heavy boots dented another part of his body. He imagined he was now full of holes and dents. He saw the fury in the man's eyes – the eyes of a user desperate for a fix. His mate watched with half-closed eyes, barely interested in the attack.

He heard something unintelligible, after which he received an almighty kick to his kidneys that wiped out all other pain. The bloke wanted him to beg for mercy. He wouldn't. His life was so shit, so what if it ended here, under the bridge? No one would miss him. There would be no one to cry at his funeral or miss him. He hadn't heard from Stacey in weeks. She'd probably chosen to forget she had a brother.

He didn't fight back or kick or curse. He lay on the ground, accepting every kick and punch. He would soon be dead. He raised a mangled face. 'Go ahead. Kill me. It won't bring back your gear.'

The man stopped in his tracks. 'You did take it. I knew it.'

He spat out gobs of blood. His entire body screamed in agony. He had never suffered pain like it. He managed to speak through bruised and bloody lips. 'Nah, I didn't. Your mate Raz took it. I saw him.'

The man pulled back. 'This true?'

Raz shook his head. 'Nah, bro, I wouldn't do nuffin' like that. Kid's a born liar. He's got your gear, that's a fact.'

'I'm just a kid. I don't do drugs. You're asking the wrong person. Ask someone who uses. Now if you're going to kill me, get on with it.'

A furrow appeared between the bloke's eyes, followed by a chuckle from his plump lips. 'You got big balls, little bro, talking to me like that.'

'They are a bit swollen,' he replied, grasping his tender groin area with one hand. He spat out more blood. The mood had changed. He was no longer getting kicked. He was going to be let go. He sat upright. Every part of him hurt. His ribs were probably broken. His dragged himself onto his knees and reached forward to push himself up. That was when he felt the smash against the back of his head. For a second he thought his head had been hit clean off. That was before the stars and the agonising, shooting pains. His eyes filled, and tears mingled with blood trickled down his chin and onto his filthy jeans.

'And that's for lying about my bro. He didn't never take none of my stuff. We know you did. You tried to sell it to Big H. but he called me and told me 'bout it. You got one chance now to stay alive. Go get my gear back.'

He hadn't tried to get the drugs back. He had run. He had run as far away from that bridge as he could, with every fibre and muscle in his shattered body screaming as he ran. He had stumbled and crawled and cried as he tried to make his escape on the towpath, until he couldn't bear it any more. He had collapsed. The next time he woke up he was in hospital, his foster parents by his bedside. He knew they wouldn't want him to live with them for much longer and he hadn't got any energy to care about that.

He rubbed his neck absent-mindedly. The incident had left more than a mark on his memory. He now suffered from incurable occipital neuralgia as the result of the injury. Over the years he had numerous treatments to help rid him of the incapacitating headaches. None had helped. One neurologist injected his neck with steroids and numbing agents, which were so painful he almost passed out. The injections were supposed to block the nerves in the neck and stop the headaches, but the pain returned a few months later and he couldn't bear any repeat injections. He had tried to live with the pain, but when it materialised, it wiped out every thought, every action and every hope. At times it was so bad he wanted to cut off his head, and many a time he had considered ending it all. That was before Harriet.

His thoughts turned once more to Harriet and Alan, the weak, lily-livered husband who had been too quick to accept money in recompense for losing his wife. He had claimed he wanted justice, then sold out for a mere one and a half million. He had accepted the paltry sum they offered almost with thanks. No amount of money was large enough to compensate for Harriet's death. The man should have taken them to the cleaners and then made sure their business was razed to the ground so an accident like this could never happen again. All those responsible should now be in jail, he raged.

Alan Worth had found out, to his cost, that money doesn't bring happiness. He smiled at the memory of stuffing money into his victim's mouth. Alan owed his wife, big time, and now he had paid that debt. He hoped the man had thought about that as he drew his last breath.

He dry-swallowed a couple of pills, then blew a kiss to his wall where she watched over him. He reflected, with sadness, that money did not bring happiness, nor did it bring back those you love.

CHAPTER FORTY-FOUR

'I'm sorry, Mr Dawson, it's for your own safety.' Following the incident with Alan Worth, she had managed to convince Mulholland that Scott needed protection.

'How many more officers are you going to require?' Mulholland had sounded decidedly annoyed on the phone. 'I don't have a problem with this as long as you are convinced you have grounds for believing your man is in danger. I have to get it cleared with Jackson and I want a persuasive argument for extracting officers from duties to babysit members of the public.'

Superintendent Jackson was a corpulent man with raised blood pressure and a temper when riled.

'I only need one for now. We're trying to contact Lord Bishton to advise him to change his travel plans. It would be better if he stays away for the time being and doesn't attend the hunt ball. If he insists on showing up, I might require more.'

It was clear from her tone that Mulholland was not happy, but she agreed to the request and ended the call.

Scott was still in shock. He sat on the desk in his office, palms resting on his thighs. 'I can't just leave. If I take any time off, I'll put my job at risk. I have responsibilities here.' He paused, taking in the reality of the situation. 'What about my family – Alex and George? Aren't they in danger too? They should be taken somewhere safe.'

'I'm sure management would be understanding.'

'No, you don't understand. I'm in line now for a permanent promotion as manager. It'll make a huge difference to my life if I get the job – no more insecurity and more money. I can't race off, no matter the reason.'

'In that case, we'll ensure there'll be a police officer outside your door 24/7. You'll be safe. However, you might feel happier if your wife and son were to leave home for the time being. It'll be less of a concern for you. How about an impromptu visit to relatives?'

Scott scrubbed at his chin, eyes roaming the office. 'I'll call Alex. Even if she agrees to this, I can't go home.'

'There'll be an officer watching at all times. Nothing will happen.'

His eyes settled on Robyn's and she could see the deep anxiety in them. 'I can't go home because I've been thrown out. We had a tremendous row yesterday and Alex wants a divorce. I tried to reason with her but she's having none of it. So, you see, I need this job. I'll soon have no house and no family. I'm going to have to start my life all over again.'

She thought he was about to cry, but instead he made a snuffling sound and sat up even straighter. 'I'd planned on staying here until I could sort out more permanent arrangements. There are a few vacant rooms.'

He lost control of his emotions and dropped his head into his hands, anguish visible in all his features, brow furrowed and eyes dampening. 'It's a bloody mess,' he mumbled.

'At the moment, your safety is our prime concern, Mr Dawson. Which room will you be staying in?'

'Twelve. It's on the top floor.'

'Anna, will you be okay to stay outside that room? Maybe Mr Dawson could organise a comfortable chair for you.'

'Sure, no problem.'

Scott shuffled off the desk. 'I'll sort out a chair.' He wandered out in a daze, leaving behind the three officers.

'Thanks, Anna.'

'Not a problem. I left my dog with my mum for a few days. I figured this case would involve long hours. Dog's delighted. He gets spoilt rotten there.'

Robyn turned to her colleagues. 'I'm concerned the killer's working really quickly – almost a murder a day. I've never known anything like it. We are rapidly running out of time. If I'm right about Miles, there's only one more invoice to be called in. So far he's murdered Rory, Linda, Jakub and tried to murder Alan. At £250,000 per invoice, he has almost reached the target of a million and a half that Alan Worth got in compensation, so we can assume he's almost at the end of his killing spree and I am at a loss as to how to catch him.' She hated the feeling that she was losing the match. The killer had been way ahead of them all the time.

Mitz had been quietly staring at a paper cup of coffee. Eventually he spoke up. 'I don't want to rain on your parade, boss, but what if Miles was not one of his targets?'

She levelled her gaze at him. 'Then I hope I've chosen the right two people to protect. I'm waiting to see if and when Lord Bishton turns up. I've left messages for him to call the station. So far there's been nothing. He's probably already on his way here.' She rang again. 'Answerphone,' she said, glancing at her phone and noticing there were several missed calls.

With a sigh she dialled the answering service, only to pull a face at the first message. David had received a call from journalist Amy Walters who had heard a rumour that Robyn and her team were searching for a serial killer. She was requesting an interview or a quote for the newspaper. The second was from the journalist herself asking for an interview. She deleted the call and listened to the third. It was Ross. She scribbled down his message and pushed the pad across to Mitz.

'Ross has found this message on a pay-as-you-go phone found in Miles's possessions. It's from someone he calls "JJ". The sender's phone is also a pay-as-you-go but is turned off. What do you make of the messages?'

Mitz read, "'*Ten minutes. That's all I ask. You know where to find me. Meet me there. Okay.*" So perhaps Mr Ashbrook had a lover who arranged to meet him prior to his death. Smacks of desperation, like when an affair has been ended. "*That's all I ask.*" That sounds like a plea. "*You know where to meet me.*" They obviously had a special location they use for their clandestine meetings.'

Anna opened her eyes in surprise. 'Could this person have been involved in his murder?'

'A text message as ambiguous as this one proves nothing. Besides, Miles was alive when he took the sauna at eleven o'clock and these messages were sent at eight ten.'

'True. Ah, I'm getting ahead of myself.'

'The message doesn't say *when* to meet. It only says, "*You know where to meet me.*" They could have met later that night.'

'I wonder who sent it. Miles Ashbrook didn't leave the premises that night, did he?'

Mitz shook his head. 'He was in his office all evening. There are various witnesses to that. DI Shearer's report showed that Miles was seen eating in the canteen at six thirty and went back to his office after that. One of the housekeepers passed his door at about seven forty-five when she went to the laundry before clocking off. His office light was on until after ten. It could be seen from the Hall entrance, and a receptionist spotted it as she left.'

Anna's dark brows rose and lowered. 'Then whoever sent the messages might be an employee or a guest.'

'Or came here and slipped in the back way and met him.' Mitz shrugged.

Robyn sighed wearily. 'There's not enough to go on, is there? All we know is Miles had a lover. If we could track "JJ" down, I'd like to interview him, although we have more important avenues to explore at the moment. Our killer is out there somewhere. Anna, stick by Scott, by the gym, or his office, wherever he is, and when he retires for the night, wait outside his room. I'll make sure a relief officer comes and takes over at eleven. Let's get going, Mitz.'

Outside in the car park, Robyn cast a concerned eye over her colleague. 'When we get back to the station, go home. You look wrecked.'

'I'm okay. I was up all night. Couldn't sleep. It's a mixture of this case and missing Granny Manju. Somehow I feel I have to solve this case for her. Illogical, but there you are.'

'She'd be proud of you for just doing a great job. We'll catch him, don't you worry.' She unlocked the car and slipped into the driving seat. 'You read Shearer's report?'

He beamed. 'Cover to cover. That man's thorough. There were lists of people present at the time of his death and details of their movements. He checked Miles's mobile and laptop too. There was nothing suspicious in any of it. Everything pointed to an accident.'

'So you still don't think Miles was murdered?'

'I think there's more to the case than we may have first believed, especially as there was a second phone, and I am banking on my boss being right. I want her to be right.'

She beamed at him. 'That's exactly what I need – some confidence in my ability.'

Once in the squad car, she rang Ross.

'I'm at Watford Gap service station. It's seven o'clock, the place is stuffed full, and I've had to park what feels like a town away from the actual service station.'

'You're not breaking your diet and chomping on an all-day breakfast, are you?'

'I wouldn't dare. I'm on my way to London, to the Hideaway Hotel. The receptionist won't give out any information over the phone. I'm going to wheedle it out of her with my charm.'

'And we both know you have bucketloads of that. If you can find out who Miles spent the night with, it'll mean I won't have to play guess who "JJ" is. I don't suppose you can send me the list of staff that were getting fired that you downloaded from the USB?'

'Sent it earlier. It should be in your inbox.'

'You're a real pro. Cheers for that.'

'Any time.'

'I'll call you later. I'm going to get back on the road now.'

She opened the email and read through the list of employees facing the sack. Some of them had already left, including Jakub's wife. She noticed the porters Charlie and Dan were down for dismissal, along with several of the beauty salon staff, two kitchen porters, one of the receptionists and, surprisingly, gym manager Scott Dawson. It appeared Scott had not yet been told about the decision to make him redundant. Although now he was overall manager, he was less likely to be fired. He still had the appearance of a man with the weight of the world on his shoulders.

She gathered her paperwork together and began by writing the names of staff who might have come into contact with Harriet Worth. She would interview them in the morning. She couldn't afford any errors. She had to eliminate them all from her enquiries.

CHAPTER FORTY-FIVE

The entrance to the Hideaway Hotel was an unassuming doorway to the right of the building, down a narrow, pedestrian-only lane off Fleet Street. Ross found the reception desk situated in what appeared to be an old living room – small and charming. With its polished wood panelling, open fires and genuine antique furniture it felt more like a private club than a boutique hotel. A girl in her twenties, with ash-blonde hair styled in a shoulder-grazing cut with gently razored ends, was behind the desk. He meandered into the room, trying not to gawp at the décor.

'I'm Ross Cunningham from R&J Associates. I spoke to Frieda earlier today.'

The girl studied his card and private investigator licence with large eyes. 'She's on her break at the moment, sir. I'll fetch her for you. Can I offer you a drink – a cup of tea, something stronger?'

Ross agreed to a coffee. The caffeine would help keep him awake for the return journey.

He plopped down on a large chair decorated in pastel colours. He was feeling jaded. Not only had traffic been heavy, but finding a free space in any of the car parks near the hotel had been a nightmare. He'd ended up parked some distance from the hotel and made the last mile of the trip on foot.

His thoughts were interrupted by the arrival of a girl with ice-blue eyes and shoulder-length hair, tied up in a blue ribbon. It had to be Frieda. She extended a hand that was cool and soft.

'I apologise for the inconvenience, Mr Cunningham. You will appreciate we have to respect our clients' privacy.'

Her voice flowed over him like a trickling stream. 'I do, Frieda.'

'I have the registration forms here.' She pulled out a sheet of paper and pointed to a line.

Ross put on his glasses. He had only recently taken to wearing them and hated that they signalled he was getting older. He squinted at it, and made out Miles Ashbrook's signature. The other was unidentifiable and little more than a scrawl.

'Is that it? I can't make it out at all.'

'After I spoke to you, I worried that might be the case, so I thought about this and checked it for you.'

She passed a large leather-bound book of guest comments to him.

He read through those on the page she showed him. He came to the third comment down and stopped, eyebrows raised in surprise.

'Can I take a copy of this?' he asked.

'Certainly, Mr Cunningham.' She gave a cat-like tilt of the head, pleased to have helped.

Ross snapped a shot of the comment with his mobile and sent it to Robyn before calling her. She sounded worn out.

'I can't get a handle on this, Ross. It's really bugging me. I'm worried that I shouldn't have insisted on keeping the case open. Shearer might have made more progress than me on it.'

'Nonsense. You're tired, that's all. Shearer would be in the same position as you. In truth, he wouldn't be anywhere as near as you are to finding this perpetrator. Come on, Robyn. It isn't like you to have self-doubts. Where's that brilliant unstoppable DI I know and care about?'

She fell silent. He could tell she was considering the question carefully.

'Let me boost your confidence. Check your email. You're in for a surprise.'

*

Robyn stared at the photo Ross had sent and berated herself. Why hadn't she suspected this? The haggard looks, the intense anxiety in his eyes and the split from his wife. The guest comment book was the evidence she needed to prove the identity of Miles's lover.

> *Thoroughly enjoyed our romantic weekend at this amazing hotel. Can't recommend it enough.*
>
> *Miles Ashbrook and Scott Dawson*

Whether the pair had been confident that no one they knew would ever read the comment remained a mystery; however one thing was for sure: Miles and Scott had been seeing each other. Scott had been at the Hall the night Miles had died. She had to speak to him immediately. She called Anna.

'Is Scott in his room?'

'I've not moved from here since he turned in for the night. The receptionist gave me a thriller to read – it's gripping, so I've been wide awake.'

'Can you bring him in? I need to question him.'

'Will do.'

Anna rang off. Robyn returned to the whiteboard in the office. There were several new photographs with connecting lines and comments – a picture of Jakub and another of Alan Worth, who was still in intensive care and causing concern to the staff at the hospital, who suspected he had brain damage. She rubbed at her sore eyes and stared at the board.

She noted the times of each attack: late at night; ten in the morning; late afternoon; and in the early hours of the morning. She pulled out a red marker pen and wrote: 'Suspect works odd hours or is unemployed.' It wasn't much to go on. She scratched her head and debated whether to go for a run or head home for a power nap and a shower. She thought about the Fiat 500 that had been spotted in Kings Bromley and read PC David Marker's note. He had got in touch with numerous owners of Fiat cars and had narrowed his search down to twenty in Staffordshire and Derbyshire who had yet to be contacted. She wrote: 'Drives Fiat 500?' Then, staring blankly at the board, wondered where Miles and Scott fitted into the picture.

The ring of her mobile cut into her thoughts. Anna was flustered. 'He's gone.'

'How?'

'Room twelve's bathroom interconnects to room thirteen's. He's sidled out via room thirteen, which faces onto another corridor. I couldn't have spotted him leaving.'

The fatigue that had been threatening to consume Robyn vanished. Scott Dawson had to be found. He was either a valuable witness to a murder or in terrible danger.

CHAPTER FORTY-SIX

Mulholland's lips were pressed so tightly together they were almost invisible. She pushed the newspaper towards Robyn without a word.

She knew what the article said. David had already shown it to her.

'It's big news now. The "Lichfield Leopard" has caught on, as I feared.'

'Oh, for crying out loud! Where do they get these inappropriate names and where did this Amy Walters get this information?'

'No one knows. I've asked about.'

She wondered if Shearer would stoop low enough to tell the journalist anything and decided that he was neither spiteful nor unprofessional. In this business, no one spoke to journalists off the record. They often did more harm than good. This was a prime example of poor reporting, a few facts mixed with conjecture and enough gory details to frighten the general public.

She read:

HAS AS THE LICHFIELD LEOPARD CLAIMED A THIRD VICTIM?

A spate of murders in the Lichfield area has shocked the public. On Saturday 19th, Rory Wallis (34) was found brutally murdered in his bar the Happy Pig in Lichfield. It is believed that Wallis was discovered with his throat cut. This was followed on Monday 21st by the murder of housewife Linda Upton (32) in Kings Bromley. Linda, wife to Robert Upton and mother to Louis (6) was drowned in her bath. Friends and neighbours have been shocked by the murder. Theresa Harris, whose daughter attends the same school as Linda's son, said, 'People are now terrified to leave their houses and it has sent a frisson of anxiety through our peaceful, quiet community. I don't know how anyone could harm Linda. We're all staying indoors until the Lichfield Leopard is caught.'

Wednesday saw the death of another local man, Jakub Woźniak, involved in a hit and run. Mrs Woźniak, who is expecting their second child, said her husband was travelling home from work when he was struck by a vehicle and died. Could this third death be connected in any way to the work of the individual people are calling the Lichfield Leopard, due to the fact he has struck stealthily and without detection?

While it has not been confirmed the deaths are con-nected, DI Robyn Carter of Staffordshire Police was spotted at the scene of all the incidents, leading to speculation that they are related. DI Carter was unavail-able to comment.

The article was accompanied by an unflattering photograph of Robyn looking gaunt and worried, taken outside the Happy Pig.

Mulholland was staring at her. 'I don't need to tell you that this is the last thing we need.'

'I agree, and I can assure you none of my team spoke to Amy Walters. We've all been flat out on this case.'

'Robyn, I can't convey how much pressure I am under to get this resolved. We can't afford to have everybody in Staffordshire terrified they're going to be bumped off by this person. I've been asked to give a press conference this afternoon to reassure the public that they are not in danger.' Louisa hated appearing in front of the cameras. Robyn knew where the conversation was going. 'I have an appointment at three so I want you to take my place.'

She loathed press conferences even more than Louisa did. 'Do I have any choice?'

'No. Keep it brief. Keep it accurate and try to get rid of this ridiculous name the Lichfield Leopard.'

Robyn felt she had hit rock bottom. She had nothing to give the press and Scott Dawson was still missing. Passing Shearer's door, she felt she ought to at least build bridges with her co-worker. Shearer was typing with two fingers. 'Don't make any comment. I can type as quickly with two as others can using all their fingers.'

'I'm not here to bandy insults. I've come to tell you I've found out that Miles Ashbrook was having an affair with Scott Dawson.'

Shearer's eyebrows arched high on his forehead. 'Well, there's a turn-up for the books.'

'They spent a night together in a hotel in London and had pay-as-you-go phones to keep their communication private.'

'And why are you are telling me? Am I wearing a dog collar? Does this look like a confessional booth?' he said, arm sweeping around the empty office.

'Lay off the jibes, Tom. I'm in so much shit I can smell it myself and I wanted to clear the air with you. Miles Ashbrook was your case until I got some information about it that I had to follow up. I voiced my concerns about Ashbrook's death and you didn't want to listen, so I had no option other than to look into it myself.'

Shearer's piercing eyes studied her cautiously.

'Mulholland is pissed off with lack of results on the murder cases and I can't say I blame her. And, to make matters worse, I went off at a tangent and delved into Miles Ashbrook's death, trying to find a link between it and the murders I'm investigating.

'I was given some personal effects belonging to Ashbrook and among them was a receipt for a night's stay at a London hotel, a pay-as-you-go mobile and a USB stick. I should have told you or handed them over to you, but instead I looked into the matter alone. There were messages on the phone that suggested Ashbrook was meeting his lover the night he died. Now I can't determine their relevance and I think I might have royally screwed up. I took my eye off what was important – catching the killer. I suspected Miles might have been killed by the same person who murdered Rory Wallis and Linda Upton.'

'The Lichfield Leopard?'

She sighed heavily. 'I wish Amy hadn't given him that nickname. Gives him a status that he certainly doesn't deserve.'

'For the record, I'm sorry about it too. I have no time for these bloody reporters who shit stir.'

'Thanks. Anyway, I wonder if trying to link the killer to Miles's death hasn't cost the lives of others. To cap it all, we had Scott under surveillance at the Hall last night and he did a runner. I'm worried he could be next.'

'You tried to track his car?'

She nodded. 'No sign of it, and we've talked to everyone we know who knows him. Where could he have gone, Tom? Where would you go if you were on the run and scared?'

'Somewhere isolated or somewhere I felt safe – family, loved ones?'

'His loved ones have chucked him out. His wife wants a divorce.'

Shearer tilted back on his chair. 'Well, I hope his turns out more amicable than mine.'

'Anyway, I wanted to apologise for pursuing the Ashbrook case. I should have let you in on what I was doing.'

'It's okay. I should apologise too for griping to Mulholland. I was bang out of order. I was out of sorts that day.'

'Forgotten.'

'Robyn, we all work on the same side, even if it doesn't feel like it some days. We want the same thing – results.'

'While you're in such a magnanimous mood, I don't suppose you feel like standing in for me at a press conference, do you? Mulholland has an appointment.'

Tom snorted. 'Not a chance in hell. You're definitely on your own with that. And I think you'll find her appointment is more a job interview.'

'Really?'

'Pretty certain.'

She lifted a hand and walked off. She now wasn't sure if she had really cleared the air with Shearer or whether he was playing games to further his career. That was the thing about Tom – you never actually knew.

CHAPTER FORTY-SEVEN

He was outside waiting for Scott Dawson. The man was later than usual. He should have left at least an hour earlier. Patience had paid off, and now Scott was scurrying to his car, keys in his hand, looking around before he jumped in and drove away.

He'd thought long and hard about how to kill Scott and had come up with the ideal way, but the wretched man was unpredictable and had not adhered to his usual routines and his plans had to be changed. While it had been easy to overpower his other victims, Scott Dawson was an expert in ju-jitsu, and would be able to fell him with one sharp kick or blow. He had the advantage of surprise, yet that wouldn't help a huge amount once Scott, like the others, decided to fight for his life.

His new plan was simple. He would wait for Scott to leave work and follow him. The dark, narrow lanes were perfect for what he had in mind. He would turn off his headlights and ease up to Scott's car before lighting them up on full beam. Scott would then be both startled and blinded by the sudden glare, and either veer off the road or press the brake – either way, he would emerge from the car at some point to assess damage, or find out what had happened. At that point, he would be recognised and he would play the dumb fool, apologising profusely until Scott suspected nothing. He would offer to pay for the damage and move towards Scott. Then he would strike. The claw hammer sat on the passenger seat. A blow to the temple would be all it would take – that or a full frontal attack, just like a real leopard. He smiled at his new name – the Lichfield Leopard. He had never felt so important in all his life. Harriet would be extremely proud of him.

Scott didn't turn in his usual direction. Instead, he cut across the A515, sticking to the back roads that led to Uttoxeter. He sighed heavily in exasperation then shrugged. At least Scott was travelling on a rural road, hardly used by traffic at this time of night. They were fast approaching Marchington Woodlands, spread out over three miles of undulating land covered by large wooded areas. It consisted mostly of farms and properties in remote, rural settings, and he would have a job tailing Scott without using his lights. He would have to act soon. He moved closer to his prey before extinguishing his headlights on a stretch of straight road, relying purely on the beam coming from Scott's vehicle. Then, without warning, lights appeared from the left as a car trundled down a lane and, not seeing his own car, pulled out in front of him and joined the road. He swore loudly. He had missed a chance. Now Scott's Toyota Rav 4 was ahead of the newcomer's.

He began to sweat. He had a moment of confusion before he could decide how to rectify the situation. The fact was, he couldn't do anything while the other car was in front. He put his lights on dipped beam and followed behind, hoping the car would pull off. He could barely see Scott's car now. He banged his steering wheel and yelled for the car in front to get a move on. Frustration mounted as he lost track of Scott's car. Then the car in front indicated and slowed, before pulling into a drive. It took an eternity for the driver to make the turn, during which time he became increasingly angry. He hurled abuse at the unsuspecting driver, and had he not been after Scott, would have dragged the man out of the car into the road and kicked him to death. He accelerated away, all the while muttering and grumbling. The road ahead was empty. He raced towards Marchington, but couldn't spot the Toyota anywhere. He let out a howl of rage. Scott had disappeared.

CHAPTER FORTY-EIGHT

Robyn checked her reflection and straightened her black and white checked cravat. She barely recognised the grim-faced woman in the mirror with her sharp cheekbones and heavy bags under her eyes. All her team had the same hollow look. This case was getting to each of them. Outside the station, a small crowd of press had gathered. She knew what she would tell them – as little as possible.

The sun shone fiercely, making her squint as she emerged from the building. She could already imagine the photographs that would appear of her, brows furrowed and face screwed up against the bright light. She cleared her throat and began, keeping her voice level and speaking with a confidence she didn't feel. 'I can confirm that we are investigating the deaths of three citizens from the Lichfield area. We are currently seeking a person, or persons, unknown in this matter. A televised appeal for assistance from the public regarding the death of Rory Wallis resulted in several leads, all of which we are following up. We are asking the public to look out for a silver Fiat 500 with a 2014 plate. It may have a sticker in the back window that reads "I Love Westies". If you own such a vehicle or know of someone who has such a car, would you please get in touch with us, so we can eliminate this person from our enquiries? I must stress that we believe the general public is not at risk, and we would like to appeal for calm. Thank you.' She surveyed them all coolly.

A journalist directly in front of her spoke up. 'Gareth Taylor, *Staffordshire Newsletter*. Does this mean only certain people are being targeted, and do you know who they are?'

'I do not believe the general public is at risk,' she repeated.

'DI Carter, are you searching for a serial killer?'

She had known the question was going to arise. She spoke directly to the young man holding a microphone bearing a logo from a local radio station. 'We are looking into each individual case, and if we establish a connection, we shall be seeking one suspect. Thank you. No further comment.'

Robyn spotted Amy Walters standing to one side, a sly smile on her face. Robyn began to move away, ignoring the stream of questions being hurled at her. As she was about to enter the building, she heard Amy Walters shouting, 'DI Carter, can you confirm that the killer left behind notes on each of the bodies?'

With her arm against the door she turned quickly. *How on earth had the woman got hold of such sensitive information?* 'No comment, Miss Walters. This is an ongoing investigation and I am not at liberty to divulge any information that may jeopardise it.'

She threw the door open and marched into the station, stopping in the corridor to take a deep breath. She'd blown it. Her reaction had been exactly what Amy Walters needed to confirm the invoices existed. She stormed to her office and rang the *Lichfield Times*. 'Tell Amy Walters to call me immediately.' She banged down the phone and paced around the room, pausing intermittently to stare at her whiteboard. Someone had told Amy about the notes. It was highly unlikely any of her team had said anything. She trusted them all implicitly. There was only one other person who could have given her that information, and that was the killer himself.

The phone rang and she snatched it from the desk. 'Carter,' she snapped. It was Matt.

'Boss, I've spoken to Harriet Worth's friends and found out something very interesting – Harriet was being stalked. According to one of her friends – Lulu Howard – Harriet was concerned about a man she'd befriended who walked his dog at Stowe Pool, a small reservoir near Lichfield Cathedral. She only lived a short distance away in Cathedral Rise at the time, and used to run there most mornings. On one occasion, the man's dog slipped its lead and ran away. She helped recover it and thereafter whenever they met, he spoke to her.

'At first she thought he was just being friendly and she would sometimes stop and chat. Then one day he came to the park without his dog – it turned out the animal had died, and he was so upset she invited him to the café for tea to help calm him down. After that he waited for her every day and would try to engage her in conversation, so Harriet stopped running in the morning to avoid him. She grew suspicious when he was in the same spot every day no matter what time she went training. This started to trouble her and she sought advice from Lulu and Linda when they met up for a fun run. The man had announced he was madly in love with her and it freaked her out. Lulu and Linda both advised her to tell her husband and report the man. Harriet didn't want Alan to get the wrong idea – in case he believed she'd been leading him on – and was going to tell him after the spa weekend.'

'I don't suppose you got a name for this man, did you?'

'Lulu didn't know that. She remembered the man had a West Highland terrier called Alfie. No description of the man though. I've got one more of Harriet's friends to see.'

'Thanks, Matt. Catch you later.'

It was only another snippet of information, but she added it to the whiteboard. The man had a West Highland terrier, and the Fiat 500 they were searching for had a sticker saying 'I Love Westies'. Surely it was no coincidence?

The phone rang again. This time it was Amy Walters.

'Who told you about the notes, Amy?'

'So there *were* notes on the body?'

'Don't box clever with me. You know how unprofessional that was, coming out with it at the press conference. Who told you?'

'I can't divulge my source, DI Carter.'

Robyn felt a surge of anger. 'Amy, this isn't some game. You want a story, I'll give you one – but not until the investigation is over. I cannot put people's lives in danger because you want a scoop. You set me up for this. This is what you wanted. Now, who was it that informed you?'

'You'll give me an exclusive on the Lichfield Leopard?'

She cringed at the name. 'Only if you divulge your source.'

'I'm recording this conversation, DI Carter, so you'd better make good on your promise.'

She mentally cursed the woman. 'I'm waiting.'

Amy's voice was triumphant. 'It was the Leopard. He rang yesterday afternoon at four ten.'

'And you didn't think to tell me?'

'I'm telling you now.'

'Amy, if he rings again, call me immediately. Record the conversation. Did you record the last one with him?'

'It happened out of the blue, so I wasn't prepared. I don't think he'll ring again.'

'What makes you say that?'

'He laughed and told me he wasn't stupid, that he wouldn't risk his plan by calling again.'

'Anything else?'

'He thanked me for his new name, declared he was very pleased with it and roared like a big cat before ringing off.'

She was furious. The woman had spoken to their killer and not alerted them to the fact. 'Withholding evidence is a crime.'

'I haven't withheld it, though, DI Carter. I've willingly shared it. And now I shall look forward to my exclusive with you. You've got my number.'

Robyn resisted raising her voice. She knew the journalist was deliberately goading her. 'I'm going to have to ask you for your mobile. We have to see if we can trace where the call came from. I'll send an officer around to collect it.'

Amy went quiet. 'How am I supposed to work without it?'

'You'll have to use a landline. Be grateful I'm not making this more difficult for you. An officer will be with you shortly.'

She slammed the phone down. *Bloody journalists!* Amy Waters had just made her life more difficult and she had agreed to talk to her after the case was solved. Mulholland was not going to be at all impressed.

CHAPTER FORTY-NINE

Sweat poured down his neck and pooled between his shoulder blades. He was having a really bad turn. His head felt like someone was drilling through his skull and into his brain, and he wanted nothing more than for it to stop. With trembling hands he reached for the pills and dry-swallowed four – double the recommended dose.

He blamed his lousy headache on the fact he'd lost Scott Dawson the night before. His perfectly thought-through plan had been ruined, and for the moment he couldn't think of a new one because of the agonising waves of pain in his head. He curled into a ball and waited for the pain to ease.

His sleep had been punctuated with nightmares from his childhood, and as he lay in his tight ball he recalled one of them…

He had been asleep in the room he shared with three other boys at the home. Stacey was in a different room, on the bottom floor, with two girls. She had settled into the home better than him, and he could feel a gulf between them as she became increasingly friendly with the girls. He had had more trouble making friends. In fact, he hadn't made any. The other boys called him a freak. With his lanky frame, he was a good bit taller than them, but the reason they called him names was down to his left ear, which was larger than the right and deformed.

The room was pitch black when he woke with a jolt. The others had surrounded his bed, and before he could react, they dragged him from his sheets and half-carried, half-pulled him towards the showers. Once there, they shoved him into a cubicle and stuffed his head down the toilet filled with excrement and urine. They held his head down in the floating mess until he thought he would drown. Finally, they yanked his head up and let him gulp in air, laughing all the while. They shoved his head in again and flushed the chain. He felt the faeces wash around his face, filling his nostrils and ears and hair. He gagged. Suddenly, the pressure was released and he lifted his head in a rush, breathed in and threw up.

The boys taunted him as he puked into the same toilet bowl he had been forced into.

'Big ears, teeny knob,' they chorused.

They left him on the floor, crying, hair reeking. After a while he stopped crying and climbed into the shower, where he stood for an hour, under scalding water, until he could no longer smell the foul odour.

Three weeks later, there was a fire in the home that started in the boys' dormitory. Apparently, the three boys had been drinking and smoking. In a drunken state, one of them had not extinguished his cigarette properly and it had set fire to his bedding while he slept. The other boys were overcome by fumes and did not make it out in time with the girls. Only one of them did – blackened by smoke, he had sobbed and wailed that he had tried to stop them. He had warned them not to drink but they had told him to shut up. He was much younger than them. They had threatened him and told him to stay quiet about their activities. It was not the first time, he told the policeman. He had woken up when the fire started and tried save his friends, but he was only ten and couldn't drag them from their beds. So he had raced downstairs and hammered on the girls' door and got them out instead. He was commended for his bravery. They never discovered that he had brought in the cigarettes and stolen bottles of whisky that had made his room-mates dopey and sent them into a deep slumber, nor that he had smothered the boys one by one as they slept before setting fire to the bedding and making good his escape.

His head began to clear a little. He took another two pills. He had to get back on track. There were only three days to go.

CHAPTER FIFTY

The call came as a surprise. 'DI Carter, it's Scott Dawson.'

'Scott, where are you?'

'I can't tell you. I'm worried. Well, to be honest, I'm terrified, and so many other things too.'

'Tell me where you are and I'll make sure you're safe from any harm.'

There was a silence and a sound like a hiccough. Scott was crying. 'I'm safe here,' he replied.

She waited until he had collected himself. 'Scott, where are you?'

'In a place where I can't be found. I have to confess something, DI Carter. I can't live with myself any more. It's eating me away at me.'

She pressed the receiver to her ear. 'Go ahead. You can tell me.'

A soft sob. 'It's about Miles. I loved him.'

'We know. We found a receipt for a stay at the Hideaway Hotel and messages on Miles's second phone.'

'Then you must know he meant the world to me. I met Miles a few years ago when I was in America. He was travelling, getting over the loss of a boyfriend who'd been tragically killed in a motorbike crash. I was young – trying to find out who I really was. I was at a specialist school learning ju-jitsu, and bumped into him one evening at a bar. We got chatting – two Brits together in a foreign country. First, it was a holiday romance. He was my first, if you know what I mean. Then it became more serious. My training course was coming to an end and we decided to part. He wasn't ready to commit to a full-time relationship again and had more travelling to do, and I felt I was too young to get involved. I wanted a career.'

Scott sounded wistful. She strained to hear any background sounds that might indicate his location.

'I came home, started work at Bromley Hall and met Alex. I think it's fair to say I've always been confused about my sexuality. I am equally happy with men and women and I fell for Alex in a different way. I hadn't planned on having a permanent relationship with her, then she fell pregnant, and I was really taken with the idea of being a father. Miles was out of my life and I hadn't felt the inclination to be with any other men. Alex was there and we had George on the way. It seemed logical – get married. Then Miles turned up at Bromley Hall. Neither of us expected it and neither of us expected to feel the way we did. We picked up where we had left off. We had to keep it secret – not just because of Alex and George, but because his job would have been at risk too. We only used pay-as-you-go phones to contact each other and initials instead of our real names in case the phones got discovered. He was "AL" for American lover and I was "JJ" because I teach ju-jitsu.'

Robyn made a non-committal noise and wondered where all this was going. She hoped it wasn't some pre-suicide confession. She thought she could detect the rumbling of a large machine in the background. It faded before she could get a handle on it. Scott was talking quietly, lost in a world of memories. She looked into the corridor, hoping to catch the attention of a passing officer. She wanted a trace on this call.

'Last Wednesday, Miles called me into his office and told me I was being fired as part of the cutbacks. The classes were being axed and the gym was going to be run by junior staff. I was being made redundant. I'm afraid I took it badly. Miles was as cool as a cucumber. It was as if our relationship meant nothing. Worse still, he hadn't mentioned a thing when we were in London. We'd had a wonderful, romantic time. Then two weeks later he announced I was going to be made redundant. He must have known about the redundancy plans and said nothing.'

She listened to his words and the puzzle pieces that had been floating about in her head for days finally came together. Scott had run away, not through fear of being murdered so much as what would happen to him when the police uncovered this information.

Scott sounded weary, the very effort of speaking squeezing the last bit of energy from him as he recounted the events of that night…

'Miles, you can't. You just can't.'

Miles, in a white shirt, sleeves rolled up, looks at him without the usual tenderness. This isn't the Miles he knows and loves. This isn't the man who held his hand across the white linen tablecloth as they sat by the window at the Hideaway Hotel, a breakfast tray of warm croissants in front of them and champagne bubbles swirling and popping in their glasses as they toasted their relationship.

The strip light in his office highlights the shadows under Miles's eyes, two half-crescents that sink to his cheekbones. 'I'm sorry,' is all he offers. 'This is out of my control, Scott. And it isn't the end of the world. You'll easily find work. You have a lot to offer. You can rest assured I'll write a good reference.'

'What about us?' he asks, already feeling the answer in the pit of his stomach. The weekend in London wasn't to celebrate their relationship – it was to end it. Miles knew all along that he was going to fire him. Miles's face says it all and he feels sick.

'Look, it was never going to last. It has been amazing and I'm so glad I found you again, but it's different this time. You're married. You have a son. I can't be responsible for breaking up your marriage. Move away. Get a new position. Enjoy your family and forget about me.'

Scott's stomach tightens and he fights back the tears. Miles puts a hand on his shoulder; the warmth of it seeps into him, yet he pulls away. His sorrow turns instantly into anger. Miles spots the change.

'Go take the class, Scott,' he says. 'You have clients waiting. We'll talk again.'

Scott can't concentrate on his exercise routines and makes mistakes. All the while he maintains a false smile. Inside, his head is in turmoil, like someone has turned him upside down and shaken his thoughts so they float about like snowflakes in a storm. As soon as the class is over he heads back to the office. The light is on. Miles is with someone else and the door is shut. He waits outside, back against the wall, wondering how he can convince Miles to take him back. Maybe they could meet again in London?

He can't wait any longer. He heads to the changing room and drops onto a bench by the lockers. He pulls out his secret phone and texts Miles. He receives no response. The wait is agonising. He debates whether or not to return to the office. Instead he strips off his kit, sweat-stained from the exercise class, and drops it on the floor. Still no reply. He stands in the shower, the water beating on his aching shoulders, and wishes Miles would respond.

He emerges, glistening, and checks his phone again before sending another plea. Clutching the phone he heads for the sauna – a place that usually relieves the tension and eases the aches he has begun to experience more often.

It is hotter than usual in the sauna, and as he breathes in the dry heat, he debates forgoing it, and then decides he is hot because his heart rate is elevated. He is stressed. He needs to take a few moments to calm down. He shuts the door and throws himself onto one of the wooden benches, face up. He studies the wooden knots in the ceiling and counts the slats as he has done many times before. There are thirty-two, and usually counting them settles his mind after a hard day. The gentle noise of the pool as the water swooshes through the skimmers does not relax him either. Sweat oozes from him, as if he is being wrung out, and the thrumming in his temples is too loud to bear. The heat is making him uncomfortable. He swings his legs off the bench and eases into a sitting position.

He is about to leave when the door bursts open and Miles stomps in.

'Scott, I've told you I'm truly sorry. The decision to fire you didn't come from me.'

Scott looks at his lover's face, a face he has caressed so many times. 'I can accept the job loss, but I can't accept losing what we have.'

Miles pulls at his collar. Dark patches of sweat have already formed under his arms. His forehead is damp, beads of sweat already forming there.

'I think it's best we call it a day,' he says, his arm stretching for the door handle. 'We both need to move on.'

Scott's right eyebrow arches in surprise. 'We need to move on? Don't you mean you *need to move on? Is there somebody else, Miles?' He leaps to his feet and in one swift movement blocks the door with his frame, legs apart, thigh muscles bulging.*

'Don't be stupid, Scott. Let me out. It's bloody hot in here.'

Scott crosses his arms. 'Not until you tell me you really loved me and all this wasn't just a bit of fun.'

Miles tugs again at his shirt and wipes a hand across his forehead. His voice is less assertive now. 'Scott, please,' he says. He opens his mouth. Nothing comes out. His head drops and he crumples to the floor. Scott is paralysed, unable to help. Miles stares up with wide eyes filled with pain and horror. His mouth opens again, the lips forming Scott's name, but no sound emerges and he falls back.

Time becomes liquid and Scott can't move; his mind is blank. By the time he drops to his knees to help, it is too late. Miles Ashbrook is dead.

Scott didn't pause for breath. 'I begged him to reconsider. He refused. I threatened to blab about our relationship and he reminded me that I had more to lose than him, that I should consider my family and the effect it would have on them to discover I was having an affair with another man. I lost my temper. I leant against the sauna door and wouldn't let him leave until he confessed he still loved me, and would do what he could to keep me on.'

Scott's voice on the phone went silent, during which time she heard the sound of an engine again. What was that? A lorry? Anna came into the room. Robyn signalled to her and mouthed, 'Trace this call.' Anna hustled into action.

'He begged me to let him out. It was too hot for him, especially fully dressed. I behaved like a petulant child and refused. Then he clutched his chest and keeled over. He died instantly. I didn't know what to do. I panicked.'

'Scott, it was an accident. You had nothing to worry about.'

'Don't you see? It was my fault. I trapped him in the sauna. My mind went crazy. After it happened, I didn't want anyone to find out about our affair, and so I tried to make it seem as if he had taken a sauna. No one other than Miles knew about my routine of going into the spa on a Wednesday. The spa is out of bounds for employees. Miles turned a blind eye to it,' he said. There was silence for a moment and Robyn thought he had hung up. Then she heard him again. 'I stripped the clothes from his body and left him in the sauna. I sat in the changing room for an hour trying to work out how to make it appear like a genuine accident, and it came to me. I knew the CCTV camera would focus on the shower outside the sauna for a few minutes, so I left my clothes in the changing room, carried Miles's clothes to the lounger, and stood under the shower. Miles and me look a bit alike, especially when I flatten my hair.' He stopped for a second. 'We *were* similar – the same height and size. I wanted to make sure no one spotted any difference, though, so I wore the pants.'

'You wore the Union Jack boxers deliberately.'

'They were a joke present from Miles. We bought them in London on our last trip and I kept them in my locker at the gym. I didn't want Alex to find them. I figured anyone looking would see the Union Jack boxers rather than the man wearing them. I kept my back to the CCTV.'

'It was very convincing.' *Not a lorry – a tractor. Scott was somewhere rural.*

The sound of gentle sobbing, then, 'I had to dress him in them afterwards. It was awful – the most dreadful thing I've ever done.'

'Scott, you can't be held responsible for his death. You didn't murder him. Either tell me where you are or come into the station. We can resolve this.'

'I've lost everything. Alex knows about Miles now. I couldn't sleep, eat or anything. I was in such a state, I told her about our affair. She doesn't know any more than that. I can't face her knowing the real truth.'

'I'm worried you're in danger, Scott. There is someone out there who wishes you harm. Please, let us help.'

'I feel better now you know about Miles. I'm sorry, I can't tell you where I am. I have a few more issues I need to address.'

'Scott, don't do anything drastic. Your marriage to Alex may be over, but you still have a little boy who needs his daddy. Don't deny him that. He needs you now and he'll need you as he grows up. This week, another little boy had his mother taken from him. Think about George.'

There was more sobbing from the other end and then the phone went dead. Robyn looked across at Anna, who shook her head in apology. They still had no idea where Scott was hiding.

CHAPTER FIFTY-ONE

Adrian Bishton had never got used to his title. He was plain old Adrian to his family and friends, and now he was fast approaching seventy he felt even less like a lord. However, one thing he enjoyed about being Lord Bishton was the annual hunt ball. Some of his dearest friends attended, and it was a great opportunity to catch up with those he hadn't seen for a while.

Bromley Hall was a far cry from his home in Thailand, where he was simply a self-made millionaire who lived in a fairly large villa with a view of the sea. Bromley Hall had been bequeathed to him; he and Kate had left their terraced home in London to take it on. It had been a labour of love at the start, with both of them keen to transform it into a prestigious location for the elite and well-to-do. Kate had exquisite taste, and it had been enjoyable travelling to Italy and France to source all the fabrics and furnishings. And once they had opened the Hall, it had been hugely entertaining to mingle with rock stars and celebrities, who'd rushed to stay there from all over the globe. After the accident in 2012, both he and Kate had lost heart in the place. The Hall lost its popularity almost overnight. It was shut for several months, and it cost them dearly to avoid being sued for millions and to keep the whole nasty affair out of the major newspapers.

He wasn't proud of his part in it, but Bromley Hall had been a major investment of time, effort and money. Every penny he had earned had been pumped into it. He couldn't allow the business to fail because of Harriet Worth's accident. Adrian had thrown any savings they had at the lawyers and at Harriet's grieving husband, to make the problem go away. Alan Worth had accepted the money and then insisted they close the pool and spa area. They had almost been ruined. Transforming the place into a large hotel spa and selling it on had been the answer. The Bishtons had kept their house in the grounds of the Hall, which they would leave to their family, along with a now very healthy financial legacy.

In part, he was looking forward to seeing the old place. It was five months since he had last been in the UK. It was a pity Kate wasn't with him. He wasn't used to travelling without his wife. She'd insisted on remaining in Thailand, where the sun shone in November and she could wear flip-flops and swimsuits instead of thermal vests, thick woollen jumpers and boots. She detested the British weather at the best of times and abhorred winter. No matter what he had said, she had flatly refused to join him, and instead packed his warmest clothes, pecked him on the cheek and told him to enjoy himself. As he waited for his luggage to come off the carousel at Heathrow airport, he checked his phone and listened to his voicemails. He was vaguely amused. Some woman claiming to be a DI Carter was advising not to travel to the UK. Who the heck was this woman? She'd left a number and a request for him to call her. His case arrived and he trundled through customs with all the other arrivals. A stern-faced officer called him to one side and asked what was in his suitcase. By the time Lord Bishton had left the airport and managed to get soaked in a heavy downpour waiting for his car to arrive, he was not in the best of moods and the phone message had been forgotten.

CHAPTER FIFTY-TWO

Robyn stood with her back to the window, arms folded, and sighed. 'No idea, just that Scott is hiding out in a rural location, and we both know how much countryside there is in Staffordshire. We're going to have to hope he calls again or hands himself in.'

Matt Higham shook his head in despair. 'Every time we get close to something significant, it escapes our grasp.' He studied the whiteboard. 'I hope the killer is thwarted too and can't find Scott. He's surely one of the potential victims on the Leopard's list.' He huffed in dismay. 'A West Highland terrier called Alfie and a silver Fiat 500. It's not much to go on, is it?'

'I agree. I've never felt so frustrated or anxious about a case, and the killer is on some ego trip knowing the press have named him the Lichfield Leopard.'

David Marker interrupted the conversation. 'There's been a call about a Fiat 500 with a sticker in the back windscreen. Someone claims his next-door neighbour has such a car.'

She picked up her hat from the desk. 'Give me the neighbour's address. I'll question him.'

'It's not a him, guv. It's a her – Stacey Turner.'

'Okay, I'll check it out. I'm going stir-crazy here.'

Delphinium Avenue may have been christened with a pretty, horticultural name, but there was nothing on this street that bore any resemblance to any larkspur Robyn had ever seen. The front paved drives were filled with clutter, cars and various broken bits of machinery. Each was a veritable scrapyard.

The semi-detached houses were dingy – built in the late sixties, they lacked paint and regular maintenance. It was as if the entire street had decided to decline into a shabby state. She pulled up outside number twelve, a house like all the others on the street, with nothing to distinguish it from its neighbours other than the number twelve stuck on the front door. She detected a figure at the window of the house next door and assumed it was the neighbour who had called the station. The curtain fell back and the figure disappeared from view, no doubt to watch the proceedings from some other less obvious vantage point.

It was seven fifteen and the street stood in darkness, save for a few pools of light. Two children were lurking under a lamp-post that gave off an orange glow, turning their faces an eerie colour. They stared at her with vacant expressions as she got out of the car. They were about the same age as Amélie, though she doubted Amélie would be allowed outside like them. Which reminded her, she really ought to phone and explain why she had not yet arranged their day out. It was becoming increasingly unlikely she would find time to spend a day with Davies's daughter.

The Fiat 500 was parked on the drive. Robyn noted the large anti-theft clamp on the steering wheel. She rang the bell and, getting no response, rapped on the door loudly. A volley of barking came from inside, followed by a shout, and once the dog became quiet she heard a bolt being drawn. The door opened a few inches to reveal a vertical slice of a hefty woman wearing a faded pink onesie. Stacey Turner gawked at her, her plain round face devoid of make-up and her hair lank and greasy. She took a moment to register the fact Robyn was a policewoman, and then her pale, insipid eyes took on a look Robyn had seen before – one of distrust.

'What d'ya want?' asked Stacey, her voice rough and low.

'Can I have a few moments to ask a couple of questions about your vehicle?'

'What about it? It's paid for. I got it with the insurance money from when my old car got bashed up. Nothin' wrong with that, is there?'

Robyn shook her head. 'Nothing at all. I'm trying to locate the driver of a Fiat 500 who was in Kings Bromley on Monday, the twenty-first of November. They might be a witness to a crime.'

'Never heard of Kings whatever-it-is. It wasn't me.' She began to shut the door but Robyn persisted.

'I have to ask you, Miss Turner, where you were that day?'

The door opened further. Stacey's outfit did little to disguise the layers of flab. She shook her hand 'I was here, in bed. I worked nights last week at the pharmaceutical factory near Derby. I pack boxes of supplies. Check with my employer. I got in at six and went to bed, all right? That enough information for you?'

'Thank you, Miss Turner.' The dog inside the house howled to be let out. 'Is that your dog? Is it a West Highland terrier?'

Stacey's face softened for a moment. 'It is.'

'I love Westies. Such nice natures.'

Stacey gave her a suspicious look. 'Love 'em or not, I have nothing more to say to you.' The dog howled again. 'Shut up, Alfie,' she shouted.

As the door was about to shut, Robyn felt a frisson of excitement at hearing the dog's name. She pushed against it, preventing it from closing. 'Miss Turner, I'm going to have make this formal and take you into the station unless you talk to me.'

Stacey hesitated, weighing up her options. Reluctantly, she held the door open. 'In that case, you'd better come in.'

CHAPTER FIFTY-THREE

It was too dark to be time to get up. Outside, the hum of the early-morning traffic had begun and he knew he would not be able to sleep. Last night he had been prowling the streets, his glossy coat shining under the lights, his teeth bared ready to chase his prey. He could feel the powerful muscles under his skin. He was invincible. He was the Lichfield Leopard.

He had caught a glimpse of his reflection in a shop window and crouched on his haunches to admire it. He was truly a magnificent creature, smaller than the other big members of the Felidae family – the tiger, lion and jaguar – but the very epitome of stealth. He knew he was the most secretive and elusive of the big cats, and also the shrewdest. The knowledge made him swell with confidence. He stared at his shoulders, upper arms, back and haunches marked with dark spots in a rosette pattern, which acted as camouflage. He was the most furtive of nocturnal predators and would never be caught.

Harriet suddenly materialised beside him. She was wearing his favourite outfit – the pink top she had worn the first day he saw her. She stroked his head and murmured into his ear. His entire body trembled at her touch and he let out a noise – a mixture of a purr and a growl.

'You have to be more careful, my love,' she whispered, her hand caressing his spine. 'You are stealthy, yet you didn't act quickly enough, and now one of our prey has escaped. It was a mistake that could put you in danger. You must go to ground and hide like the leopard you have become. That way, the hunters will never find you and you will be able to deal with the person who most deserves to suffer.'

'But I have to capture my prey that fled. I owe it to you.'

She caressed his ear for a moment and regarded him thoughtfully.

'You have made most of them pay. Dawson was fortunate to escape. If you have time after the next victim, you should seek him again and crush his skull. Now it is important you stick to the plan and prepare for the most important of all the victims. I want you to collect his payment, and then soon, so soon, you and I shall finally be together forever.'

The dream had been a sign that he ought to heed. He dragged on a pair of jeans and prepared his survival bag. He would do as Harriet suggested. He would hide until it was time to make his final kill.

CHAPTER FIFTY-FOUR

Stacey regarded her with icy-grey eyes and sat with her plump arms folded protectively over her chest, revealing a tattoo of a green and blue bird – a swallow in flight, distorted in shape and size – on her forearm.

'I'm investigating a murder, Miss Turner, and I require your cooperation. I'll ask you again – where were you on Monday last?'

There was a silence in which only the television could be heard. It was an old episode of an American sitcom, the canned laughter at odds with the sombre room itself. Inside, number twelve was as scruffy as its exterior. Stacey clearly was not house-proud: layers of dust had gathered on the stand supporting the large television screen, the fabric on the chairs was grubby and several stains were evident on the seat cushions. The room was sparsely furnished, with few ornaments and knick-knacks and only one picture – a seaside scene – on the wall. The entire place smacked of neglect and loneliness. A family-sized bag of crisps rested on the settee where Stacey had been sitting and a can of cola was perched on the arm. The dog had been allowed into the room and was sitting on one of the chairs, throwing Robyn baleful glances.

'I was here like I told you. I work shifts. Some weeks I work days and other nights. I was on nights that week so I got in at about seven a.m., let Alfie out, had some breakfast and went straight to bed. I didn't get up again until five p.m. and had to go back to work for ten.' While she was speaking, Stacey's eyes rested on the television, observing the antics of the characters on the screen, semi-oblivious to the presence of the detective sitting opposite. There was something about the way she wouldn't meet Robyn's eye that made her suspicious.

'Do you have a partner or could anyone else have driven your car that day, Miss Turner?'

Stacey's reaction was immediate and nervous. She brushed imaginary crumbs from her woollen jumper and picked at a hole in it. 'I don't have anyone in my life,' she replied. After a fraction of a second she glanced at a photograph of two children hand in hand with a woman in a sundress and large hat.

'Miss Turner, you do know I can check up on you. I can go to my car, call the station and have your details brought up on the police computer. If you are hiding anything at all, I'll know about it.'

The woman continued to pick at the hole, pulling at a loose thread and twisting it round and round into a tiny, tight ball.

'Is there anybody who has access to your vehicle?'

Stacey shrugged. 'There might be someone.'

'I can't stress how important this is. If you conceal anything that might hinder my investigation I shall have to charge you, and that will have a negative impact on your employment.'

'What? I could lose my job?'

'Employers don't take too kindly to their employees having a criminal record.'

Stacey sat for a while, wrestling with her conscience and staring at the television. Although the laughter was becoming increasingly irritating, Robyn sat quietly, calmly, waiting for Stacey to crack. She eventually did.

'I lent it to someone that day.'

She felt her heart beat faster. At last she had something significant.

'I don't want to get him into trouble.' Alfie, his head on his paws, eyes half-closed, let out what sounded like a sigh. She took a breath, her words slow and deliberate, as if each sentence were being extracted from her with force. 'My brother's car was in for a service and the garage didn't have any loan cars, so he called me. He had to get to work and asked if he could use mine. He only took it for a few hours and returned it after lunch.

'It was a one-off. I wasn't keen but he sounded desperate. He's not been lucky with work, he has a medical condition that makes it difficult for him to find a job, and he didn't want to lose this one.'

The room went quiet and the credits rolled on the television show. The dog let out a whine.

'His name's Dan and he's a doorman and porter at Bromley Hall. Be nice when you talk to him, please. I'm sure he isn't involved in anything…' The sentence hung in the air, and although she spoke the words, Stacey didn't look too certain she believed them.

'Thank you, Miss Turner. Can I ask one last question? Why do you have a different name to your brother?'

'Different fathers. We're half-brother and sister. My father left our mum and she remarried. Dan was born Williams and I kept Turner. Mum was a basket case. She had more men than hot dinners. She was into drugs too. We both ended up in care. She's dead now. Life's like that,' she added in a flat tone.

'I might need to talk to you again.'

Stacey slumped further into the settee cushion and patted the one next to her. Alfie bounded over and jumped up. She stroked him. 'Is that it?'

'Yes, for now.'

'Good. Now go. Leave me in peace.'

Stacey stared at the television. A new show was beginning. She aimed the remote control at the set and helped herself to a handful of crisps, leaving Robyn to find her own way out.

CHAPTER FIFTY-FIVE

Adrian Bishton was welcomed by his housekeeper. He kept Flo Andrews on retainer while the house was empty, to keep it clean and prepare it for each visit. He was glad to be home after the long journey. He inhaled the familiar scent of lavender and beeswax and surveyed the entrance. The same art deco lamp on the antique table in the hallway, the same hat stand with carved feet purchased in Africa, the same grandfather clock that now chimed eleven times as if to welcome its owner, leaving Adrian smiling at the familiarity of it all, its ring resonating in his ears.

Adrian had many happy memories in this house – the rooms filled with guests and laughter at dinner parties, family memories of his two children – precious times that had passed in the blink of an eye. He had been most fortunate in life and there wasn't a day when he didn't count his blessings.

The hand-carved wooden handrail that curled up the staircase had been polished to a gleaming finish. Portraits of the Bishton family lined the walls leading to the first landing. He stared at the largest of the portraits, of him and Kate, painted in the 1980s – they had been filled with youthful confidence and pride back then. The future had stretched before them and they had felt invincible. The full-length, gilt-edged mirror hanging beside the drawing-room door revealed the man of today. He hadn't aged too badly – a little grey at the temples, but still the same lean frame. Following years in the fitness industry, he maintained a vigorous exercise regime, and months living in the sunshine had given him a healthy complexion along with a deep suntan.

Adrian felt a rush of pride as he strode about, reacquainting himself with his surroundings. Flo had done a good job. He must remember to give her a Christmas bonus.

The hunt ball on Sunday evening was taking place at one of his favourite venues – Weston Hall in Stafford – a manor house built in 1550 that was now an upscale hotel. He'd been there on a few occasions and never tired of the stunning building. Now there was a property he would like to have owned. He made a call to the local chauffeur service, confirming the arrangements for Sunday evening, after which he poured a large brandy from a glass decanter and settled down in the living room in front of a roaring fire, the long journey and frustrations of the day behind him.

Mitz sounded more like his usual self as he gave directions. 'Ring road A601, past the Siddals Road car park, then first on your right, near the Intu shopping centre. That'll take you into Liversage Street, opposite the Gala Bingo hall. Should be able to park on the road. Matt's on his way.'

Robyn followed the road over the River Derwent and got her bearings. She wasn't far from Dan's flat. Feeling the adrenalin coursing through her veins, she accelerated. She wanted this to be the breakthrough she so desperately needed. They'd had no luck in locating Scott, and Alan Worth was still in a critical state and unable to assist them. Her team was worn out, and morale had been fading quickly; this was the boost they needed. Mitz confirmed Dan was not due at Bromley until the following morning. She dare not hope for too much – every turn in this case had taken her to a dead end, or given her only the slightest hint of her killer's identity. This time, she had to be right.

Mitz's voice contained a trace of excitement. 'I've got background on Dan Williams. He and his sister were taken into care in 1985. Sister went to live with a family in Lichfield, but Dan had several foster families. Ran away from one in 1987 and was admitted to hospital with significant head and back injuries. Has since been on medication for occipital neuralgia – severe and debilitating headaches. Employment history is sketchy. Held down several part-time positions in supermarkets and factories. Never lasts more than a few months. Moved into sheltered housing accommodation in Lichfield late 2012 and to new accommodation in Derby in 2015.'

'Okay, thanks. Good work.'

'You will also want to know what I came across regarding his sister. She moved to Delphinium Avenue early 2013. Before that she rented a two-bedroomed flat in Shenstone House, Hobs Road, Lichfield.'

'Is it near Stowe Pool?' Robyn's pulse raced.

'It's a twenty-minute walk.' Mitz sounded like she felt. They had most likely found their man. She found the turning and pulled up on Liversage Street. She watched for any movement. She couldn't lose him now. Matt would soon join her, and if all went to plan, she might just catch the Lichfield Leopard in his lair.

CHAPTER FIFTY-SIX

Anna waited impatiently at the station. She and Mitz had uncovered plenty of information regarding Dan Williams and Stacey Turner, and she was beginning to feel the after-effects of an adrenalin surge. She meandered into the corridor, intent on getting some air to keep her going, when she had a sudden thought.

They'd been focusing heavily on finding whoever was guilty of killing Rory, Linda and Jakub, and since Scott's confession they had ceased to think about Miles Ashbrook. Scott had told Robyn he had wanted to leave the sauna because it was too hot. She had a flashback to the shadow on the CCTV footage and dashed back to the office. She inserted the USB stick and fast-forwarded to the moment she thought she saw the shadow of a man. The time clock showed seven twenty. The shadow couldn't be Scott Dawson, as he was busy taking Scotty's Combatives at that time. This was somebody else.

'Mitz, does this look like a person's head to you?'

'Sort of. It's an odd shape though. Is that just the way the light has fallen and distorted it?'

'I can't be certain. It seems peculiar. I'm taking a few stills from the frame to put on the board with a question mark. They might have a bearing on the case, and the boss always says to leave no stone unturned.'

The moon was large and bright, flooding the roads with silver light. Robyn inhaled the crisp air and pulled her coat tighter around her. Across the road, twinkling coloured lights, a reminder of the festive season, flashed in sequence. The roads were quiet and the cold had kept people inside. Matt drew up beside her car and got out, carrying a zipped bag. She felt her neck muscles bunching and adjusted her flak vest. The desperate need to catch this man was mounting.

'Parky or what? Matt exclaimed. 'Where are we headed? I've brought the big key in case we need it.' He motioned at the bag containing an enforcer. The specially designed steel tubular battering ram was some fifty-eight centimetres long, with an angled handle at one end and a steel pad at the other. Matt was one of only two officers in her team who had completed a course on how to safely use it. He passed Robyn a pair of ear defenders.

She pointed at the flats nearest the road. 'Got the warrant?'

'In my pocket.'

'Come on, then.'

'He's not going to be hanging out in a tree waiting to pounce, is he?'

'Who?'

'The Lichfield Leopard. Leopards lurk in trees waiting to leap on unsuspecting victims and even drag their prey up there to eat. Good climbers,' he added with a smirk.

Robyn grinned in spite of herself. Matt had diffused the tension. 'His car is parked in the next street, so he ought to be in.'

They hugged the walls of the building and climbed the stairs to the second floor to Dan's flat. She put an ear to the door. It was silent inside – no television, no radio, nothing. She thumped on the door. Nothing. 'Open up, Mr Williams,' she called. 'This is the police. Please open the door.' Nothing. 'Mr Williams, for the final time, open the door.'

This wasn't right. Surely he had to be inside. He couldn't possibly have got wind of their intentions and fled. She moved aside to let Matt force entry. He removed the enforcer from the holdall and positioned himself in front of the door, swung the ram back and smashed it into the door, causing it to fly open with a loud bang. Robyn waited for tenants to appear and demand to know what was happening, but no one came to see what had produced such a noise.

Robyn and Matt walked into the bedsit. If Stacey's house was squalid, this surpassed it. There was nothing other than a couch, a table and a small television. A blanket lay in a heap on the floor. A filthy glass stood on the table. Matt let out a low whistle. 'Holy…' Her eyes followed his. On the wall were hundreds and hundreds of photographs of Harriet Worth – each exactly the same photograph of her in a pink jogging top and leggings, running around an expanse of water.

CHAPTER FIFTY-SEVEN

The lights in the office blazed brightly. Robyn sat on her desk, flak vest on the back of her chair, her head aching as she tried to fathom what to do next. They had not found Williams, even though they had waited – one inside the building, the other outside, in case he appeared. His car remained in the street. He was either somewhere else for the night or had got spooked and gone into hiding.

She had sent her officers home. There was little more to achieve and it was past midnight. She turned her attention to the whiteboard and noticed Anna had added Dan Williams and Stacey Turner to it. There was a photograph of each of them. Anna had also added Miles Ashbrook and a picture taken from the CCTV footage of a man's head. She studied it hard, then shook her head to clear it. Her thoughts were no longer coherent. She had a potential victim on the run and a killer on the loose.

One thing was certain. She was going to be too busy to take Amélie out for the day. She had to let her know. It was only fair. She logged onto her Skype account and noted that the girl was still showing as 'active' even though it was late by now. She rang and within seconds Amélie's avatar was replaced by the girl herself, wearing a cream, long-sleeved vest, her long dark hair tied up in a red ribbon. As always, she reminded Robyn of Davies.

She grinned. A light above her revealed the sprinkling of freckles across her nose. 'Hey.'

'Hi. How's it going?'

The girl shrugged. 'You know, same old.'

'Look, I'm really sorry but I've got a difficult case at the moment.'

'I know what you're going to say. We can't go out together this weekend.'

'As soon as I get some leave, I'll call you and we'll rearrange it.'

Amélie threw her a smile. 'I knew you'd call. I heard you're trying to solve a big case.'

'Who told you that?'

'I overheard Mum and Richard. I think they'd been talking to Ross. Are you after a murderer?'

'Can't discuss it, young lady.'

She grinned again. 'You're so cool. I think I'd like to be a detective when I get through school. I love mysteries and puzzles.'

'You'd be a cracking detective. How's school?'

'Same old,' she repeated, and then laughed.

'How's Florence? I was thinking, when we go out you might like to invite her too?'

A small shake of the head. Amélie suddenly looked disheartened. 'No. She's starting acting weirdly. I've tried to talk to her but she doesn't want to, not even on the phone.'

The girl's face was full of misery. Robyn couldn't remember how she dealt with relationships when she was that age, but she recalled it was a turbulent time for some, what with changes in hormones.

Robyn dragged up some old Latin from her own schooldays. '*Gradatim* – it means take it gradually, step by step. How about you look at it the same way I do when I'm working through a case?'

'She's been weird ever since she went to a big race meeting. She was excited about it cos a boy she fancies called Andy was also going, but she hasn't mentioned it since.'

Robyn rubbed her chin. 'I think that's the key. Something occurred then.'

Amélie stared at the screen. 'You think so? It makes sense. Is this what it's like being a detective?'

'Pretty much. You keep picking up pieces of a puzzle, deciding if they're important and putting them in place. Sometimes they fit together. If I were you I'd either ask Florence what happened when she went to the races, or speak to Andy.'

'Cool. I'll do that. Thanks.'

'So, I'll talk to you again soon?'

Amélie stuck up a thumb. 'You bet. Better go. It's late and Mum will be on the warpath if she hears I'm still up.'

Robyn disconnected and stared at the board once more. Davies had been the best puzzle-solver. She wasn't as quick as him, and relied more on instinct and feeling than logical deduction. She wished he were here to advise Amélie or to help her work through her own problems. But he wasn't, and no amount of wishing was going to bring him back to her.

Lord Bishton's name was on the board with a question mark beside it. He must have received her message by now. She sank onto her chair with a lengthy sigh and spun around, head tilted back, berating herself for making a mess of this case. She ought to have checked to see if Bishton had caught the flight from Thailand. He could be in the UK. That was a bad error on her part. If he was here, he could be in danger. She dialled his number but the phone was still switched off. She needed somebody to keep a watch on Bishton's place in case Williams decided to go after him. David Marker lived the closest to the Hall. It was late but she had no choice. She rang her officer.

Once she'd ended her call, she attempted to create a profile of Dan Williams in her head: an unhappy childhood, farmed out to foster families and separated from his sister; a history of ill health; apparently no serious relationships, and an unhealthy interest in Harriet Worth. What had triggered that? She would have to interview Stacey again. Her thoughts turned to Stacey and her squalid home, devoid of love or family, the only photograph one of her and her brother with their mother. She couldn't help noticing that Stacey had resembled Harriet – similar eyes, and if Robyn remembered correctly, a wisp of blonde hair much the same colour as Harriet's. Maybe that had been the catalyst. She would never know unless she unearthed Dan.

Although she had seen Dan at Bromley Hall, she had not paid much attention to him. Mitz had interviewed most of the staff, while she had tried to figure out how Miles Ashbrook had met his end. Dan had seemed a quiet, polite individual. He was tall and skinny, about six foot three, with long arms that didn't fit his porter's outfit and black hair that reached his shoulders, concealing some of his sharp features. More interested in the members of staff who had worked at the Hall when Harriet had died, Robyn had let him slip under her radar, and no doubt Mulholland would hang her out to dry for that. She stared at the photograph of him and, shutting her eyes, tilted her head back and let her mind wander. Dan was not a leopard. He was a chameleon.

Mitz found Robyn dead to the world, head on the desk. He shook her shoulder gently. 'Guv, wake up.' She sat up with a start, her mouth dry, her breath sour, and with a dreadful crick in her neck.

'Coffee?' he asked, pushing a cup in her direction. She gave him a grateful look. She checked her mobile. It was almost 6 a.m. 'What are you doing in so early?'

'Figured you'd want to swing past Miss Turner's house and have another chat with her. Thought you might like support. Didn't you say she was on day shifts? She'll be leaving for work soon.'

She downed the coffee and headed to the bathroom to spruce up. She kept a wash bag in her locker along with her gym kit, so she was able to make herself presentable in a short time before hustling out of the station towards Delphinium Avenue.

They found Stacey standing outside, watching Alfie do his business. She grimaced when she saw the squad car pull up.

'Stacey, we need your help. Dan has disappeared and I have to ask you a few more questions.'

'He's not here,' the woman replied, folding her arms across her gargantuan chest so they rested on top of her breasts.

'Can we come in for a moment?' Mitz gave her a genuine smile. She wavered, and calling for her dog, she showed them inside.

The drinks can from the night before was still on the table and in the daylight the house was even more squalid. Stacey plonked herself on a chair. 'What now?' she asked.

'Can you think of any place Dan might have gone? Was there somewhere that was special to him? Or has he any friends that might put him up for a few days?'

Stacey snorted. 'You're joking. Dan's never had any friends. He doesn't like people much. He doesn't like me much. We put up with each other cos there's no one else. I had friends when I was younger, but it's different when you're older. I only know people at the warehouse where I work, and half of them don't speak English. They're nice, like, though they're not the sort to invite you round for a drink or a meal, and people here, they keep themselves to themselves. If you haven't got any family it can feel lonely at times. That's why I got Alfie. He keeps me company. I've got online friends. I chat to them, but Dan, he's never liked anyone. He doesn't trust anyone at all. He didn't have it easy as a kid, or an adult.'

'There are no relatives, people he used to live with?'

'No. He lived with me once and that didn't work out. He gets these really bad headaches and they make him scream and cry out. It's really horrible. Then he gets in filthy moods because of the headaches. There's no one who'd take that on, believe me. Is Dan in trouble?'

Robyn could see concern on her face. She may have found it hard living with her brother but she cared about him all the same. 'We have to track him down.' Stacey shrugged, a defeated gesture.

Mitz gave the woman a kindly smile and moved away while Robyn questioned her further. She made little headway. Stacey really knew very little about Dan's life or his habits.

Stacey glanced at her phone and stood up suddenly. 'I have to get to work. I can't be late. We get points if we're late, and if we get too many points we get an official warning.'

Robyn also rose and spotted Mitz standing in front of the photograph of Stacey, Dan and their late mother.

'Stacey, this is you with Dan, isn't it?'

Her voice softened for a moment, the big sister emerging. She picked up the photograph. 'Yes, he was an ugly little sod. He was born with one ear bigger than the other. He used to get ribbed something awful about it.'

'Can I borrow this photo?'

Stacey shrugged. 'Go ahead. I don't know why I've kept it all these years. I suppose it was because it was the only picture I had of her.'

Robyn gazed at the sad little family, Dan wearing a baseball cap and shorts, barely old enough for school, his hand in his sister's. Stacey with large front teeth that she had yet to grow into, a skinny child with knobbly knees, and their mother, blonde-haired, blue-eyed, a faraway look on her tired face. She squinted at the scene. Just to the side was a shimmer of water. 'Where was it taken?'

'It's near Lichfield Cathedral, at a lake called Stowe Pool. We used to go that way to school every day. Sometimes, in the summer, we'd have a picnic there. That was before Mum really got into drugs and things went wrong. Look, I really have to go. Take the photo. Bring it back when you've finished.'

Robyn marched out to the squad car, talking rapidly to Mitz, 'The photograph, it's the clue we needed.'

Mitz nodded. 'You spotted it too?'

'What?'

'It was Dan's ear. If you close your eyes and think about it, it resembles that shadow Anna spotted on the CCTV footage. It's always struck me as peculiar. At first I thought it was the way the light had distorted the shadow, but now I think it might look like Dan's head. It's like someone's got a very large ear.'

She stopped dead and stared at him, mind whirring. Her head bobbed up and down. 'Mitz, you could be right. I was looking at their mother. She and Harriet Worth could be sisters. They look very similar.'

'Back to the station?'

She waved the photograph at him. 'Not yet, I want to check out a theory first. Stowe Pool holds a great significance for Dan. I want to check it out.'

CHAPTER FIFTY-EIGHT

David sounded as laid-back as usual as Robyn spoke to him from the squad car. 'We've had confirmation that Dan's not shown up for work today. And Lord Bishton arrived at his house late yesterday. He's not answering his phone yet. As soon as he does, we'll bring him up to date with events.

'Keep the house under watch until Lord Bishton leaves again for Thailand. He is not to attend any functions without a police escort. I want you and Matt to keep him under surveillance at all times.'

'Roger that. Matt's there now. Anna has compared the photograph you emailed across of Dan against the still she took from the CCTV footage and they match. The shadow looks a lot like Dan's head. It appears he was near the control box outside the sauna the night Miles Ashbrook died. I checked with the maintenance guy at Bromley Hall and he confirmed there were two keys to the control box and one has disappeared. He last checked the key safe on Monday the fourteenth, two days before Miles Ashbrook died.'

'Any news on Scott Dawson?'

'No sightings of him or his car, and he hasn't contacted family or friends.'

'I hope he hasn't done anything stupid, given his state of mind. Okay, we're almost at Lichfield. Talk later.'

Mitz pulled up by the cathedral. The drizzle and rain from the last few days had gone, to be replaced by a perfect winter's day, and as Robyn emerged from the car she heard the distant honking of geese on the reservoir. The three spires of the cathedral rose into the limitless cobalt sky, criss-crossed by several fat vapour trails. She had little idea where to begin her search, although she sensed she was in the right place.

They cut past the cathedral and into Dam Street with its historic buildings. No doubt David would have known the history of each of them, but Mitz was more intent on spotting possible hiding places rather than exploring the history of the city. In the car they had thrown around ideas, and decided Dan had a strong connection to Stowe Pool that might bring him here and even provide him with a hideout.

They separated at the entrance to the reservoir, Mitz heading left, and stopping at the various paths that led to winding streets to explore the backyards and alleyways behind them. Robyn stuck to Stowe Pool itself. Gaggles of geese waddled along the path in front of her, chattering noisily as they went. A sharp wind blew from behind her, forcing her to quicken her pace. She turned away from the water, ripples blowing along its surface, and scouted along the hedge that surrounded the grassed playing field. It was open space and afforded few hiding places. A group of toddlers with mothers were running about on the grass. Apart from the children's squeals of delight carried by the wind, there was nothing else to be heard.

Robyn passed the empty playground and returned to the path around the reservoir, now bordered by denser foliage. She crouched and searched under soggy-leaved bushes for signs that someone had slept under them, and found nothing other than a pile of dog excrement. Aged trees flanked the bushes, none of them viable places for someone to spend a night. She walked with deliberate steps, methodically checking every bush. She hoped, with every fibre of her being, that this wasn't going to be fruitless. As the path curved left, a bench came into view. There were several more ahead, each offering a place for someone to spend a night. She paused at the first. It was impossible to know if it had been used. Damp splodges of water stood proud on the wood where earlier rain had fallen. Her limbs felt heavy and her brain sluggish with exhaustion. Although there were no signs of him, she knew he had been here. He was like his wretched moniker – a leopard.

For an hour, Robyn and Mitz combed the site for any sign of Dan. Neither of them found anything.

She was silent on their return to the squad car, disappointment oozing from every pore. Mitz remained optimistic. 'Dan lived close to Derby railway station. What if he caught a train from Derby to Lichfield?' She pondered his idea. It was feasible.

'Drop me back at the station and check that out. Good work.'

'Guv, I should really drop you back home. You look like you're going to keel over at any moment. I've never seen you look so tired.'

She smiled at him. 'Rubbish. I always look like this when I'm working on a difficult case. I won't be able to sleep. This all feels like it's coming to a head and I want to be in position when it does.' She shut her eyes for a moment. 'Thanks for your concern though.'

'Granny Manju wouldn't want you to be ill,' he replied with a smile. Robyn acknowledged it with a smile of her own. 'But she would want this villain apprehended and brought to justice.'

'And we want to do right by Granny Manju, don't we?'

CHAPTER FIFTY-NINE

Dan sniffed his armpits and squirted them with deodorant. Leopards had their own particular smell, but he didn't want to alert anyone to his intentions by stinking like a tramp. He washed his face and drew the disposable razor down his cheek, removing the growth from the last couple of days. The station toilets were empty apart from him, and he savoured the moment as he prepared for his final day.

Overnight, he had caught the train from Derby to Lichfield. It had been a circuitous route, taking him first to Tamworth and on to Lichfield Trent Valley, some distance from the city centre. Sitting on the platform at Lichfield Trent Valley, drinking hot chocolate from a vending machine, he had come up with another perfect plan to catch his quarry.

He telephoned the chauffeur service that Lord Bishton always used. This valuable nugget of information had, like all the other information he had accrued over his time at Bromley Hall, been doled out by Charlie. Dear old Charlie, who gossiped for England and who felt sorry for his colleague – the quiet, shy, polite porter.

It was thanks to Charlie that he'd learned that Scott Dawson always took a sauna after his class on a Wednesday, and where to find the key to the box that regulated the temperature in the sauna. He felt a surge of annoyance. That part had been so well orchestrated, and Scott Dawson would have died in the sauna had Miles Ashbrook not suddenly turned up. Dan had heard him coming and hidden in a locker in the changing room, his plan to keep Scott shut in the sauna until he passed out from the heat in jeopardy. He crunched up his paper cup and threw it onto the railway line. Stupid Miles Ashbrook with his swaggering stance and superior ways. He was no loss to society. Still, it should have been Scott's body they discovered in the sauna, not Ashbrook's. Scott Dawson had more lives than a cat. Twice he had escaped Dan's clutches. Dan's vision blurred and he felt himself being pulled into a black mood. He reminded himself to breathe deeply and stay calm. He had to be in control.

He had called Bromley Chauffeurs as soon as he arrived in Lichfield, and, imitating one of the posh folk who visited Bromley Hall, he'd said, 'Sorry to trouble you at such short notice, I need to be collected from Lichfield Trent Valley at six thirty this afternoon to go to Bromley Hall. Is that possible? Thank you so much.'

He had hunkered down on the bench in the waiting room overnight, a coat over his body. It was freezing, yet with the adrenalin and excitement coursing through his veins he didn't feel the cold. Daytime was easier, as he wandered across to the flats where his sister and he had once lived. He didn't dare go to Stowe Pool yet. It wasn't time. Instead, he hung around shops and cafés, mingling with the shoppers, biding his time until evening fell.

Now he waited for the chauffeur-driven Mercedes to appear so he could put the plan into action. He could see headlights approaching the station and he held up a hand. The car drew to a halt and a man in a peaked cap got out. 'Mr Asquith?' he asked.

Dan smiled genially. 'That's me.'

The man held the door open and Dan slid in, the length of rope he intended using hidden in his hands.

'Right, sir,' said the driver, hopping into his seat. 'Bromley Hall it is. Have you been there before?'

'Oh yes,' replied Dan. 'I'm very familiar with it.'

CHAPTER SIXTY

'I've been thinking about Scott Dawson.' Shearer swigged his coffee and scowled at the liquid in his paper cup. 'This stuff doesn't improve. Or possibly my taste buds haven't yet recovered.'

Robyn rubbed the back of her aching neck, trying to rub out the knots that had formed there.

'He kept one big secret from everyone – his affair with Miles Ashbrook. If he was going to hide out, could it not be somewhere he and Ashbrook both knew? They must have had somewhere they met up for their affair. It can't all have been conducted in rooms in Bromley Hall.'

'They spent a night in London.'

'I doubt he'd go back there – it'd be too expensive to hole up at a London hotel indefinitely,' scoffed Shearer, his eyebrows dancing. 'Where did Ashbrook live?'

'In a village, three miles away from Bromley Hall. It's really close to the Hall. Surely he wouldn't be there?'

'You won't know until you look.'

'I'll check it out.'

'You're welcome.'

'I didn't say thanks.'

'You were going to.' He winked, waved and wandered off.

Back in her office, she moved towards the whiteboard. She placed the photograph of Dan Williams in the middle of the board, next to a photograph of Harriet Worth, and connected them with a red line. Around the pair, in a circle, she put photographs of all the victims so far, including Alan Worth, then added a picture of Scott and one of Lord Bishton.

She crossed her arms and closed her eyes. The puzzle was falling into place at last. They had victims, a perp and a reason for the killings, and they all hinged on Harriet Worth's death. She gathered Anna and Mitz into the office.

'I'm concerned that Dan Williams will strike again. He has become emboldened by his killings and knows we are on to him. I don't think that will deter him from his killing spree. He is without doubt on a mission, and will attempt to kill these two men.' She pointed out Scott Dawson and Adrian Bishton. 'It's imperative we protect these individuals while at the same time trying to track down our murderer before he strikes again. Our problem is, we don't know where one of them is. I want you both to try the house where Miles Ashbrook lived. He rented it and it's vacant at the moment. There's a possibility Scott is there, given he is not at his own house or with any of his known friends. I'll try and locate other places he might have holed up. And, I don't need to tell you, if Dan Williams is in the vicinity, he's a dangerous man, so exercise caution.'

'Okay, guv.' The pair went immediately, leaving Robyn with her board and Post-its. She laid the yellow pieces out on her large desk this time, with Harriet's name written on the first note, and placed in the centre of the desk. Alan Worth had accepted one and a half million pounds to stay quiet about the incident. Dan had taken that amount and shared it among the people he blamed most for Harriet's death. Those people included Alan himself. Not only had Dan attempted to murder the man, he had stuffed wads of money into his mouth. Robyn wrote:

Alan Worth
Received £1,500,000 compensation.
Money in mouth symbolic of greed.
Invoice for £250,000.

She moved on to Linda Upton, who had invited Harriet to the spa, had not prevented her from getting drunk on champagne, nor realised Harriet had left their shared room for a swim, and therefore had been deemed partly culpable for Harriet's death. Dan had undressed Linda before drowning her. Was this so she suffered a similar fate to her friend? She wrote:

Linda Upton
Guilty for inviting and not looking after Harriet.
Wearing underwear. Like Harriet, who died wearing hers?
Invoice for £250,000.

Rory Wallis had served the champagne that had made Harriet drunk. In Dan's mind, this had played a significant part in her death, hence he had not only murdered Rory Wallis, he had first made him drink a bottle of champagne. She scribbled, faster now:

Rory Wallis
Served champagne that made Harriet drunk.
Forced to drink champagne before death.
Invoice for £250,000.

Jakub Woźniak had not cleared up the water from the dripping shower head that caused Harriet to slip. He had also failed to lock the door to the spa.

Jakub Woźniak
Left spa open. Failed to clean up water that Harriet slipped on.
Invoice for £250,000.

She was left with the problem of those still likely to be attacked. Who would Dan go after next? She couldn't be certain about Scott. He wasn't to blame for the spa being left open, because Jakub had been there that night, yet Dan had a list of people he held responsible. He had worked at the Hall and spoken to colleagues. He would certainly have learned that Scott was duty manager on the night of the accident, and therefore the locking of the spa fell to him. She crossed out *Left spa open* on Jakub's note and made a new one for Scott:

Scott Dawson
Left spa open.
No invoice yet.

And finally there was Lord Bishton, who had offered Alan Worth the one and a half million pounds not to take Bromley Hall to court. It was logical Bishton would be targeted. If he was, that would take the total of the invoices to the one and a half million paid out for Harriet's accident. She stared at her notes, now arranged in a circle like the ones on the whiteboard. She jotted down the names of everyone working at the Hall who might have been there on that disastrous night. Charlie had been on duty. Surely Dan would not go after his colleague? How could he hold Charlie responsible for anything? Or Lorna, who had been in the beauty salon? Robyn nibbled at her bottom lip and wrote *Charlie?* It wasn't possible. How could Charlie be implicated in any way?

She pulled up the information on Charlie and called her cousin.

'I wondered when you'd call again,' he said. 'I figured you'd need me sooner or later.'

'How well you know me.'

'How's it going?'

'That's the reason for the call. I actually do need you. You got along very well with Charlie, the porter at Bromley Hall. As I recall, he was the source of much of the information you gave me.'

'He's a lovely old chap. Took a shine to Jeanette.'

'We've identified our killer. It's Dan Williams, one of the porters at Bromley Hall. He's disappeared off the radar for the moment and, although I can't be certain, I think Charlie may be at risk. Mulholland is not giving me any extra manpower and I could do with someone going to keep an eye on him for a couple of days, until we catch Williams.'

'Couple of days?'

'I'm seriously hoping to catch him before then. I can't afford not to. Mulholland is breathing down my neck, and is going to haul me off the case soon if I can't get a grip on it, while Shearer is hovering about in the background. I expect he's waiting to swoop in and get the glory. He's got an agenda, I can tell. It's the way his eyes glitter when he's talking to you, like he's eyeing up a prize, or prey.'

'I know him of old.' Ross had no love for the man, having crossed paths with him on a few occasions. 'I'll watch Charlie for you. I haven't got any major stuff going on here. Besides, I'm sure I still owe you some free work as thanks for our spa break. Charlie won't know I'm there.'

Robyn could hear the edge in his voice. He was excited to be involved in some police work again. She felt a surge of affection for her loyal cousin. 'If the killer turns up, no heroics. I mean it, Ross. You call it in immediately.'

'Scouts' honour,' he replied with a deep chuckle.

'If anything was to happen to you…' She left it unsaid. Ross knew how she felt. She owed him so much.

'Nothing will happen. If I see anything suspicious, I'll phone you. I won't go in.'

'Thank you. I'll text you his address. Hope there's nothing to worry about, but I ought to cover my bases.'

'I'll cover this one for you.'

She studied her notes and hoped she hadn't missed anyone who could be in danger, because if she had, that person could soon be dead.

She pulled up the information they had on Ashbrook. Where could Scott be? So far they knew he had worked in various locations in the UK, including Edinburgh, Harrogate and Devon – all too far away from Bromley Hall and Staffordshire. She was about to shut off the computer and go back to the board when she thought of Tricia and rang her.

'Tricia, I want to let you know that at this stage we believe Miles's death was suspicious. I can't tell you much more than that. It would help me greatly if you knew of any places that Miles liked to visit – maybe for a weekend, or just the day.'

'He liked the theatre and often went to London. I don't know much about his life. No, sorry, I can't think of anywhere he used to go, apart from the caravan in Matlock.'

'He has a caravan?'

'No, his parents do. Well, his mum still owns it. She hasn't used it in years. She hasn't got the heart to get rid of it. It holds too many memories. Miles's dad had a fear of flying, so they bought a static caravan in Matlock and spent holidays there. Mark spent time with Miles there. It's in the Derbyshire dales.'

Her stomach flipped. 'Tricia, thank you. You might have just helped out hugely. I'll keep you informed.' She ended the call and then dialled Mitz.

'Mitz, once you've checked out the house Miles Ashbrook rented, I want you to head to Matlock.' She gave out the information for the caravan park and sat back. She was back on course and it was the most exhilarating feeling.

CHAPTER SIXTY-ONE

Dan pulled up outside Lord Bishton's property. This was a daring plan, but he was the Lichfield Leopard, and nothing would thwart him. By now his absence at Bromley Hall would have been noted, the police would most likely have put two and two together and discovered the identity of the person responsible for killing four people. They were likely to be searching for him, so home was not an option.

It didn't matter to Dan. He wasn't going home. Today was the day he'd earmarked on his calendar with the red letter X. Once he had disposed of Lord Bishton he would be joining his beloved Harriet. He patted his trouser pocket. He'd bought the suit in a charity shop, especially for this day. It was grey and had a double-breasted jacket. It would serve not only as an ideal disguise for a chauffeur, it would make an ideal wedding suit. Harriet was going to meet him at their bench. She would wait for him to swallow all his pills that made him foggy and numb, and holding his hand, they would walk into Stowe Pool and be together forever more.

It had all been her idea. She had snuggled in his arms as he drifted in and out of consciousness.

'Dan, I know how we can be together – properly.'

He had lifted his head from the arm of the settee. He couldn't focus on the television and the bright glare from it hurt his eyes, so he closed them again, allowing the warmth of her body to seep into his own.

'You can free me from this world of not-dead, yet not alive.'

'I'd do anything for you,' he mumbled, his head swimming as he battled to stay awake and listen to her.

'If you can find all those responsible for my death, and avenge me, we can spend eternity together. I'll be with you at the end.'

He shook his head to clear it but it didn't help.

'How, my love?'

'I'll meet you at our special place, once you have done away with them all, and show you. You'll need to take extra pills, then I'll show you the door to eternity. It lies in the water at Stowe Pool, but only those who have drowned once can assist the living through it.'

His head dropped back against the arm of the settee. It was perfect. He would get a job at Bromley Hall, find out who was responsible for her death and kill each and every one of them. Then he would go with her through the watery grave doorway to paradise.

'I'll do it,' he whispered, as the fog overtook him and he drifted into a deep slumber.

It had taken over a year before he had got a job at the Hall, but making friends with old Charlie at the old man's regular pub had given him the break he needed. Charlie had told him of the opening for a porter and even recommended him to the management. Since then, he had slowly been investigating Harriet's death. No one could have suspected the quiet, invisible man – the quiet, invisible man who had since transformed into a deadly killer. He smiled at the thought.

The police knew his name, where he worked and where he lived, but they did not know Dan. He was the Lichfield Leopard, stealthy, cunning and a survivor. However, unlike a leopard, Dan could change his spots, and had managed to alter his appearance.

He checked his reflection in the rear-view mirror. He had pulled the cap well down on his head and the pencilled-on moustache made him look much older, as did the glasses with clear lenses. He looked nothing like Dan the porter. The real driver of the vehicle was trussed and knocked out on chloroform. He'd be dead to the world for ages, and if he did come around, he'd be unable to make any noise.

Dan waited, heart hammering in his chest. It was time at last for next kill. *This is for you, my love.* The door to the large house opened and Lord Bishton came out in full regalia, including a bright-red bow tie. Dan wanted to laugh, but instead he kept a serious demeanour, more befitting a chauffeur. He opened the back door to the Mercedes and stood to attention. 'Good evening, Lord Bishton.'

'Where's the usual chappy?' barked Lord Bishton, sliding into the Mercedes.

'He came down with flu suddenly.'

'Really?'

'There's a lot of it about, sir.' He wanted to shut the door, but Bishton had one leg out, a shining black dress shoe on the gravel. 'He phoned me and asked if I could stand in.'

'So you know where we're headed?'

'Weston Hall, sir.' Dan kept the smug look from his face. He had found out everything he needed to know from Charlie. This man wasn't going to catch him out.

Bishton gave him a steely look. 'Flu?'

'Yes, sir.'

'Len's got flu? Poor old chap. I expect that means Sarah will have to look after him.'

'That's right, sir. Len called me earlier. Sounded awful.' He hoped Bishton would draw in his leg. He was eager to get on the road and carry out his plan. He had the claw hammer in the glove box. He was going to beat the man senseless. The thought excited him. He coughed politely. 'I'm sure Sarah will take care of him. Ready, sir?'

Lord Bishton patted down his pockets. 'Blast! Forgotten my notes for the speech. Hang on.' He clambered back out of the car and strode to the house, where he fumbled with his key and let himself in. Yolk-yellow light flooded the entrance. Bishton moved towards the darkened lounge.

A soft whisper in his ear brought Dan to his senses. Harriet worked it out before him. The darkened room gave it away. Bishton wasn't collecting his notes. He was on to him. Somehow the police had alerted him. A curtain of rage dropped in front of his eyes, momentarily blinding him. He could still follow Bishton inside the house and smash his head open. He reached for the glovebox. He would kill him, no matter the consequences.

'No,' said Harriet, her voice harsher than normal. 'It's too late. You will never get away with that. The police are here somewhere. You haven't got much time. You have to save yourself.'

He wrestled with the idea of smashing in Bishton's skull once more before slamming the door shut and jumping back into the driver's seat, then gunning the throttle and making good his getaway. A dark car followed him out of the drive, two men in the front. It had to be the police. They had been at Bishton's house all the time. Dan smacked the steering wheel with the palm of his hand. 'No, no, no.'

There was no option now. He had to lose them. He steamed down the lane and, at the crossroads, swung a left and then pulled into a farm entrance, racing for the tin-roofed shed. He drove into it and waited, pulse thrumming in his ears. The car halted at the crossroads, then chose the right turn that led to Burton-upon-Trent. Dan let out a wheeze, only then realising he had been holding his breath for so long his lungs actually hurt. He reversed from the shed and raced off in the opposite direction.

His heart was heavy. Harriet was nowhere to be seen or heard. It was too late. He would not be able to collect the final payment. Furious and frustrated, he drove off into the dark night.

CHAPTER SIXTY-TWO

Anna rather liked Matlock. She and her dog had visited a few times and enjoyed long walks in the Peak District National Park. Matlock offered numerous tourist attractions, walks, pleasure gardens and a theme park. There was an unexpected contrast between old and new in Matlock Bath, where the amusement arcades and gift shops along the main road provided a sharp contrast with the elegant Victorian villas perched above.

Anna sighed. 'I wish I'd brought Razzle along. He loves a good outing. Got him from the dogs' home. I should never have walked into the place. Jackie insisted. We came out with Razzle, a scruffy mongrel with a beard and the loveliest brown eyes. I told Jackie it was madness, given my schedule and erratic hours. She insisted, saying it would be fine because she worked from home and so…'

Her head bobbed about as if she was reasoning with herself before she said, 'Jackie met a bloke and decided to move away – to Dubai, about as far away as she could. I was left with rent I could no longer afford, and with Razzle. To be honest, I wouldn't be without him. Flatmates are all very well, but dogs never let you down.'

'So you're renting?'

'It's hopeless trying to get a mortgage when you're single. Jackie's money meant we could live in a decent semi. I'm not sure how much longer I'll be able to afford it on my own, and agencies are really sniffy about letting to people with dogs. I might have to move back in with my mum.' She pulled a face. 'Not really what I want to do at my age.'

'How about at my age?' said Mitz, laughing. 'I'm still upstairs in the room I had when I was five.'

'I don't think I can handle being treated like a kid again. My mum doesn't seem to recognise the fact I'm grown up.'

They drove towards hills, verdant after recent rains. 'It's nice out here.'

'I used to live near Buxton. I've been here a few times.'

'Really? I didn't know.'

'I worked for a computer firm. I was a techie geek before I joined the force.'

Mitz barked a short laugh. 'No way. I had no idea. You're the best-looking geek I've ever met.' His face flushed at this declaration. 'Er, sorry.'

Her face took on a dark, serious look, then seeing him squirm, she cracked a wicked grin. 'Don't be – I'm flattered. Ah, there's the caravan park entrance.' The mood changed as both scouted the area for a glimpse of Scott.

Tranquillity Caravan Park was fifteen minutes from Matlock in ten acres of beautifully kept grounds, with colourful floral displays of rhododendrons that gave privacy to each of the hardstanding pitches. There were large grassed areas and a sign marked 'Woodland Walk', which made Anna wish once more that Razzle was with her.

They checked in at reception, housed in what was called a facility block with toilets, showers, a small kitchen and laundry, as well as a shop selling essentials and newspapers. The man on the desk had a florid complexion, a network of broken veins covering his nose, no doubt caused by walking in all weathers.

'Not many people on site at the moment,' he said. 'Picks up just after Christmas. Lots of folk turn up, intent on walking off those extra pounds they've put on.'

'We're only interested in the Ashbrook caravan.'

'Right-ho. It's got a chap staying there – friend of the family. He's been a few times with Miles. I used to see them going off down the woodland walk most days. Terrible news about the lad. I've known him since he was a nipper. His partner's jolly cut up about it. I could tell when he came in to collect the keys. Looks proper awful. I knocked on the door earlier to see if he was okay. He was out. He might be back by now. That was about an hour ago. Is everything okay?'

Anna threw Mitz a quick look of concern and said, 'We need to chat to Scott, that's all. You haven't had any strangers turn up, asking for a night or two's accommodation, have you?'

The man shook his head. 'As I said, not many people about at the moment, and nobody new.'

'You haven't spotted any cars, patrolling the site?'

'I'm only here for a few hours each day. I haven't noticed anything unusual while I've been here. We also have a keypad entry system and CCTV cameras, so it's unlikely anyone could come in without prior booking.' He gave them a suspicious look, his forehead lined with deep furrows. 'What's this all about?'

'Nothing to worry about, sir. Thank you for your time.'

Once outside, Anna turned to Mitz. 'How do you want to play this?'

'You knock on the caravan door and see if Scott's there. If he is, get inside the caravan and keep him in there. I'm going to keep a watch on the area. If there's any sign at all of trouble and Williams appears, I'll yell. If that happens, you stay and protect Scott and I'll tackle Williams.'

'What if Williams has a gun or a knife?'

'It's a chance we'll have to take. I'm not sensing that Williams is about.'

'Don't forget, he's good at hiding in the shadows. He could already be here and watching out for us.'

Mitz exhaled noisily through his nose: a tiny huff of irritation. 'We have to ensure Scott Dawson's safety. We'll exercise extreme caution. Happy with that?'

'Yes, Sarge.' She gave him a nod and a grin.

'See if he's inside the van first.'

They headed in the direction the man had indicated on a map. The Ashbrooks' caravan was well positioned, with superb views over surrounding hills. With Mitz observing the area from under a tree, Anna marched up to the caravan with its peeling paint and faded curtains now drawn to. Tall weeds had pushed up through small cracks in the hardstanding surface. It all required some attention. She put an ear to the door, straining to hear any sign of life inside. No radio or television. She rapped on the door. 'Mr Dawson. Open up, sir.'

There was no sound from within. 'Mr Dawson. It's the police.'

She shrugged at Mitz who signalled to try the door. She did, and it opened immediately. She was hit by the smell of stale air mingled with perspiration. The van was in a state: drawers open, debris on the floor as if there had been a tussle. She shouted for Mitz, who tore over to join her.

'Are we too late?'

Bedclothes were tossed onto the floor, along with the contents of a kitchen drawer. 'Either he was involved in a struggle or he went ballistic,' said Mitz, surveying the chaos.

'I can't believe Williams got here before us. Scott has to be on site.'

'But where?'

'The man on reception said he and Miles used to take the woodland walk most days. He might have gone in that direction.'

'We'll give it a shot and see if we can find him.'

The path led them away from the site on a shady route. It was lined with trees, the path damp, smelling of rotten vegetation. They had not walked too far into the woods when they spotted a figure sitting on a branch of a sturdy tree, head resting on his forearms.

Anna's mouth opened in surprise. 'Why on earth has he clambered up a tree?' Mitz pulled on her arm to prevent her from going forward. It was too late. Scott saw them.

'Don't come near me,' Scott shouted, clambering to his feet on the branch on which he had been sitting. It was then Anna spotted the rope hanging from the branch above and the knotted loop around Scott's neck.

'Mr Dawson, don't do anything hasty.'

'This isn't hasty,' he sobbed. 'Miles's death is my fault. I can't live with myself any more.'

'Sir, you weren't to blame,' shouted Anna. 'There was a third party. Somebody tampered with the control that heated the sauna.'

Scott wobbled on the branch and, arms out wide, took a moment to recover his balance. 'It doesn't matter. I was still the reason he died, and what do I have now? Nothing. Alex wants to divorce me and I can't face working at the Hall. I'll think of Miles every time I drive into the place. You say I can't do it? You can't stop me. I want to end it all.'

Anna walked forward a few paces. Mitz tugged at her forearm. She gave an imperceptible shake of her head and whispered, 'Let me talk to him.'

'Mr Dawson,' she said, smoothly. 'Don't you have a little boy?'

Scott gulped back tears. 'Yes – George.'

'You can't leave him. He's only young and, divorced or not, a boy needs his father.'

'He'll be better off without me. What example am I to him? I'll confuse him.'

Anna edged closer. 'Then who better to help him if he does become confused? You'll be able to support him and understand him in ways his mother can't. And, at the moment, you are George's world. He doesn't care about anything other than you being there for him and loving him. Do you want him to wake up on Christmas morning knowing you are dead? Isn't it better he wakes up knowing he's going to see you?'

Scott's voice wavered. 'You don't know what it's like living a double life. I hate myself. And now I have the guilt of knowing Miles has gone because of me.'

Anna stepped closer. 'It wasn't because of you. It was an accident. And I do know how you feel, because my parents divorced when I was little, probably the same age as George. My father left my mother and moved in with his best friend. I used to stay with them at weekends and we had lots of fun.' She was now a whisker away from the tree and was working out how she could reach the branch on which he was standing should she need to. Her fingers searched for and gripped a Swiss Army knife she kept in her pocket.

'Rubbish,' Scott shouted. 'You're trying to keep me talking so I can't hang myself. I'm not scared. I've been building myself up for this. Now back off – I'm going to jump.' Scott looked down at the ground, his face crumpled in anxiety. Anna continued in her soft voice. 'I didn't lose a father. I gained another. I still visit them every Christmas. I can't imagine not having had him there to support me. In my darkest hours, I might even have tried to take my own life, had it not been for him.'

Scott hesitated, then his shoulders began shaking and he slid to a seated position on the branch. Anna raised her arm, got a foothold on the tree and hauled herself up to the first branch. Then, from there, she climbed onto the same branch as Scott. She reached up and sawed through the rope with one swift movement. The end fell away and Scott put his head in his hands once more and wept.

CHAPTER SIXTY-THREE

It was a little after seven on Sunday evening when Matt called the office. Robyn's eyes opened wide in surprise. 'What? He got away. After all that, he escaped?'

Matt sounded furious, his words echoing through the receiver. 'We were in position. We were waiting for Lord Bishton to confirm the identity of the driver and follow it at a discreet distance. He absolutely refused to be driven in an unmarked car to Weston Hall.

'He suddenly moved away from the vehicle and went back into the Hall, where he phoned to say the man driving was a phoney. The man claimed the usual chauffeur had been taken ill. It didn't ring true to Lord Bishton, who only this morning had spoken to that same chauffeur to confirm pick-up times. Bishton was quick-witted, and before he got into the vehicle, voiced his concern about Len the chauffeur's health, knowing the chauffeur is not called Len. He also invented a wife called Sarah, and the chauffeur didn't question either name. Bishton declared he'd forgotten something, went inside and called us. Something spooked our man. As Bishton was speaking to us, the Mercedes set off. We lost it at a crossroads. It must have either darted down a track or gone off in another direction.'

Robyn kept her cool. This wasn't the fault of any of her officers. She stared at the whiteboard and the photographs of Dan and his victims. Everything felt like it was a film on fast-forward.

'Okay, wait for instructions.'

She paced the room, her head now aching, and stood in front of the board. The answer to this was up there. She looked again at the photograph of Dan with his sister and mother at Stowe Pool, at Harriet Worth who had run around the reservoir on a regular basis. The whole case revolved around Harriet Worth, and a man who claimed to have loved her. It had begun at Stowe Pool and the murders were linked to Harriet's accident at Bromley Hall.

She listened to the steady beat of her heart. *Stowe Pool, Harriet Worth, drowning.* The pieces were there. Dan had great affection for Stowe Pool. Harriet resembled his mother. Dan had fallen in love with Harriet. Harriet had drowned. There was a chance that Dan had gone back to where this all started – Stowe Pool. She had no proof of this, only her instinct. Mulholland would thoroughly disapprove of her actions. She heard Davies telling her to follow her instinct…

The completed crossword lies discarded on the settee and Davies has an arm around her shoulder as they watch the flames leaping and dancing in the fireplace.

She kisses his stubbly face.

'You are way better at crosswords than me. You work out the clues so patiently, little by little. I get bored too quickly. Once I can't see an immediate answer, I'm off doing something else.'

'Gradatim,' he replied with a smile. 'It means gradually, step by step. That's how conundrums are best approached. Whenever I have a problem to solve and I can't see the answer immediately, I work out a bit of it and then another until it becomes apparent. However, sometimes I am not correct and you, you impatient person, nearly always are. You see things in a completely different way to me, and you have a terrific instinct. I wish I had that.'

'Right now my instinct is telling me to leap on top of you, wrestle you into submission and have my wicked way with you.'

'As I said, DI Carter, you have terrific instinct and should always follow it.'

She had to take the chance even if she was wrong. 'Matt, head to Lichfield, and more specifically, Stowe Pool. I think Williams might be going there.'

She dashed to Mulholland's office and, without waiting, knocked and entered. 'I think our perp's headed to Stowe Pool.'

Louisa studied her. 'What makes you think that?'

'Dan Williams used to go there as a child with his mother, who looks a little like Harriet Worth. Dan met Harriet at Stowe Pool and became obsessed with her. Their meetings were always at Stowe Pool, and then there's this whole water thing. Harriet drowned. I have a feeling Dan Williams might try and drown himself too.'

'If so, why not at Bromley Hall?'

'I can't answer that, other than he can't go back to Bromley Hall. He's guessed we know his identity and will be trying to avoid all his usual haunts.'

Mulholland drew a breath. 'Robyn, you look totally exhausted. I worry that you've driven yourself too hard over this case. Are you capable of making sound judgements?'

'I hope so. I am convinced that's where he's headed. Can you get roadblocks arranged?'

'If this is a mistake—'

'It won't be.'

Robyn dashed to her car and left the car park, tyres squealing. She had to be right. This time it really was her head on the line.

The three spires of the cathedral loomed as she drove along the main road to Lichfield. Shoppers exiting a large supermarket impeded her route and she wished she had brought a squad car to move them out of the way. She rang Matt, but there was no reply.

As she got closer to the cathedral, it was evident that officers had been drafted in. A car blocked the main road by a small roundabout, and the traffic was being diverted. She wound down the passenger window, leant across brandishing her ID and shouted to be let through. The officer in charge was slow to react. All the while, her heart hammered.

She tore down the road, past the quaint historical buildings, searching for the turning to the cathedral. There, on Cathedral Close, another police car, blue lights flashing, stood by the huge pillars of the Gothic cathedral. The policeman jogged across to her. She recognised him as PC Ashton, a young officer from her station.

'He went that way, ma'am. I don't know if they caught him.'

She followed the road past the cathedral and turned right towards the town centre where she saw three squad cars behind a Mercedes, the driver's door wide open.

She ignored the policemen ahead of her hunting in shop doorways, torch beams searching out the dark corners, and raced directly to the reservoir. It was mostly in darkness, moonlight slipping through clouds to shine on the dark surface of the water. Dan had to be here. She spotted officers patrolling the playing fields, hunting under bushes and behind trees. The water shimmered as a bird flapped its wings, causing ripples that stretched out until they lapped against the path. Stowe Pool was slightly kidney-shaped, preventing her from seeing all of it. She brought to mind the photograph of Dan, his sister and mother, taken here at the reservoir. Would he come to that very spot? It seemed too obvious, but it was worth checking. She moved forward, her boots trampling damp grass. Some ducks huddled on the banks became unsettled, their angry quacking shattering the silence of the evening. Her eyes searched out any movement.

An officer searched the bushes on the other side of the reservoir, near the first exit that led into a housing estate. Williams could have taken that route and disappeared back into the streets of Lichfield. This was hopeless. There were five exits. He could easily have fled from the reservoir and they would have an almighty job finding him. She wondered if she should ask for the assistance of the police helicopter with its heat-seeking camera.

She caught a glimpse of hurried movement ahead of her and heard a shout. It was Matt. She sprinted towards him, a tight knot of anxiety in her stomach. The light from her torch bounced in front of her. Beside her, disturbed birds began to wake from their slumber and stir as she ran past. Matt was chasing someone ahead of her. She raced on, determined to catch them up. This wasn't a marathon; she needed all her reserves of energy to fly after them. The scene in front became blurred: a confusion of arms and legs, two bodies entwined; shouts, then as she drew closer, the men pulled apart and one slumped to the bench. The other drew back, hands on knees, catching his breath. The knot inside her tightened as she recognised the man to be Dan Williams.

She yelled, 'Matt.' Her voice sounded loud to her own ears but Matt did not respond. Instead, he rose and lurched forward at the shadow, now at the edge of Stowe Pool. Her torch beam picked out the dark figures, silhouetted against the water as Matt struggled to get a hold on Williams. Then came an explosive splash as both tumbled into the water and urgent thrashing sounds as they continued fighting. A group of geese became agitated, their wings beating like manic drummers, and their frightened honking filling the night sky. She called again, standing by the side of the pool, her eyes scanning the dark water, searching for the men. A cacophony of noise rose into the night as ducks joined the geese and their combined calls blotted out all other sound. She trained her torch beam on the water, finally alighting on two figures, arms flailing. She couldn't see faces. Arms and hands rose and fell, slapping against the water. Then one man rose like a demented sea serpent, dark hair slick to his deformed head, and pushed the other below the surface, pressing and holding him under the water. The Leopard was drowning Matt.

Breath coming in small puffs, she tore at her jacket and yanked it and the communications unit off, tugged at her shoes, threw everything onto the ground and dived into the water, the cold taking her breath away. She told herself it was only like taking part in a triathlon and breathed regularly, ignoring the icy fingers that gripped her legs. She was a strong swimmer. She pushed off towards Matt and Dan, ignoring the pondweed and stench. The men were no longer struggling and fighting. They had stirred up silt, making visibility impossible, but she was sure they were in the water nearby. She would have to dive down and find Matt. She wasn't losing a good man to this maniac.

She snatched a breath and dived deep, arms outstretched, eyes open. In the darkness her eyes strained to spot the slightest movement. It was hopeless. Suddenly, she made out a figure within arm's length, and powering her legs, she lurched forward and grasped his jacket, dragging him to the surface. She emerged gasping and pulled the man towards her. Her heart hammered. The man was in a suit not a uniform. A gleam of moonlight on the surface of the water confirmed her fears. His long dark hair gave it away. She had saved the wrong man. In her arms was the Lichfield Leopard.

She was about to shove him to one side and dive again for Matt when the geese fell quiet for a moment and she heard a faint splash followed by a gasp.

'Matt?'

'Here,' came the reply. 'I'm okay. I've lost him. I can't find the Leopard.'

'I've got him,' she called. Relief flooded her body, warming it. Matt was all right. As quickly as it had started, the flapping of wings ceased, and in its place came the steady strokes of someone swimming towards her. Beside her, the Leopard stirred. He was alive.

'I wasn't going to let him get away. Once was bad enough,' Matt said. He clipped the handcuffs holding their prisoner to the bench.

Dan was bent double and was groaning. Robyn ignored him as she slipped on her shoes and collected her jacket from the side of the pool. She was cold and soaking wet, but relieved. Fellow officers, their beams now trained on the three of them, were approaching. Matt, face white, uniform dripping onto the path, waited for her. She stood in front of the man they had been hunting. 'Mr Williams, you are under arrest for the murders of Rory Wallis, Linda Upton and Jakub Woźniak.'

Dan pulled himself upright, his face a mask of misery. 'Harriet didn't come. She was supposed to meet me on *our* bench and she hasn't come. We were supposed to go there together, hand in hand, to the doorway.'

Robyn glanced in the direction he indicated. Dan had always intended drowning himself in Stowe Pool.

'Harriet isn't here. She's angry with me because I didn't kill Dawson or Bishton. She wanted them all dead and I let her down. If I wait, she might still come.' Grief took him again and he sobbed – noisy, angry sobs that made his shoulders shudder.

Robyn nodded at Matt who released one cuff from the bench and hauled the man to his feet. 'She was never coming,' he said, as he forced the man's hands behind his back and clipped the handcuffs on them.

CHAPTER SIXTY-FOUR

'Scott Dawson was found alive in Matlock. We'll be looking into charging him with obstructing justice. And Lord Bishton has caught the flight back to Thailand. The driver at the chauffeur service was found unharmed, bound in the boot of his vehicle.'

Louisa Mulholland nodded her approval. 'It was a close one, Robyn. Closer than I would have liked, yet there is no doubt you have a dedicated team and you got the results. After you've interviewed Williams and got a confession, I want you to take some enforced rest. You will be no good to your team if you constantly drive yourself into the ground. Take the rest of the week off and recover.'

'Yes, ma'am.' Robyn turned to leave, then paused. 'I heard you had an interview.'

'You heard correctly. I was going to mention it to you when you had less on your mind. I decided to put myself forward for promotion and the new position we discussed. It might be time for me to move to pastures new.'

'I'll be sad to see you go.'

'It's not a done deal yet. I had rather hoped to put you up for my present position. Unfortunately, the powers that be don't feel you're ready yet. Give them reason to believe in you, Robyn. I think you'd make a very good chief inspector. Work for it.'

'Have they anyone in mind to replace you?'

'I really don't know.'

Robyn gave a short laugh. 'If it's Shearer, I'm going to request a transfer to Yorkshire.'

'Where you'd be most welcome.'

Mitz was sitting opposite Dan Williams. He spoke into the recording device. 'It is nine fifty-nine and DI Carter has just entered the room.'

The man opposite her was ghostly pale. He glanced at her then turned his look to his hands, fingers so tightly intertwined his knuckles were white.

'Mr Williams, I'm DI Carter. You know why you're here. You're being charged on several counts of murder and the attempted murder of Alan Worth. Is there anything you want to say?'

Dan studied his nails, maintaining his silence.

'Please don't make this harder for yourself. We have evidence that will prove you murdered several victims and injured others. We believe you attacked and murdered these people to avenge the death of Harriet Worth.'

He looked up then and gave a smirk that chilled her to the bone.

'We have forensic evidence that links you to all the scenes of crime. Is there anything you want to say?'

Dan sat back in his chair, the smile still on his face. 'Go on, charge me. I don't care any more. Harriet still loves me. Those people deserved to pay for her death and I made sure they did. Harriet is very proud of me.'

'I doubt it. I don't think any woman would be proud of you murdering a housewife with a small child. We have our confession. Take him to the cells.'

Outside, she leant against the door, her heart beating too fast. Shearer was watching. 'Okay?'

She nodded. 'Got the bastard.'

He smiled, small creases around his eyes. 'Well done, Carter.'

'It feels like a hollow victory. He's not right in the head, and so many people have died. I feel I should have caught him sooner.'

He put a hand on her shoulder. She felt its warmth seep into her.

'We always feel like that. You did good. You've put a nutcase out of harm's way, and tomorrow is another day.'

He left his hand there for a moment longer then pulled away. 'I'll treat you and your team to a pint at the pub later to celebrate.'

A swift drink was probably what she needed. And tomorrow was another day, one she intended spending with Amélie.

Anna was writing her report and didn't hear Robyn enter. 'Nice work, PC Shamash. I understand you talked Scott Dawson down from a tree where he intended hanging himself. That took skill.'

Anna spun to face her superior. 'When I was at university, I did part-time work for the Samaritans. I've spoken to people before that have wanted to end their lives. I thought I stood a good chance with Scott. He'd been up the tree for some time before we arrived, so I figured he wasn't too keen to do the deed. Then I talked. I'm afraid I made up some lies about my dad to get him to come down. I told him my dad had run off with another man. I worked on the premise he'd feel more comfortable if I empathised with his situation. If he hadn't believed me, I had time to leap up and free him before he did any real damage to himself. Either way, he'd have been safe.'

'So your dad didn't run off with a man?'

'Or anyone. He was a policeman in the Met. He's retired now. He's on a golfing holiday in Portugal with his golfing chums. He'll laugh his socks off when I tell him what I said about him.' She spun back and returned to her paperwork.

'I definitely owe you a spa treat. You've got a few days' leave coming up. Would you like me to arrange it?'

'If it's all the same to you, I don't think I fancy a spa break. I've gone off the idea. I'm going to Granny Manju's funeral on

Tuesday, and then I'm taking Razzle for a trip to the Peak District Park along with Mitz.'

'Mitz?'

'Can you believe it? He's lived here all his life and never been walking in the Peaks. It'll do him good to get some fresh air after all the upset.' Robyn waited in case Anna wanted to tell her more. When she remained quiet, intent on writing her report, Robyn let it drop. If there was anything going on between her officers, it was none of her business. She had her own report to write and a day out with Amélie to arrange.

CHAPTER SIXTY-FIVE

Amélie and Robyn burst free of the locked room, setting free the other members of the team. Amélie's eyes were shining. 'That was seriously the best fun I've had – being locked in a room and having to work out your escape through puzzles. It was awesome!' She shouted the last word loudly, throwing her arms open wide in excitement.

Robyn was glad she had chosen the Puzzle Room Experience as entertainment for the day. They had been introduced to their teammates and given a brief in the meeting room: 'A crucial witness who could attest for Dr Grimshaw's innocence and the existence of the terrorist organisation known as "The Ones" has died. It's now your mission to uncover his secrets, solve the puzzles and save the world. Can you unravel the mystery of his death?'

The Puzzle Room Experience had required sharp investigative and surveillance skills, quick wits and physical prowess. Amélie fast revealed herself to be a natural leader as she worked through the array of puzzles and clues that would lead to their escape. It had been wonderful to spend time with her, guiding her.

If Davies were looking down on them, he would be very proud of his daughter, who displayed her father's ability to work out conundrums, confusing problems and sequences of numbers and letters.

Amélie, face glowing, pulled on her woollen hat. The sequins on it sparkled like small diamonds. 'Florence is coming over tomorrow.'

'Ah, you've made up.'

The furry pompom on Amélie's hat wobbled up and down. 'It was so stupid. It was all over a boy. Remember the one I told you about who went to the same race meeting as Florence?'

'Andy?'

Amélie nodded again. 'Florence really fancied him and thought he liked her too. When she found out he was going to the horse race, she pestered her parents to go along too. She planned to get off with him. That's why she bought the new leggings and gear. It was to show him she wasn't a silly little schoolgirl. When she got to the races, she found him and tried flirting with him.'

'And he didn't fancy her?'

'That's right.' She squirmed and the pink flush on her cheeks flushed deeper.

Robyn smiled. 'He fancied *you*.'

'I don't know why.'

Amélie pulled a strand of dark hair away from her face. Robyn saw what Andy had fallen for. She was turning into a beauty, the perfect combination of Brigitte's French glamour and Davies's confidence. 'I do. He has great taste.'

'I don't fancy him though. It was thanks to you that Florence and I are friends again. I did what you suggested – I kept an eye on Florence and noticed she was giving me sly glances during lessons. She still wouldn't talk to me when I asked her outright, so I spoke to Andy. He explained what had happened. He said Florence was nice, but acted too young for him, and he liked me. I explained that I wasn't going to go out with anyone yet. It's not that I'm not pleased he likes me. I'm just not ready for all that stuff. I want to do well at school and be like Dad. I'd love to work in intelligence and be an undercover agent or similar. I wouldn't mind being in the police force, either.'

The girl was growing up and fast, and with that attitude had a bright future ahead of her. Robyn was proud to know her.

'I'm glad it's worked out between you and Florence. Friends are really important. Many of life's problems can be solved if you treat them like a puzzle. You just have to gather the pieces and eventually, through jiggling them about, you'll work out the answer.'

'I'll have to remember that when I'm next struggling with my homework,' said Amélie, taking Robyn's arm in her own. 'Or, I'll just Skype you for help.'

Robyn ran the last mile at full pelt on the treadmill. Her heart felt like it would explode, yet the buzz she was getting from the endorphins far outweighed the effort and strain. Her training had taken a back seat, and now she needed to refocus her energies. She had replenished her kitchen cupboards and fridge, and even cooked a wholesome stir-fry the night before. Her sleep had been dreamless, and when she awoke, she was ready to get back to a normal routine.

She slowed the treadmill little by little until it came to a complete stop. Then, dripping with sweat, she completed the stretch routine she followed after every running session. She would soon be back on top form.

As she rose to leave the gym, a figure dressed in a leather jacket and jeans appeared at the door and waved. It was Tricia. She beetled over, a smile on her face.

'Hi. I thought I'd find you here. I've left the boys decorating the tree, so Lord knows what state it'll be in when I get back. This may seem weird, especially as we hardly know each other. Would you like to spend Christmas Day with me? The twins are going to their dad's this year and I'll be alone. I thought we could wolf down a ready-made meal, or some pasta, and quaff some quality champagne and then watch some light-hearted films, or we could even play a board game. I thought we could just get to know each other a little better. It's got to be better than both of us sitting on our own, brooding over the past. That's what I normally do if I'm alone. This year, I thought I'd break the routine. What do you think?' She twisted the ends of her cream scarf and waited with an air of expectation.

Robyn wiped the sweat from her face. Christmases were a lonely time. She couldn't impose on Ross and Jeanette, and she didn't fancy another year of feeling sorry for herself. It had been two years, and she knew what Davies would want her to do. He would have hated to see her hiding away. The corners of her mouth lifted. 'I agree. It's time to start anew for both of us. Thank you. I'd love to. Sounds like a great Christmas.'

LETTER FROM CAROL

I hope you have enjoyed reading *Secrets of the Dead*. I enjoyed writing this book so much, especially as it is set so close to where I live.

The idea came to me some time ago while on my back in a sauna. It was unbearably hot in there, and as I counted the wooden slats above me, I wondered if it would be possible to murder someone in a sauna. After much research I learned that it was, and the kernel of an idea formed in my twisted mind.

My characters tend to be damaged, and Dan Williams is no exception. Many years ago, I had a stalker like Dan. I initially felt sorry for him, just as Harriet does with Dan, and engaged in conversation with him on our 'chance' meetings, but soon wished I hadn't. He followed me to work, to my house, lay in wait for me when I was shopping or at the gym, and scared me witless. If I hadn't managed to get him to see sense, it could have ended quite badly. I wonder if he might not have become a Dan.

Robyn is one of my favourite characters, and has taken to chastising me in my head when I don't write a good scene for her. I have something very gripping planned for her in the next book. So please join DI Robyn Carter again on her next case.

Can I ask one favour? If you have loved this book, would you please write a review for me? It doesn't have to be very long, but it would mean a lot to me. Thank you so much.

If you'd like to keep up-to-date with all my latest releases, just sign up at the following link. Your email address will never be shared and you can unsubscribe at any time.

www.bookouture.com/carol-wyer

Thanks
Carol

www.facebook.com/AuthorCarolEWyer

twitter.com/carolewyer

www.carolewyer.co.uk

ACKNOWLEDGMENTS

Behind every author is a fantastic team, and I am no exception. This book couldn't have been written without the assistance, advice and hand-holding from eagle-eyed Lydia Vassar-Smith, Natalie Butlin, Lauren Finger and Seán Costello, or produced without all the incredible, dedicated people at Bookouture. I am, as always, completely indebted to them.

I am also hugely grateful to all of the reviewers, bloggers and readers who read my books. Thank you. You keep me motivated when I reach a dry patch of writing and you get me through it with your generous praise.

Emma Mitchell deserves a special thank you for her words of wisdom and for checking through my script when my brain and eyes had given up!

Finally, my thanks to everyone who has written to me or posted reviews to say how much they enjoyed the first book in this series, *Little Girl Lost*. I hope you enjoy *Secrets of the Dead* as much.